THE CROSSING PLACES

THE CROSSING PLACES

Elly Griffiths

McClelland & Stewart

Cloth edition published 2009
Trade paperback edition published 2010

Library and Archives Canada Cataloguing in Publication

Griffiths, Elly
The crossing places / Elly Griffiths.

(A Ruth Galloway mystery)
ISBN 978-0-7710-3585-2

I. Title. II. Series: Griffiths, Elly. Ruth Galloway mystery.

PR6107.R53C76 2010 823'.92 C2009-905036-6

We acknowledge the financial support of the Government of Canada through the Book Publishing Industry Development Program and that of the Government of Ontario through the Ontario Media Development Corporation's Ontario Book Initiative. We further acknowledge the support of the Canada Council for the Arts and the Ontario Arts Council for our publishing program.

Printed and bound in the United States of America

McClelland & Stewart Ltd.
75 Sherbourne Street
Toronto, Ontario
M5A 2P9
www.mcclelland.com

2 3 4 5 15

For Marge

PROLOGUE

They wait for the tide and set out at first light.

It has rained all night and in the morning the ground is seething gently, the mist rising up to join the overhanging clouds. Nelson calls for Ruth in an unmarked police car. He sits beside the driver and Ruth is in the back, like a passenger in a minicab. They drive in silence to the car park near where the bones were first found. As they drive along the Saltmarsh road, the only sounds are the sudden, staccato crackle of the police radio and the driver's heavy, cold-clogged breathing. Nelson says nothing. There is nothing to say.

They get out of the car and walk across the rain-sodden grass towards the marsh. The wind is whispering through the reeds, and here and there they see glimpses of still, sullen water reflecting the grey sky. At the edge of the marshland Ruth stops, looking for the first sunken post, the twisting shingle path that leads through the treacherous water and out to the mudflats. When she finds it, half-submerged by brackish water, she sets out without looking back.

Silently, they cross the marshes. As they get nearer the sea, the mist disperses and the sun starts to filter through the clouds. At the henge circle, the tide is out and the sand glitters in the early morning light. Ruth kneels on the ground as she saw Erik doing all those years ago. Gently, she stirs the quivering mud with her trowel.

Suddenly everything is quiet; even the seabirds stop their mad skirling and calling up above. Or maybe they are still there and she just doesn't hear them. In the background she can hear Nelson breathing hard but Ruth herself feels strangely calm. Even when she sees it, the tiny arm still wearing the christening bracelet, even then she feels nothing.

She had known what she was going to find.

CHAPTER 1

Waking is like rising from the dead. The slow climb out of sleep, shapes appearing out of blackness, the alarm clock ringing like the last trump. Ruth flings out an arm and sends the alarm crashing to the floor, where it carries on ringing reproachfully. Groaning, she levers herself upright and pulls up the blind. Still dark. It's just not right, she tells herself, wincing as her feet touch the cold floorboards. Neolithic man would have gone to sleep when the sun set and woken when it rose. What makes us think this is the right way round? Falling asleep on the sofa during *Newsnight*, then dragging herself upstairs to lie sleepless over an Inspector Rebus book, listen to the World Service on the radio, count Iron Age burial sites to make herself sleep and now this; waking in the darkness feeling like death. It just wasn't right somehow.

In the shower, the water unglues her eyes and sends her hair streaming down her back. This is baptism, if you like. Ruth's parents are Born Again Christians and are fans of Full Immersion For Adults (capitals obligatory). Ruth can quite see the attraction, apart from the slight problem of not believing in God. Still, her parents are Praying For Her (capitals again), which should be a comfort but somehow isn't.

Ruth rubs herself vigorously with a towel and stares unseeingly into the steamy mirror. She knows what she will see and the knowledge is no more comforting than her parents' prayers. Shoulder-length brown hair, blue eyes, pale skin – and however she stands on the scales, which are at present banished to the broom cupboard – she weighs 175 pounds. She sighs (I am not defined by my weight, fat is a state of mind) and squeezes toothpaste onto her brush. She has a very beautiful smile, but she isn't smiling now and so this too is low on the list of comforts.

Clean, damp-footed, she pads back into the bedroom. She has lectures today so will have to dress slightly more formally than usual. Black trousers, black shapeless top. She hardly looks as she selects the clothes. She likes colour and fabric; in fact she has quite a weakness for sequins, bugle beads and diamanté. You wouldn't know this from her wardrobe though. A dour row of dark trousers and loose, dark jackets. The drawers in her pine dressing table are full of black jumpers, long cardigans and opaque tights. She used to wear jeans until she hit size sixteen and now favours cords, black, of course. Jeans are too young for her anyhow. She will be forty next year.

Dressed, she negotiates the stairs. The tiny cottage has very steep stairs, more like a ladder than anything else. 'I'll never be able to manage those,' her mother had said on her one and only visit. Who's asking you to, Ruth had replied silently. Her parents had stayed at the local B and B as Ruth has only one bedroom; going upstairs was strictly unnecessary (there is a downstairs loo but it is by the kitchen, which her mother considers unsanitary). The stairs lead directly into the sitting room: sanded wooden floor, comfortable faded sofa, large flat-screen TV, books covering every available surface. Archaeology books, mostly, but also murder mysteries, cookery books, travel guides, doctor–nurse romances. Ruth is nothing if not eclectic in her tastes. She has a particular fondness for children's books about ballet or horse-riding, neither of which she has ever tried.

The kitchen barely has room for a fridge and a cooker but Ruth, despite the books, rarely cooks. Now she switches on the kettle and puts bread into the toaster, clicking on Radio 4 with a practised hand. Then she collects her lecture notes and sits at the table by the front window. Her favourite place. Beyond her front garden with its windblown grass and broken blue fence there is nothingness. Just miles and miles of marshland, spotted with stunted gorse bushes and criss-crossed with small, treacherous streams. Sometimes, at this time of year, you see great flocks of wild geese wheeling across the sky, their feathers turning pink in the rays of the rising sun. But today, on this grey winter morning, there is not a living creature as far as the eye can see. Everything is pale and washed out, grey-green merging to grey-white as the marsh meets the sky. Far off is the sea, a line of darker grey, seagulls riding in on the waves. It is utterly desolate and Ruth has absolutely no idea why she loves it so much.

She eats her toast and drinks her tea (she prefers coffee but is saving herself for a proper espresso at the university). As she does so, she leafs through her lecture notes, originally typewritten but now scribbled over with a palimpsest of additional notes in different coloured pens. 'Gender and

Prehistoric Technology', 'Excavating Artefacts', 'Life and Death in the Mesolithic', 'The Role of Animal Bone in Excavations'. Although it is only early November, the Christmas term will soon be over and this will be her last week of lectures. Briefly, she conjures up the faces of her students: earnest, hard-working, slightly dull. She only teaches postgraduates these days and rather misses the casual, hungover good humour of the undergraduates. Her students are so *keen*, waylaying her after lectures to talk about Lindow Man and Boxgrove Man and whether women really would have played a significant role in prehistoric society. Look around you, she wants to shout, we don't always play a significant role in *this* society. Why do you think a gang of grunting hunter-gatherers would have been any more enlightened than we?

Thought for the Day seeps into her unconscious, reminding her that it is time to leave. 'In some ways, God is like an iPod ...' She puts her plate and cup in the sink and leaves down food for her cats, Sparky and Flint. As she does so, she answers the ever-present sardonic interviewer in her head. 'OK, I'm a single, overweight woman on my own and I have cats. What's the big deal? And, OK, sometimes I do speak to them but I don't imagine that they answer back and I don't pretend that I'm any more to them than a convenient food dispenser.' Right on cue, Flint, a large ginger Tom, squeezes himself through the cat flap and fixes her with an unblinking, golden stare.

'Does God feature on our Recently Played list or do we sometimes have to press Shuffle?'

Ruth strokes Flint and goes back into the sitting room to

put her papers into her backpack. She winds a red scarf (her only concession to colour: even fat people can buy scarves) round her neck and puts on her anorak. Then she turns out the lights and leaves the cottage.

Ruth's cottage is one in a line of three on the edge of the Saltmarsh. One is occupied by the warden of the bird sanctuary, the other by weekenders who come down in summer, have lots of toxic barbecues and park their 4 × 4 in front of Ruth's view. The road is frequently flooded in spring and autumn and often impassable by midwinter. 'Why don't you live somewhere more convenient?' her colleagues ask. 'There are some lovely properties in King's Lynn, or even Blakeney if you want to be near to nature.' Ruth can't explain, even to herself, how a girl born and brought up in South London can feel such a pull to these inhospitable marshlands, these desolate mudflats, this lonely, unrelenting view. It was research that first brought her to the Saltmarsh but she doesn't know herself what it is that makes her stay, in the face of so much opposition. 'I'm used to it,' is all she says. 'Anyway the cats would hate to move.' And they laugh. Good old Ruth, devoted to her cats, child-substitutes of course, shame she never got married, she's really very pretty when she smiles.

Today, though, the road is clear, with only the ever-present wind blowing a thin line of salt onto her windscreen. She squirts water without noticing it, bumps slowly over the cattle grid and negotiates the twisting road that leads to the village. In summer the trees meet over-head, making this a mysterious green tunnel. But today the trees are mere skeletons, their bare arms stretching up to the sky. Ruth, driving slightly faster than is prudent, passes the four houses and boarded-up pub that constitute the village and takes the turning for King's Lynn. Her first lecture is at ten. She has plenty of time.

Ruth teaches at the University of North Norfolk (UNN is the unprepossessing acronym), a new university just outside King's Lynn. She teaches archaeology, which is a new discipline there, specialising in forensic archaeology, which is newer still. Phil, her head of department, frequently jokes that there is nothing new about archaeology and Ruth always smiles dutifully. It is only a matter of time, she thinks, before Phil gets himself a bumper sticker. 'Archaeologists dig it.' 'You're never too old for an archaeologist.' Her special interest is bones. Why didn't the skeleton go to the ball? Because he had no body to dance with. She has heard them all but she still laughs every time. Last year her students bought her a life-size cut-out of Bones from *Star Trek*. He stands at the top of her stairs, terrifying the cats.

On the radio someone is discussing life after death. Why do we feel the need to create a heaven? Is this a sign that there is one or just wishful thinking on a massive scale? Ruth's parents talk about heaven as if it is very familiar, a kind of cosmic shopping centre where they will know their way around and have free passes for the park-and-ride, and where Ruth will languish forever in the underground car park. Until she is Born Again, of course. Ruth prefers the Catholic heaven, remembered from student trips to Italy and Spain. Vast cloudy skies, incense and smoke, darkness and mystery. Ruth likes the Vast: paintings by John Martin, the Vatican, the Norfolk sky.

Just as well, she thinks wryly as she negotiates the turn into the university grounds.

The university consists of long, low buildings, linked by glass walkways. On grey mornings like this it looks inviting, the buttery light shining out across the myriad car parks, a row of dwarf lamps lighting the way to the Archaeology and Natural Sciences Building. Closer to, it looks less impressive. Though the building is only ten years old, cracks are appearing in the concrete façade, there is graffiti on the walls and a good third of the dwarf lamps don't work. Ruth hardly notices this, however, as she parks in her usual space and hauls out her heavy backpack – heavy because it is half-full of bones.

Climbing the dank-smelling staircase to her office, she thinks about her first lecture: First Principles in Excavation. Although they are postgraduates, many of her students will have little or no first-hand experience of digs. Many are from overseas (the university needs the fees) and the frozen East Anglian earth will be quite a culture shock for them. This is why they won't do their first official dig until April.

As she scrabbles for her key card in the corridor, she is aware of two people approaching her. One is Phil, the head of department, the other she doesn't recognise. He is tall and dark, with greying hair cut very short and there is something hard about him, something contained and slightly dangerous that makes her think that he can't be a student and certainly not a lecturer. She stands aside to let them pass but, to her surprise, Phil stops in front of her and speaks in a serious voice which nevertheless contains an ill-concealed edge of excitement.

'Ruth. There's someone who wants to meet you.'

A student after all, then. Ruth starts to paste a welcoming smile on her face but it is frozen by Phil's next words.

'This is Detective Chief Inspector Harry Nelson. He wants to talk to you about a murder.'

CHAPTER 2

'Suspected murder,' Detective Chief Inspector Harry Nelson says quickly.

'Yes, yes,' says Phil, just as quickly, shooting a look at Ruth as if to say, 'Look at me talking to a real detective.' Ruth keeps her face impassive.

'This is Doctor Ruth Galloway,' says Phil. 'She's our forensics expert.'

'Pleased to meet you,' says Nelson without smiling. He gestures towards the locked door of Ruth's office. 'Can we?'

Ruth slides in her key card and pushes open the door. Her office is tiny, barely six feet across. One wall is entirely taken up by bookshelves, another by the door and a third by a grubby window with a view of an even grubbier ornamental lake. Ruth's desk squats against the fourth wall, with a framed poster of Indiana Jones – ironical, she always explains hastily – hanging over it. When she has tutorials the students frequently spill out into the corridor and she props the door open with her cat doorstop, a present from Peter. But now she slams the door shut and Phil and the detective stand there awkwardly, looking too big for the space. Nelson, in particular, seems to block out all the light as he stands, scowling, in front of the window. He looks too broad, too tall, too *grown up* for the room.

'Please ...' Ruth gestures to the chairs stacked by the door. Phil makes a great performance of giving Nelson his chair first, practically wiping away the dust with his jumper sleeve.

Ruth squeezes behind her desk, which gives her an illusion of security, of being in charge. This illusion is instantly shattered when Nelson leans back, crosses his legs and addresses her in a brisk monotone. He has a slight Northern accent, which only serves to make him sound more efficient, as if he hasn't time for the slow vowels of Norfolk.

'We've found some bones,' he says. 'They seem to be a child's but they look old. I need to know how old.'

Ruth is silent but Phil chips in eagerly. 'Where did you find them, Inspector?'

'Near the bird sanctuary. Saltmarsh.'

Phil looks at Ruth. 'But that's right where you ...'

'I know it,' Ruth cuts in. 'What makes you think the bones look old?'

'They're brown, discoloured, but they look in good condition. I thought that was your area,' he says, suddenly aggressive.

'It is,' says Ruth calmly. 'I assume that's why you're here?'

'Well, would you be able to tell if they are modern or not?' asks Nelson, again sounding rather belligerent.

'A recent discovery is usually obvious,' says Ruth, 'you can tell by appearance and surface. Older bones are more tricky. Sometimes it's almost impossible to tell fifty-year-old bones from two-thousand-year-old. You need radiocarbon dating for that.'

'Professor Galloway is an expert on bone preservation.' This is Phil again, anxious not to be left out. 'She's worked in Bosnia, on the war graves ...'

'Will you come and look?' Nelson interrupts.

Ruth pretends to consider but, of course, she is utterly fascinated. Bones! On the Saltmarsh! Where she did that first unforgettable dig with Erik. It could be anything. It could be a find. It could be ...

'You suspect it's a murder?' she asks.

Nelson looks uncomfortable for the first time. 'I'd rather not say,' he says heavily, 'not at the present time. Will you come and look?'

Ruth stands up. 'I've got a lecture at ten. I could come in my lunch break.'

'I'll send a car for you at twelve,' says Nelson.

Much to Ruth's secret disappointment, Nelson does not send a police car complete with flashing blue light. Instead he appears himself, driving a muddy Mercedes. She is waiting, as agreed, by the main gate, and he does not even get out of the car but merely leans over and opens the passenger door. Ruth climbs in, feeling fat, as she always does in cars. She has a morbid dread of the seatbelt not fitting around her or of some invisible weight sensor setting off a shrill alarm. 'One hundred and seventy-five pounds! One hundred and seventy-five pounds in car! Emergency! Press ejector button.'

Nelson glances at Ruth's backpack. 'Got everything you need?'

'Yes.' She has brought her instant excavation kit: pointing trowel, small hand shovel, plastic freezer bags for samples, tapes, notebook, pencils, paint brushes, compass, digital camera. She has also changed into trainers and is wearing a reflective jacket. She is annoyed to find herself thinking that she must look a complete mess.

'So you live out Saltmarsh way?' Nelson says, pulling out across the traffic with a squeal of tires. He drives like a maniac.

'Yes,' says Ruth, feeling defensive though she doesn't know why. 'New Road.'

'New Road!' Nelson lets out a bark of laughter. 'I thought only twitchers lived out there.'

'Well, the warden of the bird sanctuary is one of my neighbours,' says Ruth, struggling to remain polite while keeping one foot clamped on an imaginary brake.

'I wouldn't fancy it,' says Nelson. 'Too isolated.'

'I like it,' says Ruth. 'I did a dig there and never left.'

'A dig? Archaeology?'

'Yes.' Ruth is remembering that summer, ten years ago. Sitting around the campfire in the evenings, eating burnt sausages and singing corny songs. The sound of birdsong in the mornings and the marsh blooming purple with sea lavender. The time when sheep trampled their tents at night. The time when Peter got stranded out on the tidal marsh and Erik had to rescue him, crawling on his hands and knees across the mudflats. The unbelievable excitement when they found that first wooden post, proof that the henge actually existed. She remembers the exact sound of Erik's voice as he turned and shouted at them across the incoming tide, 'We've found it!'

She turns to Nelson. 'We were looking for a henge.'

'A henge? Like Stonehenge?'

'Yes. All it means is a circular bank with a ditch around it. Usually with posts inside the circle.'

'I read somewhere that Stonehenge is just a big sundial. A way of telling the time.'

'Well, we don't know exactly what it was for,' says Ruth, 'but it's safe to say that it involves ritual of some kind.'

Nelson shoots a strange look at her.

'Ritual?'

'Yes, worship, offerings, sacrifices.'

'Sacrifices?' echoes Nelson. He seems genuinely interested now; the faintly condescending note has disappeared from his voice.

'Well, sometimes we find evidence of sacrifices. Pots, spears, animal bones.'

'What about human bones? Do you ever find human bones?'

'Yes, sometimes human bones.'

There is silence and then Nelson says, 'Funny place for one of those henge things, isn't it? Right out to sea.'

'This wasn't sea then. Landscape changes. Only ten thousand years ago this country was still linked to the continent. You could walk from here to Scandinavia.'

'You're joking!'

'No. King's Lynn was once a huge tidal lake. That's what Lynn means. It's the Celtic word for lake.'

Nelson turns to look sceptically at her, causing the car to swerve alarmingly. Ruth wonders if he suspects her of making the whole thing up.

'So if this area wasn't sea, what was it?'

'Flat marshland. We think the henge was on the edge of a marsh.'

'Still seems a funny place to build something like that.'

'Marshland is very important in prehistory,' explains Ruth. 'It's a kind of symbolic landscape. We think that it was important because it's a link between the land and the sea, or between life and death.'

Nelson snorts. 'Come again?'

'Well, marsh isn't dry land and it isn't sea. It's a sort of mixture of both. We know it was important to prehistoric man.'

'How do we know?'

'We've found objects left on the edge of marshes. Votive hoards.'

'Votive?'

'Offerings to the Gods, left at special or sacred places. And sometimes bodies. Have you heard of bog bodies? Lindow Man?'

'Might have,' says Nelson cautiously.

'Bodies buried in peat are almost perfectly preserved, but some people think the bodies were buried in the bogs for a purpose. To appease the Gods.'

Nelson shoots her another look but says nothing. They are approaching the Saltmarsh now, driving up from the lower road towards the visitor car park. Notices listing the various birds to be found on the marshes stand around forlornly, battered by the wind. A boarded-up kiosk advertises ice-creams, their lurid colours faded now. It seems impossible to imagine people picnicking here, enjoying ice-creams in the sun. The place seems made for the wind and the rain.

The car park is empty apart from a solitary police car.

The occupant gets out as they approach and stands there, looking cold and fed up.

'Doctor Ruth Galloway,' Nelson introduces briskly, 'Detective Sergeant Clough.'

DS Clough nods glumly. Ruth gets the impression that hanging about on a windy marshland is not his favourite way of passing the time. Nelson, though, looks positively eager, jogging slightly on the spot like a racehorse in sight of the gallops. He leads the way along a gravel path marked 'Visitor's Trail'. They pass a wooden hide, built on stilts over the marsh. It is empty, apart from some crisp wrappers and an empty can of Coke lying on the surrounding platform.

Nelson, without stopping, points at the litter and barks, 'Bag it.' Ruth has to admire his thoroughness, if not his manners. It occurs to her that police work must be rather similar to archaeology. She, too, would bag anything found at a site, labelling it carefully to give it a context. She, too, would be prepared to search for days, weeks, in the hope of finding something significant. She, too, she realises with a sudden shiver, is primarily concerned with death.

Ruth is out of breath before they find the spot marked out with the blue and white police tape that reminds her of traffic accidents. Nelson is now some ten yards ahead, hands in pockets, head forward as if sniffing the air. Clough plods behind him, holding a plastic bag containing the rubbish from the hide.

Beyond the tape is a shallow hole, half-filled by muddy water. Ruth ducks under the tape and kneels down to look. Clearly visible in the rich mud are human bones.

'How did you find this?' she asks.

It is Clough who answers. 'Member of the public, walking her dog. Animal actually had one of the bones in its mouth.'

'Did you keep it? The bone, I mean.'

'It's at the station.'

Ruth takes a quick photo of the site and sketches a brief map in her notebook. This is the far west of the marsh; she has never dug here before. The beach, where the henge was found, is about two miles away to the east. Squatting down on the muddy soil, she begins laboriously bailing out the water, using a plastic beaker from her excavation kit. Nelson is almost hopping with impatience.

'Can't we help with that?' he asks.

'No,' says Ruth shortly.

When the hole is almost free from water, Ruth's heart starts to beat faster. Carefully she scoops out another beakerful of water and only then reaches into the mud and exposes something that is pressed flat against the dark soil.

'Well?' Nelson is leaning eagerly over her shoulder.

'It's a body,' says Ruth hesitantly, 'but ...'

Slowly she reaches for her trowel. She mustn't rush things. She has seen entire excavations ruined because of one moment's carelessness. So, with Nelson grinding his teeth beside her, she gently lifts away the sodden soil. A hand, slightly clenched, wearing a bracelet of what looks like grass, lies exposed in the trench.

'Bloody hell!' murmurs Nelson over her shoulder.

She is working almost in a trance now. She plots the find on her map, noting which way it is facing. Next she takes a photograph and starts to dig again.

This time her trowel grates against metal. Still working slowly and meticulously, Ruth reaches down and pulls the object free from the mud. It gleams dully in the winter light, the sixpence in the Christmas cake: a lump of twisted metal, semi-circular in shape.

'What's that?' Nelson's voice seems to come from another world.

'I think it's a torque,' says Ruth dreamily.

'What the hell's that?'

'A necklace. Probably from the Iron Age.'

'The Iron Age? When was that?'

'About two thousand years ago,' says Ruth.

Clough lets out a sudden bark of laughter. Nelson turns away without a word.

Nelson gives Ruth a lift back to the university. He seems sunk in gloom but Ruth is in a state of high excitement. An Iron Age body, because the bodies must surely be from the Iron Age, that time of ritual slaughter and fabulous treasure hoards. What does it mean? It's a long way from the henge but could the two discoveries possibly be linked? The henge is early Bronze Age, over a thousand years before the Iron Age. But surely another find on the same site can't simply be coincidence? She can't wait to tell Phil. Perhaps they should inform the press; the publicity might be just what the Department needs.

Nelson says suddenly, 'You're sure about the date?'

'I'm pretty sure about the torque, that's definitely Iron Age and it seems logical that the body was buried with it. But we can do carbon 14 dating to be sure.'

'What's that?'

'Carbon 14 is present in the earth's atmosphere. Plants take it in, animals eat the plants, we eat the animals. So we all absorb carbon 14 and, when we die, we stop absorbing it and the carbon 14 in our bones starts to break down. So, by measuring the amount of carbon 14 left in a bone, we can tell its age.'

'How accurate is it?'

'Well, cosmic radiation can skew the findings – sun spots, solar flares, nuclear testing, that sort of thing. But it can be accurate within a range of a few hundred years. So we'll be able to tell if the bones are roughly from the Iron Age.'

'Which was when exactly?'

'I can't be that exact but roughly seven hundred BC to forty-three AD.'

Nelson is silent for a moment, taking this in, and then he asks, 'Why would an Iron Age body be buried here?'

'As an offering to the Gods. Possibly it would have been staked down. Did you see the grass around the wrist? That could have been a rope of some kind.'

'Jesus. Staked down and left to die?'

'Well maybe, or maybe it was dead before they left it here. The stakes would be just to keep it in place.'

'Jesus,' he says again.

Suddenly Ruth remembers why she is here, in this police car, with this man. 'Why did you think the bones might be modern?' she asks.

Nelson sighs. 'Some ten years ago there was a child that went missing. Near here. We never found the body. I thought it might be her.'

'Her?'

'Her name was Lucy Downey.'

Ruth is silent. Having a name makes it all more real somehow. After all, hadn't the archaeologist who discovered the first modern human given her a name? Funnily enough, she was called Lucy too.

Nelson sighs again. 'There were letters sent to me about the Lucy Downey case. It's funny, what you said earlier.'

'What?' asks Ruth, rather bemused.

'About ritual and that. There was all sorts of rubbish in the letters but one thing they said was that Lucy had been a sacrifice and that we'd find her where the earth meets the sky.'

'Where the earth meets the sky,' Ruth repeats. 'But that could be anywhere.'

'Yes, but this place, it feels like the end of the world somehow. That's why, when I heard that bones had been found ...'

'You thought they might be hers?'

'Yes. It's hard for the parents when they don't know. Sometimes, finding a body, it gives them a chance to grieve.'

'You're sure she's dead then?'

Nelson is silent for a moment before replying, concentrating on overtaking a lorry on the inside. 'Yes,' he says at last. 'Five-year-old child, goes missing in November, no sign of her for ten years. She's dead alright.'

'November?'

'Yes. Almost ten years ago to the day.'

Ruth thinks of November, the darkening nights, the wind howling over the marshes. She thinks of the parents, waiting, praying for their daughter's return, jumping at every phone call, hoping that every day might bring news. The slow ebbing away of hope, the dull certainty of loss.

'The parents,' she asks. 'Do they still live nearby?'

'Yes, they live out Fakenham way.' He swerves to avoid a lorry. Ruth closes her eyes. 'Cases like this,' he goes on, 'it's usually the parents.'

Ruth is shocked. 'The parents who killed the child?'

Nelson's voice is matter-of-fact, the Northern vowels very flat. 'Nine cases out of ten. You get the parents all distraught, news conferences, floods of tears and then we find the child buried in the back garden.'

'How awful.'

'Yes. But this case, I don't know, I'm sure it wasn't them. They were a nice couple, not young, been trying for a baby for years and then Lucy came along. They adored her.'

'How dreadful for them,' says Ruth inadequately.

'Dreadful, yes.' Nelson's voice is expressionless. 'But they never blamed us. Never blamed me or the team. They still send me Christmas cards. That's why I –' He falters for a second. 'That's why I wanted a result for them.'

They are at the university now. Nelson screeches to a halt outside the Natural Sciences building. Students hurrying to lectures turn and stare. Although it is only two-thirty, it is already getting dark.

'Thanks for the lift,' says Ruth slightly awkwardly. 'I'll get the bones dated for you.'

'Thanks,' says Nelson. He looks at Ruth for what seems to be the first time. She is acutely aware of her wild hair and mud-stained clothes. 'This discovery, might it be important for you?'

'Yes,' says Ruth. 'It might be.'

'Glad someone's happy.' As soon as Ruth is out of the car he drives off without saying goodbye. She doesn't think she will ever see him again.

CHAPTER 3

Nelson cuts across two lanes of traffic as he heads into King's Lynn. His car is unmarked but he makes it a point of honour always to drive as if he is pursuing a suspect. He enjoys the expressions on the faces of the clueless uniforms when, after pulling them in for speeding, he flourishes his warrant card. In any case, this route is so familiar that he could drive it in his sleep: past the industrial park and the Campbell's soup factory, along the London Road and through the archway in the old city wall. Doctor Ruth Galloway would be sure to tell him exactly how old this wall is: 'I can't be that exact but I estimate that it was built before lunch on Friday 1 February 1556'. But, to Nelson, it just represents a final traffic jam before he reaches the police station.

He is no fan of his adopted county. He is a northerner, born in Blackpool, within sight of the Golden Mile. He went to the Catholic grammar school, St Joseph's (Holy Joe's as it was known locally) and joined the police as a cadet, aged sixteen. Right from the start, he'd loved the job. He loved the camaraderie, the long hours, the physical exertion, the sense of doing something worthwhile. And, though he would never admit it, he'd even liked the paperwork. Nelson is methodical, he likes lists and schedules, he is excellent at cutting through crap. He'd risen through the ranks and soon had a pretty good life: satisfying work, congenial mates, pub on Friday nights, the match on Saturdays, golf on Sundays.

But then the job in Norfolk had come up and his wife, Michelle, had been on at him to take it. Promotion, more money, and 'the chance to live in the country'. Who in their right mind, thinks Nelson, thinking of the Saltmarsh, would want to live in the bloody country? It's all cows and mud and locals who look like the result of several generations of keeping it in the family. But he'd given in and they had moved to King's Lynn. Michelle had started working for a posh hairdressing salon. They'd sent the girls to private schools and they'd come back laughing at his accent ('It's not bath, Daddy, it's ba-arth ...'). He'd done well, become a detective inspector in double quick time; people had even talked of higher things. Until Lucy Downey went missing.

Nelson turns, without indicating, into the station car park. He is thinking of Lucy and of the body on the marsh. He had always been sure that Lucy was buried somewhere near the Saltmarsh, and when the bones were found he thought that he was near an ending at last. Not a happy ending, but at least an ending. And now this Doctor Ruth Galloway tells him that the bones are from some bloody Stone Age body. Jesus, all that stuff she'd spouted about henges and burials and being able to walk to Scandinavia. He'd thought she was taking the piss at first. But, when they got to the site, he could see she was a professional. He admired the way that she did everything slowly and carefully, making notes, taking photos, sifting the evidence. It's the way that police work should be done. Not that she'd ever make a policewoman. Too overweight, for one thing. What would Michelle say about a woman so out-of-condition that she is out of breath after a five-minute walk? She would be genuinely horrified. But, then, he can't think of any situation in which Michelle would meet Doctor Ruth Galloway. She's not likely to start popping into the salon, not from what he could see of her hair.

But she interests him. Like all forceful people (he calls it forceful rather than bullying), he prefers people who stand up to him, but in his job that doesn't happen often. People either despise him or kowtow to him. Ruth had done neither. She had looked him in the face, coolly, as an equal. He thinks he's never met anyone, any *woman*, quite as sure of themselves as Ruth Galloway. Even the way she dresses – baggy clothes, trainers – seemed to be a way of saying that she doesn't care what anyone thinks. She's not going to tart herself up in skirts and high heels just to please men. Not that there's anything wrong with pleasing men, muses Nelson, kicking open the door to his office, but there's something interesting, even refreshing, about a woman who doesn't care whether or not she's attractive.

And the things she said about ritual were interesting too. Nelson is frowning as he sits behind his desk. Talking about ritual and sacrifice and all that crap has brought it all back: the days and nights spent in fingertip searches, the anguished meetings with the parents, the gradual, unbearable shift from hope to despair, the station full to bursting point, teams brought in from six different forces, all dedicated to finding one little girl. All in vain.

Nelson sighs. However much he tries not to, he knows

that, before he goes home tonight, he will read through the Lucy Downey files.

It is pitch black by the time Ruth drives home, edging her car carefully along New Road. There are ditches on both sides of the road and the merest twitch on the wheel can send you plunging ignominiously downwards. This has happened to Ruth once before and she is not keen to repeat the experience. Her headlights illuminate the raised tarmac of the road; the land drops away on either side so that she seems to be driving into nothingness. Nothing but the road ahead and the sky above. *Where the earth meets the sky.* She shivers and turns on the car radio. Radio 4, soothing, civilised and slightly smug, fills the car. 'And now for the News Quiz ...'

Ruth parks outside her broken blue fence and pulls her backpack out of the trunk. The weekenders' house is in darkness but the warden has a light on upstairs. She assumes he goes to bed early so as to be up for the dawn chorus. Flint appears on her doorstep mewing piteously for admittance even though he has his own cat-flap and has, in fact, been snoozing inside all day. Remembering she hasn't yet seen Sparky, Ruth feels a pang of anxiety as she opens the door. But Sparky, a small black cat with a white nose, is sleeping safely on the sofa. Ruth calls her but she stays put, flexing her claws and shutting her eyes. Sparky is a reserved character, quite unlike Flint who is now weaving ecstatically around Ruth's legs.

'Stop it, you stupid cat.'

She drops her backpack on the table and puts down food for the cats. Her answerphone light is flashing. She has a feeling that it won't be good news and when she presses

PLAY she is right. Her mother's voice, aggrieved and slightly breathless, fills the room.

'... whether you're coming for Christmas. Really, Ruth, you could be a bit more considerate. I heard from Simon weeks ago. I assume you'll be coming because I can't imagine you'll want to spend Christmas on your own in that awful ...'

Ruth clicks DELETE, breathing hard. In just a few short sentences her mother has managed to encapsulate years of irritation and subtle put-down. The accusation of inconsiderate behaviour, the comparison with the perfect Simon, the implication that, if she doesn't visit her parents, Ruth's Christmas will consist of a Marks & Spencer meal for one in front of the TV. Angrily sloshing wine into a glass (her mother's voice: 'How are your units Ruth? Daddy and I are worried you're getting dependent ...'), Ruth composes a reply. She will never give it in person but it is comforting to stomp around the kitchen, cutting her mother down to size with thin slices of logic.

'The reason I haven't told you about Christmas is that I dread coming home and hearing you drone on about the Christ child and the true meaning of Christmas. Simon has been in touch because he's a creep and an arse-licker. And if I don't come home I'll be with my friends or on some tropical island, not alone slumped in front of *The Vicar of Dibley*. And my house isn't awful, it's a hundred times better than your Eltham semi with its pine cladding and vile china ornaments. And Peter didn't finish with me, I finished with him.'

She has added the last one because she knows from experience that her mother will bring up the subject of

Peter sometime over Christmas. 'Peter sent us a card ... Such a shame ... Do you ever hear? ... You know he's married now?' That her daughter could voluntarily end a relationship with a nice-looking, eligible man is something that Ruth's mother will never be able to accept. Ruth noticed the same tendency in her friends and colleagues when she announced that she and Peter were no longer together. 'I'm so sorry ... Has he found someone else? ... Don't worry, he'll come back ...' Ruth explained patiently that she had ended the relationship five years ago for the simple, yet surprisingly complicated, reason that she no longer loved him. 'That's right,' people would say, ignoring her, 'he'll soon get bored with the new woman. In the meantime, pamper yourself, have a massage, maybe even lose some ...'

To cheer herself up, Ruth boils the water for some nice, fattening pasta and rings Erik. Her first university tutor, Erik Anderssen, predictably nicknamed Erik the Viking, was the man responsible for getting her into forensic archaeology. He has been a huge influence on her life and is now a close friend. Smiling, she conjures him up: silver-blond hair pulled back in a ponytail, faded jeans, unravelling sweater. She knows he will be passionately interested in today's find.

Erik the Viking has, appropriately enough, moved back to Norway. Ruth visited him last summer, in his log cabin by the lake – freezing morning swims followed by steaming saunas, Magda's wonderful food, talking to Erik about Mayan civilisation as the stars came out at night. Madga, his wife, a voluptuous blonde goddess whose beauty manages to make you feel better, not worse, about yourself, is another good friend. *She* never once mentioned Peter, even though she had been there that summer when Ruth and Peter first fell in love; had, in fact, by her tact and gentle benevolence, actually brought them together.

But Erik is out. Ruth leaves a message and, feeling restless, gets the battered lump of metal out of her backpack and examines it. Still in its freezer bag, carefully dated and labelled, it stares back at her. Phil wanted her to leave it in the Department safe but she refused. She had wanted to bring the torque home, to the Saltmarsh, at least for one night. Now she examines it under her desk light.

Stained dark green from its long immersion in the marsh, the metal nonetheless has a burnished sheen that looks like it might be gold. A gold torque! How much would that be worth? She thinks of the so-called 'marriage torc' found near here, at Snettisham. That had been a wonderful, elaborate object, showing a human face with a ring through its mouth. This piece is more battered; perhaps it has been broken by ploughing or digging. However, squinting closely, she can just see a twisted pattern, almost like a plait. The piece in her hand is barely fifteen centimetres long but she can imagine it as a full half-circle, imagine it round the neck of some savage beauty. Or round the neck of a child, a sacrificial victim?

She remembers Nelson's bitter disappointment when he learnt that the bones were not those of Lucy Downey. What must it feel like to have those deaths, those ghosts, forever on your mind? Ruth knows that for him the Iron Age bones are an annoyance, an irrelevancy, but for her they are as real as the five-year-old girl who went missing all those years ago. Why were the bones left on the edges of the marsh? Was she (from their size, Ruth thinks the bones are female but she cannot be sure) left for dead, sinking in the treacherous mud? Or was she killed somewhere else and buried at the start of the marshland, to mark the beginning of the sacred landscape?

When her pasta is cooked Ruth eats it at the table by the window, Erik's book *The Shivering Sand* propped up in front of her. The title is from *The Moonstone* by Wilkie Collins and Ruth turns again to the first page where Erik quotes Collins' description of the sands:

> The last of the evening light was fading away; and over all the desolate place there hung a still and awful calm. The heave of the main ocean on the great sand-bank out in the bay, was a heave that made no sound. The inner sea lay lost and dim, without a breath of wind to stir it. Patches of nasty ooze floated, yellow-white on the dead surface of the water. Scum and slime shone faintly in certain places, where the last of the light still caught them on the two great spits of rock jutting out, north and south, into the sea. It was now the time of the turn of the tide: and even as I stood there waiting, the broad brown face of the quicksand began to dimple and quiver – the only moving thing in all the horrid place.

Collins, surely, had understood about the ritual landscape of the sea and land and of the haunted, uncanny places that lie between the two. Ruth remembers that at least one character in *The Moonstone* meets their death on the sands. She remembers another phrase, 'What the Sand gets, the Sand keeps forever.' But the Saltmarsh had given up some of its secrets; first the henge and now this body, just waiting there for Ruth to discover them. Surely there *must* be a link.

Reading again about the discovery of the henge (Erik wrote at least three books on the strength of the find), Ruth remembers how eerie it had looked in that first morning light, like a shipwreck that had risen silently to the surface, the wooden posts forming a sombre ring, black against the sky. She remembers Erik telling fireside stories about Norse water spirits: the Nixes, shape-shifters who lure unwary travellers into the water; the Nokke, river sprites who sing at dawn and dusk. Water as a source of life and a place of death. Water is also often associated with women; women with vengeance in their hearts, luring men to a watery grave. Drowned spirits, their hair flowing green around them, their webbed hands reaching out above the turning tide ...

Ruth reads on, her pasta forgotten. She has no lectures tomorrow; she will go back to the place where the bones were buried.

But in the morning it is raining, driving, slanting rain that batters against the windows and envelops the marsh in an impenetrable grey haze. Frustrated, Ruth busies herself with work: writing up lecture notes, ordering books from Amazon, even cleaning out her fridge. But she keeps coming back to the torque lying in its freezer bag on the table by the window. Sensing her interest, Flint jumps up and sits heavily on the bag. Ruth pushes him off. She doesn't want Phil to notice the cat hairs. He is apt to be whimsical about the cats, calling them 'Ruth's familiars'. She grits her teeth. He is not going to be whimsical about this find. Phil has always been rather sceptical about Erik the Viking and his views on ritual landscape. For the Iron Age people the henge was already ancient, probably as much of a mystery to them as it is to us. Did they bury this body in the mud to symbolise the beginning of this mystic landscape? Or was the victim ritually killed to appease the water spirits? If Ruth can prove a link between the body and the henge, then the whole area becomes significant. Saltmarsh could become a major archaeological site.

By lunchtime she thinks that the weather is improving slightly. She goes out as far as the gate and the rain is soft and friendly on her face. It is ridiculous really, because the trench will have filled with water and she can do no real work on her own, but she makes up her mind to walk to the site. It's not far, maybe a mile away, and the exercise will do her good. She tells herself this briskly as she puts on the sou'wester and waders she'd bought for a dig in the Outer Hebrides, puts a flashlight in her pocket and shrugs her pack onto her back. She's just going for a look, that's all. A nice brisk walk before it gets dark. Better than sitting at home wondering and eating biscuits.

At first it is quite pleasant. She is walking with her back to the wind and the sou'wester keeps her nice and dry. In her pocket she has the very same ordnance survey map that they used on the henge dig. Looking at it earlier, she saw the henge marked in yellow, with green stickers where other pieces of prehistoric wood were found. They seemed to form a line radiating out from the henge and

Erik thought at the time that they might have been part of a path, or causeway. Could the path be leading to Ruth's bones?

Rather than following the road to the car park, Ruth strikes out west, keeping to a path intended for bird watchers. As long as she sticks to the path she will be fine. The marsh lies on either side of her, huge clumps of reed and mile upon mile of wind-swept grass. The ground looks solid enough but she knows from experience that it is full of hidden pools, treacherous and deep. When the tide comes in, the sea will come halfway up the marsh, covering the ground swiftly and silently. It was here that Peter was marooned all those years ago, stuck between the tidal and the freshwater marshes, lying on his face in the muddy water, clinging to a piece of driftwood while Erik crept towards him across the mudflats shouting words of encouragement in Norwegian.

Ruth plods along the path. It is very narrow here and the mist means that she can only see a few yards in front of her. She doesn't want to be lured onto the marsh. The rain falls steadily and the sky is heavy and grey. Once, she disturbs a flock of snipe, who rise zigzagging crazily into the air, but otherwise she is quite alone. She hums as she walks, thinking of Erik and Peter and of the enchanted summer on the Saltmarsh. She thinks of the druids who came and camped out by the henge. Erik had been on their side, she remembers. After all, he had said, this is what it was built for, not for scientific study in a museum. But the university, which was sponsoring the dig, had wanted the timbers moved. They were being eroded by the tide, they had argued, they needed to be moved for their own safety. 'But they were *meant* to be eroded,' Erik had argued. 'Life and death, ebb and flow, that's what it's all about.'

But Erik had lost and the timbers were removed, slowly and painstakingly, to the university laboratory. Now Ruth feels a stab of regret for the timber circle that had lain buried in the sand for two thousand years. It belongs here, she thought, wading through muddy puddles, hands deep in her pockets. What the Sand gets, the Sand keeps forever.

At last she can see the hide where Nelson ordered Clough to bag up the litter. She can even see the car park, deserted now of course. The ground is firmer here and she walks quickly despite being out of breath (she really *must* start going to the gym in January). The police tape is still fluttering in the breeze and Ruth, ducking underneath it, thinks of Nelson, his eagerness, his disappointment when the bones did not turn out to be those of Lucy Downey. He was an odd man, she thought, brusque and unfriendly, but it seemed as if he had really cared about that little girl.

As she suspected, the trench is now almost entirely filled with water. This is the major problem with excavating marshy, tidal sites. In archaeology, it is essential to get a 'context', a clear view of where something is discovered. With sites like this, the very ground is changing beneath your feet. Ruth takes out her beaker and starts to scoop away some of the water. She cannot hope to empty the trench but she just wants to see if there is anything else visible in the soil. Phil has promised to send a team from the university to excavate properly but she wants to see it first. This is her discovery.

After about half an hour, maybe more, she thinks she sees something. A dull, bronze-green gleam in the rich, dark soil. Gently she brushes away soil from its edges. It looks like another torque. Trembling, she takes out her original plan of the site and marks in the new find. A second torque could mean the beginnings of a hoard, a ritual depositing of treasure.

It is definitely another torque, battered and scrunched up as if crushed by a huge hand. But, looking closely, Ruth can see that it is intact. She can see both ends, rounded and smooth compared with the plaited quality of the rest of the metal. Ruth is sure it is from the same period, early to middle Iron Age. Is this a votive hoard? One find looks like chance, two starts to look like a ritual.

She sits back on her heels, her arms aching. It is only then that she realises how dark it has become. She looks at her watch. Four o'clock! The walk can only have taken half-an-hour so she has been squatting here in the mud for nearly two hours. She must be getting back. She straightens up, puts the bag containing the torque in her pocket and pulls up her hood. The rain, which had settled into a fine mist, now suddenly gathers in strength, hitting her in the face as she starts the climb back up towards the path. Ruth puts her head down and ploughs onwards; she has never been stuck on the marsh in the dark and she doesn't mean to start now.

For about twenty minutes she plods on, head down against the driving rain. Then she stops. She should have reached the gravel path by now. It is almost completely dark, with just a faint phosphorescent gleam coming from the marsh itself. Ruth gets out her flashlight but its shaky light shows her only flat marshland in all directions. Far off, she can hear the sea roaring as it thunders inland. She tries to get out her map but it is blown back in her face. It is too precious to lose so she packs it away again. She can hear the sea but from which direction? She gets out her compass. She is heading too far to the east. Slowly, trying not to panic, she revolves on the spot until she is facing south, then sets out again.

This time she stops because her foot steps into nothingness. Literally one minute she is on dry land and the next she has sunk knee-high into the bog. She almost falls on her face but manages to save herself, rocking backwards until she is sitting on the firm ground. With an effort she pulls her leg from the liquid mud. It comes free with a horrible squelching sound but her wader, thank God, stays on. Panting, she takes a step backwards. Firm ground. Step forwards. Oozing mud. To the right, more mud. To the left, firmer ground. She starts to edge to the left, her flashlight held out in front of her.

After a few yards, she falls headlong into a ditch. Putting out her hands to save herself, she encounters icy water. She raises a hand to her lips. Salt. Oh God, she must have wandered right out to the tidal marsh. Scrambling to her feet she wipes mud off her face and checks her compass again. Due east. Has she missed the path altogether? Is she heading straight out to sea? The roaring in her ears is so loud now that she cannot tell if it is the sea or just the wind. Then a wave breaks right over her feet. There is no mistaking it, a freezing, briny-smelling swell of water. She is on the tidal mudflats, possibly at the very spot where Peter called for help all those years ago. But there is no

Erik to save her. She will be drowned right here on the desolate marshland with a priceless Iron Age torque in her pocket.

She is sobbing now, her tears mingling with the rain and sea water on her face. Then she hears something so miraculous that she almost discounts it as a mirage. A voice. Calling her. She sees a light, a shaky hand-held light coming towards her. 'Help!' she shouts frantically, 'Help!'

The light comes nearer and a man's voice shouts, 'Come this way. Towards me.' Almost on all fours, she crawls towards the light and the voice. A figure looms out of the mist, a thick-set figure wearing a reflective jacket. A hand reaches out and grabs hers. 'This way,' says the voice, 'this way.'

Clinging on to the yellow waterproof sleeve as if it were a lifebelt, she stumbles along beside the man. He seems familiar somehow but she can't think about that now. All she can do is follow him as he traces a circuitous path, first left and then right, now into the wind, now away from the wind, through the mudflats. But whatever route he is taking seems a remarkably effective one. Her feet are on firm ground almost all the time, and before too long she can see the blue and white police tape and the car park where a battered Land Rover is waiting.

'Oh my God.' She lets go of the man and leans over to catch her breath.

The man steps back, shining his flashlight into her face. 'What the hell were you playing at?' he demands.

'I was trying to get home. I got lost. Thank you. I don't know what I would have done if you hadn't come along.'

'You'd have drowned, that's what you would have done.'

Then his voice changes. 'You're the girl from the university, aren't you?'

Ruth looks at him, taking in close-cropped grey hair, blue eyes, official-looking jacket. It is her neighbour, the warden of the bird sanctuary. She smiles. Despite her feminist principles, she quite likes being called a girl.

'Yes. You're my neighbour, aren't you?'

He holds out a hand. 'David.'

She shakes hands, smiling again at the strangeness of it. A few moments ago she was clinging on to his sleeve, sobbing hysterically. Now they are behaving as if they have just met at a cocktail party.

'I'm Ruth. Thanks again for saving me.'

He shrugs. 'That's OK. Look, we'd better get you home. My car's over there.'

In the Land Rover, a blessed oasis of warmth and safety, Ruth feels almost elated. She isn't dead, she is about to be driven home in comfort and she has the torque in her pocket. She turns to David, who is coaxing the engine into life.

'How did you know the way back? It was amazing, the way you twisted and turned across the marsh.'

'I know this place like the back of my hand,' says David, putting the car into gear. 'It's weird. There are wooden posts sunk into the ground. If you follow them, it leads you on a safe path through the marsh. I don't know who put them there but, whoever did, they knew the land even better than I do.'

Ruth stares at him. 'Wooden posts ...' she whispers.

'Yes. They're sunk deep into the ground, sometimes half-submerged, but if you know where they are they'll lead you through the treacherous ground, right out to sea.'

Right out to sea. Right out to the henge. Ruth touches the freezer bag in her pocket but says nothing. Her mind is working furiously.

'What were you doing out on a night like this anyway?' asks David as they drive along the Saltmarsh Road. The windscreen wipers are almost buckling under the weight of water.

'We found something. Over by the car park. I wanted to take a second look. I know it was stupid.'

'You found something? Something old? You're an archaeologist, aren't you?'

'Yes. Some Iron Age bones. I think they might be linked to the henge. Do you remember, ten years ago, when we found the henge?' She dimly remembers David watching the excavations that summer. How terrible that they haven't spoken since.

'Yes,' he says slowly, 'I remember. That chap with a ponytail, he was in charge wasn't he? He was a good bloke. I had a lot of time for him.'

'Yes, he is a good bloke.' Funnily enough, there is something about David that reminds her of Erik. Perhaps it's the eyes, used to scanning far horizons.

'So, will there be all sorts of people here again? Druids and students and idiots with cameras?'

Ruth hesitates. She can tell that David thinks the Saltmarsh should be left to him and the birds. How can she say that she hopes there will be a major excavation, almost certainly involving students and idiots with cameras, if not druids.

'Not necessarily,' she says at last. 'It's very low key at the moment.'

David grunts. 'The police were here the other day. What were they after?'

Ruth is not sure how much she should say. Eventually she says, 'It was because of the bones, but when they turned out to be prehistoric they lost interest.'

They have reached Ruth's blue gate now. David turns to her and smiles for the first time. He has very white teeth. How old is he, she wonders. Forty? Fifty? Like Erik, he has an ageless quality.

'But you,' says David, 'you're more interested now, aren't you?'

Ruth grins. 'Yes I am.'

As she opens her front door, the phone is ringing. She knows, beyond any doubt, that it will be Erik.

'Ruthie!' Erik's singsong voice echoes across the frozen miles from Norway. 'What's all this about a find?'

'Oh Erik,' says Ruth ecstatically, standing dripping onto the rug. 'I think I've found your causeway.'

It is dark but she is used to that. She stretches out a hand to see if she can touch the wall and encounters cold stone. No door. There is a trapdoor in the roof but she never knows when that will open. And sometimes it is worse when it does. No use screaming or crying; she has done this many times before and it never helps. Sometimes, though, she likes to shout just to hear her own voice. It sounds different somehow, like a stranger's voice. Sometimes it's almost company, this other voice. They have long talks, sometimes, whispering in the dark.

'Don't worry.'

'It'll all come right in the end.'

'Darkest before dawn.'

Words she can't even remember hearing, though now they seem lodged in her brain. Who was it who told her once that it was darkest before dawn? She doesn't know. She only knows that the words give her a warm, ticklish feeling, like being wrapped in a blanket. She has an extra blanket when it's cold but even then she shivers so much that in the morning her whole body aches. Sometimes it's warmer and a little light shines through the edges of the trapdoor. Once he opened the window in the roof. Usually it's only open at night when the sky is black, but this time it was bright and blue and it made her eyes hurt. The bars on the window turned into a little yellow ladder. Sometimes she dreams about climbing the ladder and escaping to … where? She doesn't know. She thinks of the sun on her face and being in a garden where there are voices and cooking smells and cool water falling. Sometimes she walks through the water and it's like a curtain. A curtain. Where? A beaded curtain that you run through, laughing, and on the other side there's the warm light again and the voices and someone holding you tight, so tight; so tight they will never let you go.

And, other times, she thinks there is nothing there at all, beyond these walls. Only more walls and iron bars and cold, concrete floors.

CHAPTER 4

Ruth leaves her parents' house as soon as she decently can after Christmas. Phil is having a New Year's Eve party and, though in truth she would rather chew her own arm off than attend, she tells her parents that it is her duty to go. 'It would be bad for my career. After all, he is head of department.' They understand this alright. They understand that she might go to a party to further her career. It's enjoying herself they wouldn't understand.

So, on 29 December, Ruth is driving along the M11 to Norfolk. It is mid-morning and the frost has gone so she drives fast and happily, singing along to her new Bruce Springsteen CD, a Christmas present to herself. According to her brother Simon, Ruth has the musical taste of a sixteen-year-old boy. 'A tasteless sixteen-year-old boy.' But Ruth doesn't mind. She loves Bruce and Rod and Bryan. All those ageing rockers with croaky voices and faded jeans and age-defying hair. She loves the way they sing about love and loss and the dark, soulless heart of America, and it all sounds the same; crashing guitar chords against a wall of sound, the lyrics lost in a final, frenzied crescendo.

Singing loudly, she takes the A11 towards Newmarket. It hadn't been such a bad Christmas really. Her parents hadn't nagged her too much about not going to church and not being married. Simon hadn't been too irritating and her nephews were at quite interesting ages, eight and six, old enough to go to the park and play at being Neolithic hunters. The children adored Ruth because she told them stories about cavemen and dinosaurs and never noticed when their faces needed washing. 'You've got quite a gift with kids,' said her sister-in-law Cathy accusingly. 'It seems a shame …' 'What's a shame?' Ruth had asked, although she knew only too well. 'That you haven't any of your own. Though, I suppose, by now …'

By now I have resigned myself to spinsterhood and godmotherhood and slowly going mad, knitting clothes for my cats out of my own hair, thinks Ruth, neatly overtaking an overburdened minivan. She is nearly forty and although it is not impossible that she should still have a child she has noticed people mentioning it less and less. This suits her fine; when she was with Peter the only thing more annoying than people hinting about possible 'wedding bells' was the suggestion that she might be 'getting broody'. When she bought the cats her mother asked her straight out if they were 'baby substitutes'. 'No,' Ruth had answered, straight-faced. 'They're kittens. If I had a baby it would be a cat substitute.'

She reaches the Saltmarsh by mid-afternoon and the winter sun is low over the reed beds. The tide is coming in and the seagulls are calling, high and excited. When Ruth gets out of her car she breathes in the wonderful sea smell, potent and mysterious, and feels glad that she is home. Then she sees the weekenders' monster car parked outside their cottage and feels a stab of irritation. Don't say they have come here for New Year's. Why can't they stay in London like everyone else, flocking to Trafalgar Square or having bijou little parties at home? Why do they have to come here to 'get away from it all'? They'll probably let off fireworks and scare every bird for miles around. Imagining David's reaction, she smiles grimly.

Inside her cottage, Flint leaps on her, mewing furiously. Sparky, sitting on the sofa, steadfastly ignores her. Ruth's friend Shona has been coming in to feed the cats and Ruth finds welcome home flowers on the table as well as milk and white wine in the fridge. God bless Shona, thinks Ruth, putting on the kettle.

Shona, who teaches English at the university, is Ruth's best friend in Norfolk. Like Peter, she had been a volunteer on the henge dig ten years ago. Fey and Irish, with wild Pre-Raphaelite hair, Shona declared herself in sympathy with the druids and even joined them for an all-night vigil, sitting on the sand chanting until the tide forced them inland and Shona was lured away by the promise of a Guinness in the pub. That was the thing about Shona – she may have her New Age principles but you could nearly always overcome them with the promise of a drink. Shona is in a relationship with a married lecturer and sometimes she comes over to Ruth's cottage, weeping and flailing her hair around, declaring that she hates men and wants to become a nun or a lesbian or both. Then she will have a glass of wine and brighten up completely, singing along to Bruce Springsteen and telling Ruth that she is a 'dote'. Shona is one of the best things about the university.

Her answerphone shows four messages. One is a wrong number, one is Phil reminding her about the party, one is her mother asking if she's home yet and one … one is distinctly surprising.

'Hello ... er ... Ruth. This is Harry Nelson speaking, from the Norfolk Police. Can you ring me? Thank you.'

Harry Nelson. She hasn't spoken to him since the day they found the Iron Age bones. She sent him the results of the carbon 14 dating, confirming that the body was probably female, pre-pubescent, dating from about 650 BC. She heard nothing back and didn't expect to. Once, before Christmas, when she was shopping dispiritedly in Norwich, she saw him striding along, looking discontented and weighed down with carrier bags. With him was a blonde woman, slim in a designer tracksuit, and two sulky-looking teenage daughters. Lurking in Borders, Ruth hid behind a display of novelty calendars and watched them. In this female environment of shopping bags and fairy lights, Nelson looked more inconveniently macho than ever. The woman (his wife surely?) turned to him with a flick of hair and a smile of practised persuasiveness. Nelson said something, looking grumpy, and both girls laughed. They must gang up on him at home, Ruth decided, excluding him from their all-girl chats about boyfriends and mascara. But then Nelson caught up with his wife, whispered something that brought forth a genuine laugh, ruffled his daughter's careful hairstyle and sidestepped neatly away, grinning at her cry of rage. For a moment they looked united; a happy, teasing, slightly stressed family in the middle of their Christmas shopping. Ruth turned back to the calendars. The Simpsons' grinning yellow faces smirked back at her. She hated Christmas anyway.

Why was Harry Nelson ringing her now, at home? What was so important that he had to speak to her this minute?

And why is he so arrogant that he can't even leave a phone number? Irritated but intensely curious, Ruth rifles through the phone book to find a number for the Norfolk police. Of course it is the wrong one. 'You want CID,' says the voice at the end of the phone, sounding slightly impressed. Eventually she gets through to a flunky who connects her, somewhat reluctantly, to DCI Nelson.

'Nelson,' barks an impatient voice, sounding more Northern and even less friendly than she remembers.

'It's Ruth Galloway from the university. You rang me.'

'Oh yes. I rang you some days ago.'

'I've been away,' says Ruth. She's damned if she's going to apologise.

'Something's come up. Can you come into the station?'

Ruth is nonplussed. Of course, she wants to know what has come up but Nelson's request sounds more like an order. Also there is something a bit frightening about coming 'into the station'. It sounds uncomfortably like 'helping the police with their enquiries'.

'I'm very busy –' she begins.

'I'll send a car,' says Nelson. 'Tomorrow morning alright?'

It is on the tip of Ruth's tongue to say no, tomorrow is not alright. I'm off to a very important jet-set conference in Hawaii so I'm far too busy to drop everything just because you order me to. Instead she says, 'I suppose I could spare you an hour or two.'

'Right,' says Nelson. Then he adds, 'Thank you.' It sounds as if he hasn't had much practice in saying it.

CHAPTER 5

The police car arrives at Ruth's door promptly at nine. Expecting this (Nelson seems like an early riser to her) she is dressed and ready. As she walks to the car, she sees one of the weekenders (Sara? Sylvie? Susanna?) looking furtively out of the window, so she waves and smiles cheerfully. They probably think she is being arrested. Guilty of living alone and weighing over 140 pounds.

She is driven into the centre of King's Lynn. The police station is in a detached Victorian house which still looks more like a family home than anything else. The reception desk is obviously in the middle of the sitting room and there should be framed family portraits on the walls rather than posters telling you to lock your car safely and not to exceed the speed limit. Her escort, a taciturn uniformed policeman, ushers her through a secret door beside the desk. She imagines the defeated-looking people waiting in reception wondering who she is and why she deserves this star treatment. They climb a rather beautiful swirling staircase, now marred with institutional carpeting, and enter a door marked CID.

Harry Nelson is sitting at a battered Formica desk surrounded by papers. This room was obviously once part of a bigger one; you can see where the plasterboard partition cuts into the elaborate coving around the ceiling. Now it is an awkward slice of a room, taller than it is wide, with a disproportionately large window, half-covered by a broken white blind. Nelson, though, does not seem a man who bothers much about his surroundings.

He stands up when she enters. 'Ruth. Good of you to come.'

She can't remember telling him to call her by her first name but now it seems too late to do anything about it. She can hardly ask him to go back to Doctor Galloway.

'Coffee?' asks Nelson.

'Yes please. Black.' She knows it will be horrible but somehow it feels rude to refuse. Besides it will give her something to do with her hands.

'Two black coffees, Richards,' Nelson barks at the hovering policemen. Presumably he has the same problem with 'please' as with 'thank you'.

Ruth sits on a battered plastic chair opposite the desk. Nelson sits down too and, for a few minutes, seems just to stare at her, frowning. Ruth begins to feel uncomfortable. Surely he hasn't just asked her here for coffee? Is this silent treatment something he does to intimidate suspects?

The policeman marches back in with the coffees. Ruth thanks him profusely, noticing with a sinking heart the thin liquid and the strange wax film floating on the surface. Nelson waits until the door has shut again before saying, 'You must be wondering why I asked you to come in.'

'Yes,' says Ruth simply, taking a sip of coffee. It tastes even worse than it looks.

Nelson pushes a file towards her. 'There's been another child gone missing,' he says. 'You'll have read about it in the press.'

Ruth stays silent; she doesn't read the papers.

Nelson gives her a sharp look before continuing. He looks tired, she realises. There are dark circles around his eyes and he obviously hasn't shaved that morning. In fact, he looks more like a face on a 'wanted' poster than a policeman.

'There's been a letter,' he says. 'Remember I told you about the letters that were sent during the Lucy Downey case? Well, this looks to be from the same person. At the very least someone's trying to make me think it's from the same person, which may be stranger still.'

'And you think this person may be the murderer?'

Nelson pauses for a long time before replying, frowning darkly into his coffee cup. 'It's dangerous to make assumptions,' he says at last, 'that's what happened with the Ripper case, if you remember. The police were so sure the anonymous letters came from the killer that it skewed the whole investigation and they just turned out to be from some nutter. That may well be the case here. Nothing more likely, in fact.' He pauses again. 'It's just ... there is always the chance that they *could* be from the killer, in which case they could contain vital clues. And I remembered what you said, that day when we found the bones, about ritual and all that. There's a lot of that sort of thing in the letters, so I wondered if you'd take a look. Tell me what you think.'

Whatever Ruth had been expecting, it wasn't this. Gingerly, she takes the file and opens it. A typewritten letter faces her. She picks it up. It seems to have been written on standard printer paper using a standard computer, but she assumes the police have ways of checking all that. It's only the words that concern her:

Dear Detective Nelson,

To everything there is a season, and a time to every purpose under the heaven. A time to be born and a time to die; a time to plant and a time to pluck up what has been planted. A time to kill and a time to heal. A time to cast away stones and a time to gather stones together.

She lies where the earth meets the sky. Where the roots of the great tree Yggdrasil reach down into the next life. All flesh is grass. Yet in death are we in life. She has become the perfect sacrifice. Blood on stone. Scarlet on white.

In peace.

There is no signature.

'Well?' Nelson is watching her closely.

'Well, the first bit's from the Bible. Ecclesiastes.' Ruth shifts in her chair. She feels slightly queasy. The Bible always does this to her.

'What's all that about a tree?'

'In Norse legend, there's a tree called Yggdrasil. Its roots are supposed to stretch down to hell and up to heaven. There are all sorts of legends attached to it.' As she says this she remembers Erik, that great teller of Norse tales, sitting by the campfire, his face radiant in the half light, telling them about Odin and Thor, about Asgard, the home of the Gods, and Muspelheim, the land of fire.

'The letter says its roots reach *down* into the next life.'

'Yes.' This was the first thing to strike Ruth. She is surprised to find Nelson so perceptive. 'Some people think that prehistoric man may have believed that heaven was below the earth, not above. Have you heard of Seahenge?'

'No.'

'It was found on the coast, near the Saltmarsh, at Holme-Next-the-Sea. A wooden henge, like the one at Saltmarsh, except there was a tree buried in the centre of it. Buried upside down. Its roots upwards, its branches going down into the earth.'

'Do you think this guy' – he picks up the letter – 'may have heard of it?'

'Possibly. There was a lot of publicity at the time. Have you thought that it might not be a man?'

'What?'

'The letter writer. It might be a woman.'

'It might, I suppose. There were some handwritten letters the first time. The expert thought the handwriting was a man's but you never know. The experts aren't always right. One of the first rules of policing.'

Wondering where this leaves her, Ruth asks, 'Can you tell me something about the child? The one who's gone missing.'

He stares at her. 'It was in the papers. Local and national. Bloody hell, it was even on *Crimewatch*. Where have you been?'

Ruth is abashed. She seldom reads the papers or watches TV, preferring novels and the radio. She relies on the latter for the news, but she's been away. She realises she knows far more about happenings in the prehistoric world than in this one.

Nelson sighs and rubs his stubble. When he speaks, his voice is harsher than ever. 'Scarlet Henderson. Four years old. Vanished while playing in her parents' front garden in Spenwell.'

Spenwell is a tiny village about half a mile from Ruth's house. It makes the whole thing seem uncomfortably close.

'Scarlet?'

'Yes. Scarlet on white. Blood on stone. Quite poetic, isn't it?'

Ruth is silent. She is thinking about Erik's theories of ritual sacrifice. Wood represents life, stone death. Aloud she asks, 'How long ago was this?'

'November.' Their eyes meet. 'About a week after we found those old bones of yours. Almost ten years to the day since Lucy Downey vanished.'

'And you think the cases are connected?'

He shrugs. 'I've got to keep an open mind, but there are similarities, and then this letter arrives.'

'When?'

'Two weeks after Scarlet vanished. We'd done everything. Searched the area, drained the river, questioned everyone. Drawn a complete blank. Then this letter came. It got me thinking about the Lucy Downey case.'

'Hadn't you been thinking about it already?' It is an innocent enough enquiry but Nelson looks at her sharply, as if scenting criticism.

'I thought about it, yes,' he says, slightly defensively. 'The similarities were there – similar age child, same time of year – but there were differences too. Lucy Downey was taken from inside her own home. Terrible thing. Actually snatched from her bed. This child was on her own, in the garden ...'

There is a faint edge of censure in his voice that leads Ruth to ask, 'What about the parents? You said ... it's sometimes the parents ...'

'Hippies,' says Nelson contemptuously, 'New Agers. Got five children and don't look after any of 'em properly. Took them two hours to notice that Scarlet was missing. But we don't think they did it. No signs of abuse. Dad was away at the time and Mum was in a bloody trance or something, communing with the fairies.'

'Can I see the other letters?' asks Ruth. 'The Lucy Downey letters. There might be something there, about Yggdrasil or Norse mythology or something.'

Nelson is obviously expecting this enquiry because he hands over another file which is lying on the desk. Ruth opens it. There are ten or more sheets inside.

'Twelve,' says Nelson, reading her mind. 'The last one was sent only last year.'

'So he hasn't given up?'

'No.' Nelson shakes his head slowly. 'He hasn't given up.'

'Can I take these home and read them tonight?'

'You'll have to sign for them, mind.' As he roots around on the desk, looking for a form, he surprises her by asking, 'What about the bones we found. What's happened to them?'

'Well, I sent you the report ...'

Nelson grunts. 'Couldn't make head nor tail of it.'

'Well, basically it said it was probably the body of a young girl, between six and ten, pre-pubescent. About two thousand, six hundred years old. We excavated and found three gold torques and some coins.'

'They had coins in the Iron Age?'

'Yes, it was the start of coinage actually. We're going to do another dig in the spring when the weather's better.' She hopes Erik will be able to come over for it.

'Do you think she was murdered?'

Ruth looks at the detective, who is leaning forward across his untidy desk. It seems strange to hear the word 'murdered' on his lips, as if her Iron Age body is suddenly going to form part of his 'enquiries', as if he is planning to bring the perpetrator to justice.

'We don't know,' she admits. 'One strange thing – half her hair was shaved off. We don't know what that means but it may have been part of a ritual killing. There were branches twisted around her arms and legs, willow and hazel, as if she was tied down.'

Nelson smiles, rather grimly. 'Sounds pretty conclusive to me,' he says.

As Nelson escorts her out, he leads her through a room full of people, all working intently, crouched over phones or frowning at computer screens. On the wall is what looks like a roughly drawn mind map, full of arrows and scrawling writing. At the centre of it all is a photograph of a little girl with dark, curly hair and laughing eyes.

'Is that her?' Ruth finds herself whispering.

'That's Scarlet Henderson, yes.'

No one in the room looks up as they pass through. Perhaps they are pretending to work hard because the boss is there, but Ruth doesn't think so somehow. At the door she turns and Scarlet Henderson's smiling face looks back at her.

Once home, she pours herself a glass of Shona's wine and puts the file with the letters in front of her. Before she looks at them, though, she clicks on her computer and googles

Scarlet Henderson. Reference after reference spews onto her screen. Nelson is right, how can she have missed this? 'Heartache of Scarlet's Parents' screams an article from the *Telegraph*. 'Police Baffled in Henderson Case' says *The Times*, rather more soberly. Ruth scrolls down the article: 'Detective Chief Inspector Harry Nelson of the Norfolk Police admitted yesterday that there are no new leads in the case of missing four-year-old Scarlet Henderson. Sightings in Great Yarmouth of a child answering Scarlet's description are said by police to have been ruled out of the enquiry ...'

Scarlet's face, poignant in black and white, looks up from the edge of the page. Is she dead, this bright-eyed, smiling child? Ruth doesn't like to think about it but she knows that, sooner or later, she will have to. Somehow she has become involved.

To stave off the moment when she will have to look at the letters, Ruth types 'Lucy Downey' into the search engine. Fewer references this time; Lucy disappeared before the ubiquity of the internet. She is listed, though, on a couple of websites for missing children and there is an article from the *Guardian* headed 'Ten Years On, the Never-ending Nightmare'. 'Alice and Tom Downey,' she reads, 'meet me in their neat Norfolk home, full of pictures of the same, smiling five-year-old. Ten years ago, Lucy was sleeping in her bed in this same house when an intruder scaled the garage wall, opened the window and snatched the child while the parents were still sleeping ...' Jesus. Ruth stops reading. Imagine that. Imagine coming to wake your little girl in the morning and finding she wasn't there. Imagine looking under the bed, searching, with increasing panic, downstairs, in the garden, back in the bedroom. Imagine seeing the open window, the curtains (she imagines them pink featuring Disney princesses) blowing in the breeze. Ruth can imagine all this, the hairs lifting on the back of her neck, but she can't imagine what Alice Downey felt, is still feeling, ten years later. To lose your child, to have her spirited away like something from a fairy tale, surely that must be every mother's nightmare.

But Ruth isn't a mother; she is an archaeologist and it is time she got to work. Nelson needs her professional help and professional is what she must be. Closing down the computer, she opens the file containing the letters. First she puts them in date order, rather surprised to find that Nelson has not already done this, and examines the paper and the ink. Ten of the twelve letters seem to be on the same standard printer paper as the Scarlet Henderson letter. This doesn't necessarily mean anything, she tells herself. Nine out of ten people with printers must use this sort of paper. Similarly the typeface looks very ordinary, Times New Roman she thinks. But two of the letters are handwritten on lined paper, the sort that comes from a refill pad, complete with a narrow red margin and holes for filing. The letters are written with a thin felt-tip, what used to be called a 'handwriting pen' when Ruth was at school. The writing itself is legible but untidy and slopes wildly to the left. A man's writing, the expert said. It occurs to her that she hardly ever sees handwriting these days; her students all have laptops, her friends send her emails or texts, she even edits papers on-line. The only handwriting she can recognise is her mother's, which usually comes inside inappropriately sentimental cards. 'To a special daughter on her birthday ...'

The handwritten letters come in the middle of the sequence. Ruth puts them back into order and starts to read:

November 1997

Nelson,

You are looking for Lucy but you are looking in the wrong places. Look to the sky, the stars, the crossing places. Look at what is silhouetted against the sky. You will find her where the earth meets the sky.

In peace.

December 1997

Nelson,

Lucy is the perfect sacrifice. Like Isaac, like Jesus, she carries the wood for her own crucifixion. Like Isaac and Jesus she is obedient to the father's will.

I would wish you the compliments of the season, make you a wreath of mistletoe, but, in truth, Christmas is merely a modern addition, grafted onto the great winter solstice. The pagan festival was here first, in the short days and long nights. Perhaps I should wish you greetings for St Lucy's day. If only you have eyes to see.

In peace.

January 1998

Dear Detective Inspector Harry Nelson,

You see, I am calling you by your full name now. I feel we are old friends, you and I. Just because Nelson had only one eye, it doesn't follow that he couldn't see. 'A

man may see how the world goes with no eyes.'
In peace.

January 1998

Dear Harry,
'A little touch of Harry in the night.' How wise Shakespeare was, a shaman for all time. Perhaps it is the wise men – and women – you should be consulting now.
For you still do not look in the right places, the holy places, the other places. You look only where trees flower and springs flow. Look again Harry. Lucy lies deep below the ground but she will rise again. This I promise you.
In peace.

March 1998

Dear Harry,
Spring returns but not my friend. The trees are in bud and the swallows return. For everything there is a season.
Look where the land lies. Look at the cursuses and the causeways.

Ruth stops and reads the last line again. She is so transfixed by the word 'cursuses' that it is a few minutes before she realises that someone is knocking on the door.

Apart from the postman making his surly visits to deliver Amazon parcels, unannounced visitors are almost unheard of. Ruth is irritated to find herself feeling quite nervous as she opens the door.

It is the woman from next door; the weekender who watched her drive off in the police car that morning.

'Oh ... hello,' says Ruth.

'Hi!' The woman flashes her a brilliant smile. She is older than Ruth, maybe early fifties, but fantastically well preserved: highlighted hair, tanned skin, honed figure in low-slung jeans.

'I'm Sammy. Sammy from next door. Isn't it ridiculous that we've hardly ever spoken to each other?'

Ruth doesn't think it is ridiculous at all. She spoke to the weekenders when they first bought the house about three years ago and since then has done her best to ignore them. There used to be children, she remembers, loud teenagers who played music into the early hours and tramped over the Saltmarsh with surfboards and inflatable boats. There are no children in evidence on this visit.

'Ed and I ... we're having a little New Year's party. Just some friends who are coming up from London. Very casual, just kitchen sups. We wondered if you'd like to come.'

Ruth can't believe her ears. It's been years since she's been invited to a New Year's party and now she has two invitations to refuse. It's a conspiracy.

'Thank you very much,' she says, 'But my head of department's having a party and I might have to ...'

'Oh, I do understand.' Sammy, like Ruth's parents, seems to have no difficulty in understanding that Ruth might want to go to a party from motives of duty alone. 'You work at the university, don't you?'

'Yes. I teach archaeology.'

'Archaeology! Ed would love that. He never misses *Time Team*. I thought you might have changed jobs.'

Ruth looks at her blankly, though she has a good idea what is coming.

Sammy laughs gaily. 'The police car! This morning.'

'Oh, that,' says Ruth. 'I'm just helping the police with their enquiries.'

And with that, she thinks grimly, Sammy will have to be content.

That night, in bed, Ruth finishes the Lucy Downey letters.

She was halfway through the letter dated March 1998, with its surprising mention of cursuses and causeways. A cursus is a fairly obscure archaeological term meaning a shallow ditch. There is a cursus at Stonehenge, older even than the stones.

> ... Look at the cursuses and the causeways. We crawl on the surface of the earth but we do not know its ways, or divine its intent.
> In peace.

> April 1998
>
> Dear Harry,
> Happy Easter. I do not think of you as a Christian somehow. You seem to belong to the older ways.
> At Easter, Christians believe Christ died on the cross for their sins but did not Odin do this before him, sacrificing himself on the Tree of All Knowledge? Like Nelson.
> Odin had only one eye. How many eyes do you have Detective Inspector? A thousand, like Argus?

Lucy is buried deep now. But she will flower again.
In peace.

Now come the two handwritten letters. They are undated but someone (Nelson?) has scribbled the date they were received:

Received 21 June 1998

Dear Harry,
Greetings of the summer solstice be with you. Happy Litha time. Hail to the Sun God.
Beware the water spirits and light bonfires on the beach. Beware the wicker man.
Now the sun turns southwards and evil spirits walk abroad. Follow the will o'the wisps, the spirits of the dead children. Who knows where they will lead you?
In peace.

Received 23 June 1998

Dear Harry,
Compliments of St John's Day. Sankt Hans Aften. Herbs picked on St John's Eve have special healing powers. Did you know that? I have so much to teach you.
You are no nearer to Lucy and that makes me sad. But do not weep for her. I have rescued her and raised her up. I have saved her from a life of the mundane, a life spent worshipping false Gods. I have made her the perfect sacrifice.
Weep rather for yourself and for your children and your children's children.
In peace.

Now the letters revert to typewriting and the tone changes. No longer is there the half affectionate teasing, the assumption that Nelson and the writer are 'old friends' and share a special bond. Now the writer seems angry, resentful.

There is a gap of four months before the next letter and the date is predictable:

31st October 1998

Dear Detective Inspector Nelson,

Now is the time when the dead walk. Graves have yawned and yielded up their dead. Beware the living and the dead. Beware the living dead. We who were living are now dying.

You have disappointed me, Detective Inspector. I have shared my wisdom with you and still you are no nearer to me or to Lucy. You are, after all, a man bound to the earth and to The Mundane. I had hoped for better things of you.

Tomorrow is the Feast of All Saints. Will you find St Lucy there in all the holy pantheon? Or is she, too, bound to the earth?

In sadness.

25th November 1998

Dear Detective Inspector Nelson,

It is now a year since Lucy Downey vanished. The world has turned full circle and what have you to show for it? Truly you have feet of clay.

A curse on the man who puts his trust in man, who relies on the things of flesh, whose heart turns from the

Lord. He is like dry scrub in the wastelands, if good comes, he has no eyes for it.
In sadness.

December 1998

Dear Detective Inspector Nelson,
I nearly did not write to wish you compliments of the season but then I thought that you would miss me. But, in truth, I am deeply disappointed in you.
A girl, a young girl, an innocent soul, vanishes but you do not read the signs. A seer, a shaman, offers you the hand of friendship and you decline it. Look into your own heart, Detective Inspector. Truly it must be a dark place, full of bitterness and regret.
Yet Lucy is in light. That I promise you.
In sadness.

The last letter is dated January 2007:

Dear Detective Inspector Nelson,
Had you forgotten me? But with each New Year I think of you. Are you any nearer to the right path? Or have your feet strayed into the way of despair and lamentation?
I saw your picture in the paper last week. What sadness and loneliness is etched in those lines! Even though you have betrayed me, still I ache with pity for you.
You have daughters. Do you watch them? Do you keep them close at all times?
I hope so, for the night is full of voices and my ways

are very dark. Perhaps I will call to you again one day? In peace.

What did Nelson think, wonders Ruth, when he read that open threat to his own children? Her own hair is standing on end and she is nervously checking the curtains for signs of lurking bodies. How did Nelson feel about receiving these letters, over months and years, with their implication that he and the writer are in some way bound together, accomplices, even friends?

Ruth looks at the date on the last letter. Ten months later Scarlet Henderson vanishes. Is this man responsible? Is he even responsible for Lucy Downey? There is nothing concrete in these letters, only a web of allusion, quotation and superstition. She shakes her head, trying to clear it.

She recognises the Bible and Shakespeare, of course, but she wishes she had Shona for some of the other references. She is sure there is some T.S. Eliot in there somewhere. What interests her more are the Norse allusions: Odin, the Tree of All Knowledge, the water spirits. And, even more than that, the signs of some archaeological knowledge. No layman, surely, would use the word 'cursuses'. She lies in bed, rereading, wondering ...

It is a long time before she sleeps that night, and, when she does she dreams of drowned girls, of the water spirits and of the ghost lights leading to the bodies of the dead.

CHAPTER 6

'So what do you think? Is he a nutter?'

Ruth is once again sitting in Nelson's shabby office, drinking coffee. Only this time she brought the coffee herself, from Starbucks.

'Starbucks eh?' Nelson had said suspiciously.

'Yes. It's the closest. I don't normally go to Starbucks but ...'

'Why not?'

'Oh, you know,' she shrugged, 'too global, too American.'

'I'm all for America myself,' said Nelson, still looking doubtfully at the froth on his cappuccino. 'We went to Disney World Florida a few years ago. It was champion.'

Ruth, for whom the idea of Disney World is sheer unexpurgated hell, says nothing.

Now Nelson puts down his cup and asks again, 'Is he a nutter?'

'I don't know,' says Ruth slowly. 'I'm not a psychologist.'

Nelson grunts. 'We had one of those. Talked complete bollocks. Homoerotic this, suppressed that. Complete crap.'

Ruth who had, in fact, thought she noticed a homoerotic subtext to the letters (assuming, of course, that the writer is male), again says nothing. Instead she gets the letters out of her bag.

'I've categorised the references in the letters,' she says. 'I thought it was the best way of starting.'

'A list,' says Nelson approvingly. 'I like lists.'

'So do I.' She gets out a neatly typed sheet of paper and passes it to Nelson.

Religious
Ecclesiastes
Isaac
Christmas
Christ dying on cross/Easter
St Lucy
St Lucy's Day (21 December)
St John's Day (24 June)
All Saints' Day (1 November)
Jeremiah

Literary
Shakespeare:
King Lear: 'A man may see how the world goes with no eyes.'
Henry V: 'A little touch of Harry ...'
Julius Caesar: 'Graves have yawned and yielded up their dead.'
T.S. Eliot, *Ash Wednesday*: 'There, where trees flower, and springs flow, for there is nothing again.'
The Waste Land: 'We who were living are now dying.'

Norse legend
Odin
The Tree of All Knowledge (the World Tree, Yggdrasil)

Pagan
Summer solstice
Winter solstice
Litha (Anglo-Saxon word for the solstice)
Wicker Man
Sun God
Shamanism
Will o'the wisps
Mistletoe

Greek legend
Argus

Archaeological
Cursuses
Causeways

Nelson reads intently, his brows knitted together. 'It's good, seeing it all spread out like this,' he says at last, 'otherwise you can't tell which is a quote and which is just mumbo jumbo. "We who were living are now dying," for example. I thought that was just more spooky stuff. I never realised it was an actual quote.'

Ruth, who has spent hours trawling through Eliot's *Collected Poems*, feels gratified.

Nelson turns back to the list. 'Lots of biblical stuff,' he says, 'we spotted that straight off. Psychologist thought he might even be a lay preacher or an ex-priest.'

'Or maybe he just had a religious upbringing,' says Ruth. 'My parents are Born Again Christians. They're always reading the Bible aloud, just for kicks.'

Nelson grunts. 'I was brought up a Catholic,' he says, 'but my parents weren't really into the Bible. It was more the saints, praying to this one or that one, saying Hail Marys. Jesus – a decade of the rosary every bloody day! It seemed to take hours.'

'Are you still a Catholic?' asks Ruth.

'I had the girls baptised Catholic, more to please my mum than anything else, but Michelle's not a Catholic and we never go to church. Don't know if I'd say I was a Catholic or not. A lapsed one maybe.'

'They never let you get away, do they? Even if you don't believe in God, you're still "lapsed". As if you might go back one day.'

'Maybe I will. On my death bed.'

'I won't,' says Ruth fiercely, 'I'm an atheist. After you die, there's nothing.'

'Shame,' says Nelson with a grin, 'you never get to say I told you so.'

Ruth laughs, rather surprised. Perhaps Nelson regrets this foray into levity because he turns back, frowning, to the list.

'This guy,' he says, 'what does *he* believe?'

'Well,' says Ruth, 'there's a strong theme of death and rebirth, the seasons, the cycle of nature. I would say his beliefs were more pagan, though. There's the mention of mistletoe, for instance. The druids considered that mistletoe was sacred. That's where the tradition of kissing under the mistletoe comes from.' She pauses. 'Actually, our Iron Age girl. She had traces of mistletoe in her stomach.'

'In her stomach?'

'Yes, maybe she was forced to eat it before they killed her. As I said, ritual sacrifice was quite common in the Iron Age. You find bodies that have been stabbed, strangled, clubbed to death. One body found in Ireland had its nipples sliced through.'

Nelson winces. 'So does our guy know about all this Iron Age stuff?'

'It's possible. Take this stuff about sacrifice, the wicker man. Some people think that Iron Age man made human sacrifices every autumn to ensure that spring came again the next year. They put the victim in a wicker cage and burnt it.'

'I saw the film,' says Nelson. 'Christopher Lee. Great stuff.'

'Well, yes. It was sensationalised, of course, but there's a theme of sacrifice that runs through all religions. Odin was hung on the World Tree to gain all the knowledge of the world. Christ was hung on the cross. Abraham was prepared to sacrifice his son Isaac.'

'What did that mean, "Like Isaac, like Jesus, she carries the wood for her own crucifixion."'

'Well, Isaac carried the wood on which he was to be burnt. There's a clear echo of Christ carrying his cross.'

'Jesus.' There is a silence. Ruth suspects that Nelson is thinking of Lucy Downey, condemned, perhaps to carry the instruments of her own death. She thinks of her Iron Age body. Was she really staked down and left to die?

'Actually,' says Ruth, 'there's one very interesting Bible reference. This one from Jeremiah. "A curse on the man who puts his trust in man."'

'I didn't even realise that was from the Bible.'

'Well, it is. One of the prophets. Anyway, I looked it up and guess how the next bit goes ...' She recites it for him:

> A curse on the man who puts his trust in man,
> who relies on the things of flesh,
> whose heart turns from the Lord.
> He is like dry scrub in the wastelands,
> if good comes, he has no eyes for it,
> he settles in the parched places of the wilderness, *a salt land, uninhabited.*

Nelson looks up. 'A salt land?'

'Yes.'

'The Saltmarsh,' says Nelson, almost to himself. 'I always wondered about that place ...'

'Actually, I think there are a few things that might point to the Saltmarsh,' says Ruth. She reads from one of the letters, '"Look to the sky, the stars, the crossing places. Look at what is silhouetted against the sky. You will find her where the earth meets the sky." Erik – an archaeologist I know – he says that prehistoric man may have built structures on flat landscapes like the fens or the marshes because they would stand out so much, be silhouetted against the sky. He thinks that's one reason why the henge was built on the Saltmarsh.'

'But other places are flat. Specially in this Godforsaken county.'

'Yes, but ...' How can she explain that she thinks the letter writer shares Erik's views about a ritual landscape, about marshland being the link between life and death. 'Remember what I said about marshland?' she says at last.

'We quite often find votive offerings or occasionally bodies buried there. Maybe this man' – she gestures to the letters – 'maybe he knows that too.'

'You think he's an archaeologist?'

Ruth hesitates. 'Not necessarily but there's this word, cursuses.'

'Never heard of it.'

'Exactly! It's a very technical word. It means a parallel ditch with banks on the inner sides. They're often found within early ritual landscapes but we don't know what they were used for. At the Maxley Cursus, for example, they found shamans' batons.'

'Shamans' what?'

'Pieces of decorated deer antler. They would have been used by the shaman, the holy man.'

'What for?'

'We don't know, maybe as part of some ritual ceremony. Maybe they were like magic wands.'

'This guy' – Nelson points to the letters – 'he talks about a shaman.'

'Yes, it's quite a popular idea amongst modern New Age thinkers. A holy man who works with natural magic.'

Nelson looks back at the list. 'What about causeways? Now I've heard *that* word.'

'Causeways are early pathways, often leading across marsh or water.' She pauses. 'Actually, I think I've found one at the Saltmarsh, leading to the henge. It's a sort of hidden path marked out by sunken posts. It's very exciting.'

Nelson looks as if he will take her word for that. 'So our

man may be a pagan, he may be a New Ager, he may be a religious nutter, he may be an archaeologist.'

'He may be all four, or maybe he just knows a bit about all of them. He strikes me as someone who hoards nuggets of knowledge. The bit about the will o'the wisps, for example.'

'Yes, what was all that about?'

'Will o'the wisps are lights, often seen on marshland and often on the night of the summer solstice. They lead travellers onto dangerous ground and so to their deaths.' As she says this, Ruth thinks of the weird phosphorous glow over the marsh on the night that she was lost. Without David, would she have died? 'There are lots of legends about will o'the wisps. In some stories they're named after a wicked blacksmith who sold his soul to the devil in return for a flame from the fires of hell. He roams below the earth trying to find his way to the surface, lighting his way by the flame. Other stories say that they're the souls of murdered children.'

'Murdered children,' says Nelson grimly. 'That's what this is all about.'

Ruth arrives home to find the phone ringing. She snatches it up and is rewarded by the voice of her favourite Viking.

'Ruthie! What news on the causeway?'

She tells him that no one else knows of her discovery. However, when she visited David to give him a bottle of whisky as a thank-you present, he gave her a map of the Saltmarsh with the posts clearly marked in his own hand.

'Excellent,' purrs Erik. 'Don't let Techno Boy see anything until I get there.' Techno Boy is his nickname for

Phil, who is addicted to all kinds of archaeological technology.

'When will that be?'

'That's why I'm ringing. Very good news. I've managed to get a sabbatical for next term.'

'That's wonderful!'

'Yes, I know. Magda's very jealous. It's the long nights, you know, a real killer in the winter. Anyway, I hope to be with you in a week or so.'

'Wonderful!' says Ruth again. 'Where will you stay?'

Erik laughs. 'Don't worry; I won't be after your sofa. I don't fancy sharing it with the cats. I'm sure they would put the evil eye on me. I remember a nice B and B quite near you. I'll book there.'

'I'll book it for you, if you want,' offers Ruth, wondering why she doesn't mind Erik making jokes about her cats.

'No problem, baby. I've got the internet for that. Techno Boy would be proud of me.'

'I doubt it. Erik?'

'What?'

'There's just a chance you might get a call from someone called Detective Inspector Harry Nelson ...'

Nelson had asked her if there was anyone she remembered hanging around the dig ten years ago, anyone fascinated by archaeology and mythology. Ruth could, in fact, remember one name. A man who called himself Cathbad and who was the leader of the group of druids who wanted to save the henge. After a moment's hesitation, she had offered Nelson this name, which was met with a snort of contempt. Did Ruth have any idea what his real name was? No. Did she know anyone who might know? So Ruth had given him Erik's name. She remembers, many times, seeing Erik deep in conversation with Cathbad, the latter's purple cloak flying out behind him as they stood on the mudflats looking out to sea. Cathbad had been fairly young, she remembers. He would only be in his late thirties or early forties now.

She explains the situation to Erik, telling him about the disappearance of Scarlet Henderson and the earlier case of Lucy Downey.

Erik whistles softly. 'So. You are helping the police with this case?'

'Well, only slightly. There are some letters, you see. They were sent when Lucy Downey vanished and Nelson thinks ... Well, he'll explain if he speaks to you.'

'You sound as if you've got quite friendly with him.' There is an odd note in Erik's voice. Ruth remembers that he doesn't much like the police.

'I'm not friendly with him,' she hurries to defend herself. 'I don't know him very well.' Erik is silent so she goes on, 'He's odd, complicated. He seems very Northern and brash. Thinks archaeology is rubbish and mythology is nonsense and all New Agers should be shot but, I don't know, there's something else too. He's bright, brighter than you think at first. And he's interesting, I suppose.'

'I look forward to speaking to him,' says Erik politely. 'Am I to understand that I am a suspect?'

Ruth laughs. 'Of course not! It's just ... he was asking whether I remembered anyone from the henge dig, anyone who was interested in druids. And I thought of Cathbad.'

'Cathbad.' Erik takes a deep breath, she can hear it all

the way across the North Sea. 'Cathbad. I haven't thought of him for years. I wonder what he's doing now.'

'What was his real name?'

'Something Irish, I think. He was into the Celtic stuff too. Malone. Michael Malone.'

'Could he have been involved?'

'Cathbad? God, no. He was a real innocent. A simple soul. I think he really had magic powers, you know.'

After they have said goodbye and Ruth is bustling around, feeding herself and the cats, she reflects that Erik has a way of bringing you up short with something like that. Mentioning magic in the same quiet authoritative way that he talks about carbon dating or geophysics. Can Erik really believe that Cathbad, alias Michael Malone, has magical powers?

She doesn't know but, before she goes to bed that night, she looks up Malone in the local phone book.

CHAPTER 7

Ruth did not intend to go to Sammy's New Year's Eve party. In fact, nothing could have been further from her thoughts. Having successfully pleaded a cold as an excuse to Phil, she planned to go to bed early with the new Rebus, a surprisingly thoughtful Christmas present from Simon. Shona had been furious with her. 'Please come, Ruth,' she had wailed over the phone. 'I've got to go because Liam's going but he'll be with his wife and without you I'll just get drunk and fall over ...' But Ruth had stood firm. She thought Shona would probably get drunk anyway and the thought of an evening discussing aromatherapy with Phil's wife while trying to steer an increasingly unsteady Shona away from Liam did not appeal as a way of marking the New Year. She thinks of the Lucy Downey letters. *But with each New Year I think of you*. Briefly she wonders how Nelson is spending the evening.

As she lies in bed with Rebus propped in front of her (why are hardbacks so heavy?) and listens to the steady thump of music coming from next door, she feels oddly restless. She makes herself a hot drink but, downstairs, the lights from Sammy's house seem brighter, more tempting. Like will o'the wisps, she thinks suddenly. She sees Flint's tail disappearing through the cat flap and reflects that even her cat is going out on New Year's Eve. Why was she so pleased to think that she would be on her own? Why is her first reaction to invitations always to think of a way of refusing them? Her mother would say that she is becoming a sad spinster and she is probably right.

Ruth goes back upstairs but the words of the book dance in front of her and she can't lose herself in the wonderfully gothic streets of Edinburgh. Almost without knowing it, she gets up and dresses in black trousers and a black T-shirt. Then, as an afterthought, she adds a red silk shirt given to her years ago by Shona. She collects a bottle of red from her small store of wine and, still almost sleep-walking, she finds herself knocking on her neighbours' front door.

Sammy is thrilled to see her. 'Ruth! How lovely. I didn't think you could come.'

'No. Well, I had a bit of a cold so I thought I'd stay home, then I heard your music and –'

'I'm delighted to see you. *We're* delighted. Ed! Look who's here!'

Ed, a small, bright-eyed man who seems to be perpetually walking on tiptoe, bounds forward to shake Ruth's hand.

'Well, well, well, our mysterious neighbour. I'm very pleased you've come. I've been wanting to chat to you for ages. I'm a bit of an archaeology buff myself. Never miss *Time Team*.'

Ruth murmurs politely. Like most professional archaeologists she regards *Time Team* as at best simplistic, at worst deeply irritating.

'Come through.' Ed steers her into the house. Even with Ruth wearing her flat shoes, he only comes up to her chin.

The weekenders' house is larger than Ruth's because they have added a double-storey extension – she remembers the noise and irritation when it was built, three years ago. Even so, it is on the cosy side for a party. The sitting room feels crowded even though there are actually only about five or six people in it.

'These are our friends Derek and Sue, up from London,' says Ed, bobbing up and down beside Ruth. He really does make her feel very large. 'And this is Nicole and her husband Roger who live in Norwich, and this is, well you must know each other, this is our mutual neighbour David.'

Ruth turns in surprise to see David, the warden of the bird sanctuary, sitting uneasily on the sofa, a pint of beer held out in front of him like a shield.

'Hello,' says David smiling, 'I was hoping you'd come.'

'Oh ho,' says Ed jovially, 'what have we here? Romance blossoming on the mudflats?'

Ruth can feel herself blushing. Luckily the room is dark. 'David and I only really met a few weeks ago,' she says.

'Aren't we dreadful neighbours?' says Ed, striking himself theatrically on the forehead. 'All these years and we're only just getting to know each other. What'll you have to drink, Ruth? Red? White? Beer? I think there's even some mulled wine left.'

'White would be lovely, thanks.'

Ed prances away and leaves Ruth sitting next to David on the sofa, still holding her bottle of red.

'Oh dear,' she says, 'I meant to give this to Ed. Now it looks as if I'm planning to drink it all myself.'

'I was worse,' says David. 'I brought some sloe gin. It

was in a Lucozade bottle. I think they thought it was a bomb.'

Ruth laughs. 'I love sloe gin. Did you make it yourself?'

'Yes,' says David, 'the sloes are wonderful in autumn. And the blackberries. One year I made blackberry wine.'

'Was it good?'

'I think so, but I'm not much of a drinker. And I didn't really have anyone to offer it to.'

Ruth feels a sudden tug of understanding. She too has weekends when she doesn't speak to anyone but her cats. This is her choice and, by and large, she doesn't mind, it's just that meeting someone else solitary seems odd somehow. Like two lone round-the-world sailors suddenly coming face-to-face at the Cape of Good Hope. They understand each other but, due to the nature of their lives, will probably never become friends.

Ed is back, carrying a huge glass of white wine. Ruth gives him the red and he makes such a fuss of it that she suspects it must be rubbish.

'So, Ruth.' Ed stays standing beside her; she thinks he likes the sensation of looking down on someone for a change. 'Found any buried treasure recently?'

Ruth finds she does not want to tell Ed about the body in the mud or about the torques or even about the henge. She doesn't know why, she just feels that the secrets belong with the Saltmarsh for just a bit longer. David doesn't count; he is almost part of the marsh itself.

'I teach at the university,' she says at last. 'We don't really do many digs. At least the students do a dig every spring but they always find the same things.'

'Why's that?' asks Ed.

'Because we know what is there,' explains Ruth. 'They have to find something, after all. The Americans would ask for their money back if they didn't.'

'Americans,' says David suddenly. 'Dreadful people. We had some last year, trying to catch a sanderling. Apparently they thought it was wounded.'

'What's a sanderling?' asks Ed.

David looks astonished. 'It's a bird. Quite common. They run up and down the beach by the edge of the water, trying to catch sea creatures. These Americans, they thought it was hurt because it wasn't flying.'

'There must be some interesting birds round here,' says Ed, sounding less than interested himself. He starts bobbing up and down again, looking for someone else to talk to.

But David is transformed. 'Wonderful,' he says, his eyes shining. 'The mudflats are like heaven for them. So nutritious. You see whole flocks stopping by on their migration routes, just to feed here.'

'Like a motorway service station,' says Ruth.

David laughs. 'Exactly! In the winter, the Saltmarsh can be covered with birds, all trying to find something to eat on the mudflats. Sometimes there are as many as two thousand pink-footed geese, for example, coming from Iceland and Greenland and there are lots of native waterfowl too: golden eye, gadwell, goosander, shoveller, pintail. I've even seen a red-backed shrike.'

Ruth feels slightly dazed by all these names but she likes the sound of them, and she likes being with another expert, someone else whose job is their enthusiasm. Ed, meanwhile, has drifted quietly away.

'I recognise snipe,' she offers. 'And I think I've heard a bittern. They've got such a sinister call.'

'Yes, we've a nesting pair on the marsh,' says David. 'Must have been the male you heard. They call in the morning, first thing. It's a kind of hollow boom; echoes for miles.'

They are silent for a moment but Ruth is surprised how comfortable she feels with the silence. She doesn't feel compelled to fill it with a cute anecdote about the cats. Instead, she takes a sip of wine and says, 'About those wooden posts on the marsh ...'

David looks surprised and is about to say something but, just at that moment Sammy bustles up and tells them that there is food in the kitchen.

'Then we've got to get you two mingling. Can't have you sitting here in silence all evening, can we?'

They both get up obediently and follow her to the kitchen.

Nelson too is at a party. His is rather more glamorous than Ruth's, and certainly noisier. It is being held in rooms above a wine bar and sparkling wine is flowing like water. Discordant music blasts from the speakers and evil little canapés are circulating. Nelson, who arrived straight from work, has eaten about twenty and now feels slightly sick. His last selection, a prawn in puff pastry, is floating forlornly in a nearby ice sculpture. He is dying for a cigarette.

'Alright?' His wife Michelle drifts by, elegant in a metallic gold dress.

'No. When can we go home?'

She laughs, pretending this is a joke. 'It's a New Year's Eve party so it's kind of the idea to stay until midnight.'

'I've got a better idea. Let's go home and get a take-away.'

'I'm enjoying myself.' She smiles widely to prove this and flicks her long blonde hair over her shoulder. She does look fantastic, he has to admit.

'And besides' – her face hardens – 'how would it look to Tony and Juan?' Tony and Juan are Michelle's bosses, joint owners of the hairdressing salon she manages. They are gay, which is fine by Nelson as long as he doesn't have to go to their parties. He considers this attitude quite enlightened and is hurt when Michelle says he is prejudiced.

'They won't notice. The place is packed.'

'They will notice, and anyway I don't want to leave. Come on Harry.' She puts a hand on his arm, running a manicured nail up his sleeve. 'Relax. Let your hair down.'

He is softening. 'I haven't got much hair. I'm the only person here without highlights.'

'I like your hair,' she says. 'It's very George Clooney.'

'Grey, you mean?'

'Distinguished. Come on, let's get you another drink.'

'Have they got any beer?' Nelson asks plaintively. But he allows himself to be led away.

Ruth and David are at the conservatory window, watching Ed and Derek trying to light fireworks. The conservatory, another new addition to the house, faces towards King's Lynn and they can already see other small explosions in the sky as people greet the New Year. Ed, though, is having difficulty. It is drizzling and his safety lighter won't work.

Sammy keeps shouting helpful hints from the window and people are getting restive. It is ten minutes to midnight.

'Interesting tradition,' says David, 'lighting fireworks at the start of the new year.'

'Isn't it meant to symbolise lighting the way for the new year?' says Ruth.

'Or setting fire to the old?' suggests Sue, Derek's wife.

'What about a tall, dark man crossing the threshold at midnight,' says Sammy. 'We must have that.'

'Have we got any tall dark men?' asks Sue with a laugh.

'Well, Ed's dark ...' giggles Sammy disloyally.

'What about you?' Sue turns to David who is visibly trying to disappear into the shiny pine floor.

'I'm going a bit thin on top, I'm afraid,' he says.

'Nonsense. You'll do.'

'Isn't he meant to be carrying a lump of coal?' says Nicole, who hasn't yet spoken. She is petite and French and makes Ruth feel like an elephant.

'I'm afraid we're all oil-fired here,' says Sammy. 'But he could carry a pot of Marmite.'

'Marmite!' Nicole shudders extravagantly. 'What a terrible English taste.'

'Well it's black, that's all that matters,' says Sammy.

Ruth thinks suddenly of the will o'the wisps, and the doomed blacksmith wandering the underworld with his lump of coal from the devil's furnace. Outside, a firework finally leaps into life. The sky is filled with green and yellow stars. Everyone cheers. In the background, on the television, excitable crowds of C-list celebrities count down alongside Big Ben.

'Ten, nine, eight ...'

In the garden, Ed's capering figure looks suddenly demonic, outlined against the red glow of the fireworks.

'Seven, six, five ...'

Sammy thrusts a Marmite pot into David's hand. He looks at it helplessly. As he turns to Ruth, he too is lit by technicolour flares. Red, gold, green.

'Four, three, two, one ...'

'Happy New Year,' says David.

'Happy New Year,' echoes Ruth.

And, as Big Ben tolls mournfully in the background, the old year dies.

Nelson has sloped out to smoke a cigarette and text his daughters. Tony and Juan, too cool for Big Ben and the C-list celebs, have organised their own countdown with the help of Juan's Rolex. Unfortunately Juan's Rolex is five minutes slow so they have, technically, already missed the New Year. Laura, Nelson's eighteen-year-old, is out with her boyfriend. Rebecca, sixteen, is at a party. He thinks grimly of young lads like he had once been, using the chimes of New Year as a chance for a snog. Or worse. A text message from their old dad might be just the thing to break the mood.

Happy New Year luv, he texts twice, with scrupulous fairness. Then, glancing down the menu, he sees the name after Rebecca's. Ruth Galloway.

He wonders what Ruth is doing tonight. He imagines her at a dinner party with some other lecturers, all being very clever and intellectual, word games over the brandy, that type of thing. Does she have a boyfriend? A partner, she'd probably call it. She never mentions anyone but he thinks Ruth is the sort of person to guard her privacy. Like him. Maybe she has a girlfriend? But she doesn't look like his idea of a lesbian (which veers between shaven head and dungarees and the lipsticked porn-film version). Anyway, she might not dress for men but he doesn't think she dresses for women either. She looks, he searches for the word, *self-sufficient*, as if she doesn't much need other people. Maybe she's spending the evening on her own.

He wonders, for the hundredth time, if he's ever going to solve this case. Earlier in the evening he had heard two women talking about Scarlet Henderson. 'Still haven't found her ... Terrible for the parents ... Of course the police are doing nothing.' Nelson had had to control a murderous urge to storm over, seize the women by their surgery-enhanced necks and bellow: 'I'm working twenty-four hours a day on the case. I've cancelled all leave for my team. I've followed up every lead. I've looked at that little girl's face until it's imprinted on my eyelids. I dream about her at night. My wife says I'm obsessed. Every morning when I wake up, she's the first thing I think about. I haven't prayed since I was at school but I've prayed for her. Please God let me find her, please God let her be alive. So don't tell me I'm doing nothing, you emaciated bitches.' But, instead, he had just moved away, looking so thunderous that Michelle accused him of ruining everyone's evening. 'It's just selfish, Harry, can't you see that?'

Nelson sighs. From inside he can hear the sounds of champagne corks popping accompanied by an elderly soprano's rather dodgy high notes as she warbles 'Auld

Lang Syne'. He looks down at his mobile phone with its glowing green numbers. On an impulse he texts quickly, **Happy New Year HN**, and presses SEND. Then he walks slowly back to the party.

She watches the square of light in the roof turn green and then gold and then red. There are bangs too and sudden whizzing noises. At first she is frightened and then she thinks she has heard these sounds before. When? How many times? She doesn't know. She thinks, once before, he spoke to her and told her not to worry. It was only ... What? She doesn't remember the word.

Usually she only hears the birds. The first ones come when it's still dark: long, wavy noises that she imagines like streamers wrapping themselves around everything. Party streamers, red, gold and green, like the lights in the sky. Then there are the low sounds, deep down, like a man clearing his throat. Like him, when he coughs in the dark and she doesn't know where he is. The sounds she likes best are the ones very high up, twisting and turning in the sky. She imagines herself flying up to meet them, high up where it's blue. But the window is shut during the day so she never sees the birds themselves.

She looks up at the trapdoor. She wonders if he will come down again. She thinks she hates him more than anyone in the world but, then again, there isn't anyone else in the world. And sometimes he is kind. He gave her the extra blanket when it was cold. He gives her food though sometimes he is angry when she doesn't eat. 'We have to build you up,' he says. She doesn't know why. The words remind her of an old, old story, locked away long ago in that other time, the time she thinks must be a dream. Something about a witch and a house made of sweets. She remembers sweets, little chocolate pebbles that you put on your tongue and they melted into thick sweetness, so sweet that you almost couldn't bear it.

She thinks he gave her chocolate once. She was sick and the stone floor smelt of it and she lay down and her head hurt and he gave her water to drink. The glass had chattered against her teeth. She's got more teeth now. He took the old ones; she doesn't know why. The new teeth feel crowded and odd in her mouth. She tried to see her reflection once, in a metal tray, but this horrible creature stared back at her. A ghost face, all white with wild black hair and terrible staring eyes. She doesn't want to look again.

CHAPTER 8

'We've found him.'

There is nothing more annoying, thinks Ruth, than someone who thinks they don't have to introduce themselves on the phone, who assumes that you must recognise their voice because it is so wonderfully individual. But, then again, she *has* recognised his voice. Those flat Northern vowels, the air of suppressed impatience, are unmistakable. Still, just to teach him a lesson, she says, 'Who is this?'

'It's Nelson. Harry Nelson. From the police.'

'Oh. Who have you found exactly?'

'Cathbad. Of course, that's not his real name. He's called Michael Malone.'

I knew that, Ruth wants to say. Instead she asks, 'Where did you find him?'

'He's still in Norfolk. Lives in a caravan at Blakeney. I'm going to see him now. I wondered if you'd like to come.'

Ruth is silent for a moment. Of course, part of her wants very much to come. She is more involved in this investigation than she likes to admit. She has spent hours rereading the letters, looking for clues, chance words, *anything* that might lead her to their author. She feels oddly close to Lucy and Scarlet and to the unnamed Iron Age girl found on the Saltmarsh. In her mind they are intrinsically linked to each other – and to her. She is also curious about Cathbad and, given that she was the one who gave his name to Nelson, also feels slightly responsible for him. On the other hand, Nelson's assumption that she would be ready to drop everything at a moment's notice is rather insulting. She is actually rather busy preparing lecture notes and updating her slides. Term starts next week. But, then again, there is nothing that can't wait a few hours.

'Hello? Ruth?' Nelson is saying impatiently.

'OK,' says Ruth, 'I'll meet you in half an hour. At the car park in Blakeney. Be careful, though, it floods at high tide.'

Blakeney is famous for its seals. At Blakeney Point, the land juts out into the sea, forming a shingle spit which is a breeding ground for seals. A number of local fishermen offer trips out to watch them, and in summer you can see the little boats shuttling to and fro all day from Blakeney Harbour to the spit, filled with excitable tourists wielding giant cameras. The seals take it all with commendable calm. They lie on the beach in companionable heaps looking, Ruth always thinks, like drunks who have been chucked out of a pub. She is less tolerant and usually tries to avoid Blakeney in the summer but today the car park contains only a few vehicles, one of them Nelson's dirty Mercedes, parked as far from the sea as possible. Ruth pulls up her Renault next to Nelson's car and gets her Wellingtons out of the trunk. She has lived in Norfolk long enough to know that it is almost always advisable to wear Wellingtons.

'You're late,' Nelson greets her.

'Actually I'm early. It's only twenty-five minutes since you rang,' she counters.

As she pulls on her boots, Ruth wonders exactly why Nelson has invited her today. It is not as if he will need her archaeological knowledge and, unlike Erik, she barely knows Cathbad. Nelson is a mystery altogether. Coming home late from Sammy's party, she had not been that surprised to see her mobile phone flashing. Calls are always delayed on New Year's Eve and she expected it to be one of her friends, perhaps Shona, ringing from a drunken party. The first message had indeed been from Shona: **Happy New Year. I h8 Liam**. The second had been from Erik but the third, intriguingly, had declared itself 'caller unknown'. Pressing READ Ruth had at first wondered who HN could be. It was not until she had read the fourth message that it had come to her. Harry Nelson. Detective Chief Inspector Harry Nelson. Ringing to wish her a Happy New Year. What did it all mean?

The fourth message had been from Peter.

'It's over there,' says Nelson, pointing.

Ruth sees a decrepit caravan parked right at the top of the beach. It is surrounded by upturned fishing boats and is partly covered by a tarpaulin. In fact, it almost looks like another boat apart from the fact that it is painted purple and has a lightning rod attached to the roof.

Ruth looks quizzically at Nelson.

Nelson shrugs. 'Perhaps he's afraid of lightning.'

Or he wants to attract it, thinks Ruth.

They plod across the stony beach, Ruth's boots holding up better than Nelson's brogues. Two fishermen sitting on the harbour wall look at them curiously. As they reach the caravan, Nelson raises his hand to knock on the door but it is opened before he can connect. A figure wearing a long purple cloak and carrying a staff stands outlined in the doorway.

Cathbad. Ruth's first thought is that he hasn't changed much in ten years. Then, his hair had been long and dark, sometimes tied back in a ponytail, sometimes hanging loose about his shoulders. Now it is shorter and streaked with grey. He has grown a beard which, strangely, remains jet black, so that it looks rather like a disguise, as if it is attached with elastic around the ears. His eyes are dark too and suspicious now as he watches them. Ruth remembers him as nervous, edgy, always likely to explode in either rage or laughter. Now he seems calmer, more in control. Ruth notices, though, that the hand gripping the staff is white around the knuckles.

'Michael Malone?' Nelson greets him formally.

'Cathbad.'

'Mr Malone, also known as Cathbad, I'm Detective Chief Inspector Nelson from Norfolk Police. Can we come in?' As an afterthought, he adds. 'And this is Doctor Ruth Galloway from North Norfolk University.'

Cathbad turns his dark gaze on Ruth.

'I know you,' he says slowly.

'We met at a dig,' says Ruth, 'on the Saltmarsh, ten years ago.'

'I remember,' says Cathbad slowly. 'You were with a man. A red-headed man.'

To her annoyance Ruth finds herself blushing. She is sure Nelson is looking at her.

'Yes,' she says, 'I was.'

'Can we come in?' asks Nelson again.

Silently, Cathbad stands aside to let them into the caravan.

Inside, the first sensation is of being in a tent. Midnight blue draperies hang from the ceiling and cover every piece of furniture. Ruth can just make out a bunk bed with cupboards under it, a cooker, covered with rust and food stains, a wooden bench seat and a table, this time covered with billowing red material. The blue drapes give a strangely dreamlike feeling, as do the twenty or so dream-catchers twinkling gently from the ceiling. The air is thick and musty. Ruth sees Nelson sniffing hopefully but she doesn't think it is cannabis. Joss sticks, more likely.

Cathbad gestures them towards the bench before seating himself in a high-backed wizard's chair. First point to him, thinks Ruth.

'Mr Malone,' says Nelson. 'We're investigating a murder and we'd like to ask you a few questions.'

Cathbad looks at them calmly. 'You're very abrupt,' he says. 'Are you a Scorpio?'

Nelson ignores him. From his pocket he pulls out a photograph and puts it on the table in front of Cathbad. 'Do you recognise this girl?' he asks.

Ruth looks curiously at the picture. She has never seen a picture of Lucy Downey and is struck by the resemblance to Scarlet Henderson. The same dark, curling hair, the same smiling mouth. Only the clothes are different. Lucy Downey is wearing a grey school uniform. Scarlet, in the picture Ruth saw, had been wearing a fairy dress.

'No,' says Cathbad shortly. 'What's all this about?'

'This little girl vanished ten years ago,' says Nelson, 'when you and your mates were getting all worked up about that henge thing. I wondered if you'd seen her.' Unexpectedly, Cathbad is angry. Ruth remembers his ability to change emotions in a second. Now, his face dark in the blue light, he looks like his younger self.

'That henge thing,' he says in a voice shaking with rage, 'was a holy site, a place dedicated to worship and sacrifice. And Doctor Galloway's *friends* proceeded to destroy it.'

Ruth is rather shocked to find herself under attack. Nelson, though, positively quivers at the words 'worship and sacrifice'.

'We didn't destroy it,' Ruth says, rather lamely. 'It's at the university. In the museum.'

'The museum!' mimics Cathbad savagely. 'A dead place, full of bones and corpses.'

'Mr Malone,' cuts in Nelson. 'Ten years ago, you were ... how old?'

'I'm forty-two now. Not that I count the years on the temporal plane.'

Nelson ignores this. 'So, ten years ago you would have been thirty-two.'

'Full marks for the maths, Detective Chief Inspector.'

'What were you doing ten years ago, aged thirty-two?'

'Looking up at the stars, listening to the music of the spheres.'

Nelson leans forward. He doesn't raise his voice but suddenly Ruth feels the temperature in the caravan drop. She is suddenly aware of an undercurrent of violence in the room. And it isn't coming from Cathbad.

'Look,' says Nelson softly, 'either you answer my questions civilly or we go down to the station and do it there. And, I promise you, when it gets out that you've been questioned in connection with this case, you won't be looking at the stars. You'll be looking at a gang of vigilantes trying to burn your bloody caravan down.'

Cathbad looks at Nelson for a long moment, drawing his cloak around him as if for protection. Then he says, in a low monotone, 'Ten years ago I was living in a commune near Cromer.'

'And prior to that?'

'I was a student.'

'Where?'

'Manchester.' Cathbad suddenly looks at Ruth and smiles, rather oddly. 'Studying archaeology.'

Ruth lets out an involuntary gasp. 'But that's where –'

'Erik Anderssen taught. Yes. That's where I met him.'

Nelson seems uninterested in this but Ruth's mind is racing. So Cathbad knew Erik long before the henge dig. Why hadn't Erik mentioned it? Erik had been her tutor when she did her doctorate at Southampton but she knew that previously he had been a lecturer at Manchester. Why hadn't Erik told her that he had been Cathbad's tutor too?

'So, what did you do, on this commune? Did any of you do any real work?'

'Depends what you mean by real,' says Cathbad with a flash of his old spirit. 'We grew vegetables, we cooked them, we made music, we sang, we made love. And I was a postman,' he adds, as an afterthought.

'A *postman*?'

'Yes. Is that real enough for you? Early starts, it suited me fine. I love the dawn, leaves you with the rest of the day free.'

'Free to disrupt the henge dig?'

'Disrupt!' The fire is definitely back in Cathbad's eyes.

'We were trying to save it! Erik understood that. He wasn't like the rest of those ...' He pauses for an epithet strong enough. 'Those ... *civil servants*. He understood that the site was holy, sacred to the place and to the sea. It wasn't about carbon dating and crap like that. It was about being at one with the natural world.'

Nelson cuts in again. Ruth can tell he stopped listening at about the word 'holy'. 'And when the dig finished?'

'Life went on.'

'You went on being a postman?'

'No. I got another job.'

'Where?'

'At the university. I still work there.'

Nelson looks at Ruth who stares at him blankly. All these years, Cathbad has been working beside her at the university. Did Erik know?

'Doing what?'

'Lab assistant. My first degree was in chemistry.'

'Did you hear about the disappearance of Lucy Downey?'

'I think so. There was a lot in the papers, wasn't there?'

'And Scarlet Henderson?'

'Who? Oh, the little girl who went missing recently. I heard about it, yes. Look Inspector ...' Suddenly his voice changes and he draws himself up in the wizard's chair. 'What's all this about? You've got nothing that links me to these girls. This is police harassment.'

'No,' says Nelson mildly, 'just routine enquiries.'

'I won't say anything more without a solicitor present.'

Ruth expects Nelson to argue (something along the lines that only guilty men need solicitors) but instead he stands up, hitting his head on a dream-catcher. 'Thank you for your time, Mr Malone. Just one thing. Can I have a sample of your handwriting?'

'My handwriting?'

'Yes. For our enquiries.'

Cathbad looks as if he is about to refuse but then he slowly gets up and goes to a filing cabinet which is sitting incongruously in a corner of the caravan. He unlocks a drawer and pulls out a sheet of paper. Ruth wonders why a man living in a caravan full of dream-catchers would also have a locked filing cabinet.

Nelson looks down at the writing and, just for a second, his face darkens. Ruth sees his jaw muscles clench and wonders what's coming. But instead Nelson smoothes out the paper and says in a bland, social voice, 'Thank you very much, Mr Malone. Good day.'

'Goodbye,' says Ruth weakly. Cathbad ignores her.

Ruth and Nelson scrunch away over the shingle. The fishermen are still sitting on the harbour wall. The tide is coming in, bringing with it a heady, briny smell and a host of seagulls, calling and crying overhead.

'Well?' says Nelson at last. 'What do you think?'

'I can't believe he works at the university.'

'Why not? It's full of weirdos, that place.'

Ruth can't tell if he is joking or not. 'It's just ... if Erik knew, he didn't tell me.'

Nelson looks at her. 'Are you close then, you and this Erik bloke?'

'Yes,' says Ruth, rather defiantly.

'He's coming to England soon, isn't he?'

'Next week.'

'I'll look forward to meeting him.'

Ruth smiles. 'He said the same about you.'

Nelson grunts sceptically. They have almost reached their cars, which are still on dry land although the water is lapping round some unfortunate vehicles parked lower down.

'It'll play havoc with their suspension,' says Nelson.

'What about his writing?' asks Ruth. In reply, Nelson hands her the piece of paper. It seems to be a poem entitled 'In Praise of James Agar'.

'Who's James Agar?' she asks.

'Bastard who killed a policeman.'

'Oh.' She begins to see why Cathbad chose this particular piece of paper. She glances down the lines. The handwriting is extravagant, full of swirls and loops. It is nothing like the writing in the Lucy Downey letters.

'It's not the same,' she says.

'Doesn't mean he's off the hook.'

'Do you suspect him then?'

Nelson pauses, one hand on his car door. 'I'm not ruling him out,' he says at last. 'He's a slippery character. He was in the area at the time and he knows all about that mystic stuff. He's clever too, and he's got something to hide. Why was that cabinet locked? I'm going to come back with a search warrant.'

'Will you get one?'

'Probably not. He was right when he said I had nothing on him. That's why I say he's clever.'

Not quite knowing why she says it, Ruth volunteers, 'Erik says he has magic powers.'

This time Nelson laughs out loud. 'Magic powers!

Nothing magic about him that a kick up the arse won't cure.' He gets into his car but pauses before putting the key in the ignition. 'Mind you,' he says, 'he did get one thing right. I am a Scorpio.'

CHAPTER 9

As Ruth turns into New Road she sees a familiar red sports car parked in front of her house. Shona often explains that her car is a penis substitute and, like the real thing, is often unreliable. Ruth hasn't seen Shona since before Christmas and wonders what new dramas she will have to report. She quite enjoys Shona's love life – second hand, she wouldn't want to live it herself, just as she wouldn't drive a scarlet Mazda. Fat chance of either, she thinks, as she parks behind Shona's car – number plate: FAB 1.

Shona, huddled up in a sheepskin coat, is standing looking out over the Saltmarsh. Dark clouds are gathering over the sea, which gives the whole place an ominous feel. Shadows race over the mudflats and the seagulls are flying inland, sure sign of a storm to come.

'Jesus, Ruth,' says Shona, 'I don't know how you can live here. This place gives me the creeps.'

'I like it,' says Ruth mildly. 'I like being able to look right out to the horizon, with nothing in the way.'

'No people, no shops, no Italian restaurants.' Shona shudders. 'It wouldn't do for me.'

'No,' agrees Ruth. 'Do you want some lunch?'

In the cottage they are greeted ecstatically by Flint. Ruth goes into the kitchen and arranges cheese, pate and salami on a plate. Shona sits at the table by the window, talking.

'I'm definitely going to end it with Liam. He says he loves me but he's obviously never going to leave Anne. Now she's got to have an operation and he can't do anything to upset her. I bet it's just a tummy tuck, anything to avoid making a decision. It was awful on New Year's Eve. Liam kept shoving me into cupboards and saying he loved me and trying to feel me up, then next minute he was back with his arm round Anne talking about their extension. And Phil kept asking me if I'd got a bloke yet. Wanker. Just because I wouldn't go to bed with him. And Phil's awful wife telling me that I'd got a mauve aura. Bloody cheek, I hate mauve; it clashes with my hair.'

She pauses to eat a piece of bread, shaking out her red-gold hair so that it shimmers in the dim afternoon light. Ruth wonders what it must be like to be so beautiful. Exhausting, to judge from what Shona says. Yet it must be exciting too – imagine if every man you met wanted to go to bed with you. Briefly, she flicks through a mental card index of the men in her life: Phil, Erik, her students, Ed next door, David, Harry Nelson. She can't really imagine any of them panting with desire for her. The thought is absurd and oddly disturbing –

'Ruth!'

'What?'

'I was asking what you did on New Year's Eve.'

'Oh, well, I had a cold, like I told you, so I decided to stay home but next door were having a party and the music was so loud that I gave in and went round.'

'Did you? What was it like?'

'Pretty boring. My neighbour kept asking annoying questions about archaeology.'

'Anyone interesting or were they all smug marrieds?'

'Mostly couples. There was another neighbour, David, the bird warden.'

'Oh.' Shona perks up at the thought of an unattached man. Unconsciously she rakes her fingers through her hair so that it falls more seductively across her face. 'What was he like?'

Ruth considers. 'OK. Quiet. Interesting, though a bit obsessive about birds.'

'How old?'

'My age, I think. Fiftyish.'

'Ruth! You're not forty yet.'

'I will be in July.'

'We must have a party,' says Shona vaguely, licking her finger to pick up cheese crumbs. 'And what about this highly mysterious police work you've been doing?'

'Who told you about that?'

'Phil.'

'Oh, well it's not very mysterious really. This policeman asked me to look at some bones he'd found but they weren't modern, they were Iron Age.'

'Why did he think they might be modern?'

'He was looking for the body of a girl who disappeared ten years ago.'

Shona whistles. 'There's been another little girl gone missing recently, hasn't there?'

Ruth nods. 'Scarlet Henderson.'

'Are you involved in that too?'

Again, Ruth hesitates. She is not sure how much she wants to tell Shona. Shona is always so *interested* in everything, she is sure to make Ruth say more than she wants to.

Nelson has told her that the contents of the letters are confidential ('Don't want the press getting hold of it') but, then again, Shona is the literature expert.

'A little. There are some letters ...'

Sure enough, Shona leans forward immediately, intrigued by the mention of the written word.

'Letters?'

'Yes, written after the first disappearance and now after Scarlet Henderson. This policeman, he thinks they might be linked.' Has she said too much?

'What do the letters say?'

'I don't think I can tell you,' says Ruth. She feels uncomfortable under the ultraviolet glare of Shona's interest.

Shona looks at her speculatively, as if wondering how much information she can extract. But then she seems to change her mind, tossing back her hair and looking out of the window where the sky is now a brooding purple colour.

'This policeman, what's his name?'

'Nelson. Harry Nelson.'

Shona swings round to look hard at Ruth. 'Are you sure?'

'Yes. Why?'

'Oh nothing.' Shona goes back to the window. 'It's just that I think I heard something about him once. Something about police brutality, I think. God, look at that sky! I'd better get home before it tips down.'

Ten minutes after Shona has left, the storm breaks. Rain and hail hurl themselves at the windows until Ruth feels as if she is under siege. The wind is roaring in from the sea with a noise like thunder and she feels as if her whole cottage is shaking, tossed to and fro like a ship at sea. She is used to storms, of course, but she still finds them disconcerting. This house has stood for over a hundred years, she tells herself, it'll take more than a winter storm to blow it away. But the wind howls and wails as if it is trying to disprove her and the windows rattle under the onslaught. Ruth draws the curtains and turns on the lights. She'll do some work; that'll take her mind off the weather.

But instead of clicking onto Lectures 08, Ruth finds her finger hovering over the tempting, multicoloured Google logo. After a few seconds' inward struggle, she gives in and types in the words Harry Nelson. ENTER. A stream of Nelsons floods the screen, including a US chess champion and a professor of physics. Harry Nilsson is there too, the guy who sang 'Without You'. Ruth hums it now, scrolling down the screen. There he is. DI Harry Nelson, decorated for bravery in 1990. And again, Harry Nelson (back row, second left) in a police rugby team. Ruth has another idea and clicks onto Friends Reunited, a rather guilty late-night fix of hers. Yes, here he is. Henry (Harry) Nelson at a Catholic grammar school in Blackpool. What does he say about himself? His contribution is brief in the extreme: 'Married to Michelle, two daughters. Living in Norfolk (God help me).'

Ruth ponders this. No mention of the police. Does Nelson think his old friends in Blackpool will despise him for becoming a policeman? And it is interesting that he refers to his wife by name but not his daughters. Maybe he is scared of paedophiles on the internet. He would, surely, know more than most about the dark side of human nature.

Still, it must be significant that his marriage to Michelle is the first thing he mentions, as if it were the achievement of his life. Perhaps it is. Ruth thinks back to that sighting before Christmas. Michelle certainly looked attractive enough, a definite prize for a man who is letting himself go a bit, a man who doesn't look as if he has a gym membership or spends more than five pounds on a haircut. And Michelle looked, Ruth struggles to put her finger on it, like a woman who knows her own worth, as if she knows the value of her good looks and how to use them for her own purposes. She remembers seeing her laughing up at Nelson, her hand on his arm, soothing, cajoling. She looked, in short, like the sort of woman Ruth dislikes intensely.

What else? Well, he doesn't like Norfolk much. Ruth has already gathered as much from his references to 'this Godforsaken county'. Godforsaken. And God gets a mention here too, even if the police force doesn't. *God help me*. It is meant light-heartedly, Ruth knows, but the fact remains that Nelson has one thing in common with the mysterious letter writer. He too likes to mention God.

Ruth scrolls back and clicks on the first mention, the decoration for bravery. She sees a much younger Nelson, less battered and wary-looking. He is holding a certificate and looking embarrassed. She reads:

> PC Harry Nelson was awarded the Police Medal for Bravery in connection with the poll tax riots in Manchester. The riots, which quickly became violent, culminated in the death of a policeman, PC Stephen Naylor. PC Nelson, at great risk to his own life, broke through the lines of protestors to carry away PC

> Naylor's body. PC Naylor later died of his injuries. A twenty-four-year-old man, James Agar, was charged with the murder.

James Agar. Ruth looks at the name, clicking through her internal search engine. Then it comes to her. Cathbad's poem, 'In Praise of James Agar'. No wonder Nelson's face had turned black when he read it. No wonder Cathbad had been so careful to choose this particular example of his handwriting. Manchester. That must have been when Cathbad was a student. Maybe he was involved in the riots. Lots of students were. She remembers similar riots when she was a student in London, watching from a window at University College, sympathising with the cause but too prudent to join in. Cathbad, typically, would have shown no such reserve. And James Agar was convicted. She wonders on whose evidence.

Sure enough, Ruth clicks on 'James Agar' and finds page after page of tributes to James Agar – 'framed by the police for the killing of PC Stephen Naylor'. There had been one key witness at Agar's trial: PC Harry Nelson.

Ruth clicks back onto her lecture notes. The wind continues to howl across the marshes. Flint, his fur soaked flat, dashes in through the cat flap and sits on the sofa looking martyred. Sparky is nowhere to be seen. She is probably hiding somewhere. She hates rain.

Ruth adds a few desultory notes about soil erosion and is just about to make herself a compensatory sandwich (compensating for what?) when the phone rings. She snatches it up like a lifeline.

'Ruth! How are you?'

It is Peter.

After they split up Peter made a concerted attempt to stay in touch. He was living and working in London but he used to phone a lot, and once or twice came up to see her. On these occasions they invariably ended up in bed together and this felt so right that Ruth came to the conclusion that it must be wrong. If we're apart, we must stay apart, she had said, it's no good carrying on like this. Apart from anything else, it'll stop either of us finding someone new. Peter had been terribly hurt. But I want to be with you, he had said. Don't you see, if we can't stay away from each other, it must mean that we were meant to be together? But Ruth had been adamant and eventually Peter had stormed back to London in a fury, swearing undying love all the way. Six months later he had married someone else.

That had been five years ago. Ruth had heard very little from Peter in that time, a Christmas card, once a copy of an article he had written. She knew that he and his wife, Victoria, had had a baby, a boy called Daniel. He must be about four now. After Daniel's birth (she sent a teddy), Ruth had heard nothing until the text message on New Year's Eve. **Happy New Year love Peter**. Nothing more, but just for a second Ruth had felt her heart contract.

'Peter. Hello.'

'Bit of blast from the past, eh?'

'You could say that, yes.'

A brief silence. Ruth tries to imagine Peter at the other end of the phone. Is he calling from work? From home? She imagines Victoria, whom she has never met, sitting by his side with Daniel on her lap. 'What's Daddy doing?' 'Shh darling, he's ringing his ex-girlfriend.'

'So.' Very hearty. 'How've you been, Ruth?'

'I've been fine. How about you?'

'Fine. Working hard.'

Peter teaches history at University College, London, where Ruth did her first degree. She imagines him there: the view of dusty plane trees, of bicycles chained against railings, of London buses, and tourists wandering lost around Gordon Square.

'Still at UCL?'

'Yes. What about you?'

'Still at North Norfolk. Still digging up bones and fighting with Phil.'

Peter laughs. 'I remember Phil. Is he still keen on his geophys gadgets?'

'I think he's shortly going to mutate into a machine.'

Peter laughs again but this time the laugh ends rather abruptly. 'Look Ruth. The thing is, I've got a sabbatical next term –'

'You too?' The words are out before she can stop them.

'What do you mean?'

'Oh, it's just – Erik's got a sabbatical too. He's coming over next week.'

'Erik! The old Viking himself! So you're still in touch?'

'Yes.' Slightly defensively.

'Well, the thing is … I'm writing a book on Nelson.'

'*Who*?'

A confused pause. 'Horatio Nelson. Admiral Nelson. You remember, I did my postgraduate research on the Napoleonic Wars.'

'Oh ... yes.' The other Nelson in her life has temporarily caused her to forget the most famous Nelson of all. Of course, he was from Norfolk too, there are hundreds of pubs named after him.

'Well, I'm planning to visit Burnham Thorpe. You know, where he was born. I'm renting a cottage nearby and I thought I could pop over and see you.'

Several things cross Ruth's mind. You must have been to Burnham Thorpe before, without 'popping over' to see me, why is this different? Will your wife be there? Is this only about research? Why ring me after all this time?

Aloud she says, 'That would be great.'

'Good.' Peter sounds relieved. 'And I'd like to see the Saltmarsh again. God, I remember that summer. Finding the henge in the mud, those hippies who kept putting spells on us, old Erik telling ghost stories around the campfire. Do you remember when I nearly drowned?'

'Yes.' Peter is suffering from an attack of nostalgia, she knows the symptoms. She mustn't join in otherwise she'll be swept away too, drowning in a quicksand of the past.

Peter sighs. 'Well, I'll be in touch. It'll probably be next week or the week after. Will you be around?'

'Yes, I'll be around.'

'Great. Bye then.'

'Bye.'

Ruth replaces the receiver thoughtfully. She doesn't know why Peter is coming to see her; she only knows that the past seems to be converging on her. First Erik, then Cathbad, now Peter. Before she knows it, she will have gone back in time ten years and will be walking along the beach, hand-in-hand with Peter, her hair six inches longer and her waist four inches thinner. She shakes her head. The past is dead. She, as an archaeologist, knows that better than most. But she knows too that it can be seductive.

Rain is still drumming against the windows. Getting up, she strokes Flint, who is now stretched out on the sofa, eyes shut, pretending she isn't there. She'd better check that Sparky isn't outside meowing to be let in – although she has a cat flap, Sparky really prefers having the door opened for her. Ruth opens the door.

The rain flies in her face, blinding her. Spluttering, she wipes her eyes on her sleeve. And then she sees it. Sparky is on the doorstep but she isn't meowing or making any other sound. She is lying on her back and her throat has been cut.

CHAPTER 10

Nelson is, for once, driving slowly. It is still raining hard, turning the narrow lanes into treacherous gullies, but Nelson isn't usually the sort of driver who worries about weather conditions. No, Nelson is dawdling because he has just been to see Scarlet's parents and feels he needs some time to recover before getting back to the station. He has had to tell the parents, Delilah and Alan, that not only has the investigation made no progress, but the police want to bring sniffer dogs to search the family garden. *Cases like this, it's usually the parents.* That's what he told Ruth and although maybe he had been trying to shock her, in his experience it has often proved true. One of his first cases involved a missing child in Lytham. Hundreds of police hours spent searching, a young mother very eloquent and moving at the press conference and then Nelson, a young PC, making a routine call at the house, had noticed a strange smell in the downstairs loo. He'd called for reinforcements but, before they arrived, had already found the tiny corpse, stuffed into the cistern. 'She gets on my nerves,' said the mother, apparently unrepentant. 'She's a little devil.' The present tense. It still gets to him. He'd been commended for his work on that case but he remembers weeks, months, of sleepless nights afterwards, retching as he remembered the smell, the sight of the water-bloated body.

He's ruling nothing out but he doesn't really suspect Scarlet's parents. Alan was away anyway and Delilah – Delilah is a fading flower child in bare feet and fringed skirts. She irritates the hell out of him but he can't really imagine her as a killer. Never assume, he tells himself. 'Never assume', his first boss, Derek Fielding, used to say, laboriously. 'It makes an ass out of you and me. Get it?' He'd got it, but he wasn't going to give Fielding the satisfaction of laughing; probably why it took so long for the old bastard to promote him, despite the commendation. But the point is a good one. Never make assumptions about people or circumstances. Delilah Henderson could have killed her daughter. She was in the right location and probably had the means to hand. It had taken her three hours to report Scarlet missing. 'I thought they were just playing hide and seek,' she had sobbed. Nelson disapproves (what sort of mother would not notice, for three hours, that her four-year-old was missing?) but, on balance, he puts it down to the sort of lackadaisical parenting of people like the Hendersons. And she had been distraught, God knows, when she finally realised that Scarlet had gone. She was still distraught, weeping today and clutching an old photo of Scarlet, heartbreakingly happy astride a pink bike with training wheels. Delilah had hardly taken in the news about the garden, had just clutched at Nelson, begging him to find her baby. Nelson slows down almost to walking pace as the windscreen wipers battle against the onslaught of water. Sometimes he hates his job. Christ, he could do with a cigarette but it's only January, a bit early to break his New Year's resolution.

When his phone rings he almost doesn't answer; not for safety reasons – Nelson thinks hands-free phones are for wimps – but because he just can't be bothered with anything else today. When he does press RECEIVE an almost inhuman sound greets him, a sort of sobbing wail. Nelson squints at the caller identification. *Ruth Galloway.* Jesus.

'Ruth? What is it?'

'She's dead,' wails Ruth.

Now Nelson does stop the car, almost skidding into a water-logged ditch.

'Who's dead?'

'Sparky.' Long, gulping pause. 'My cat.'

Nelson counts to ten. 'Are you ringing me up to tell me about a dead cat?'

'Someone cut her throat.'

'*What*?'

'Someone cut her throat and left her on my doorstep.'

'I'll be right over.'

Nelson turns his car, with maximum tire skidding, and heads back towards the Saltmarsh. Ruth's dead cat could be a message from the abductor or the letter writer or both. It seems just the sort of warped thing the letter writer would do. Never assume, he tells himself, overtaking a lorry, half-blinded by spray. But cutting an animal's throat, that is definitely sick. Might be able to get some DNA though. He will have to be sensitive ('sensitive' he repeats to himself – the word has a wet, *Guardian*-reader sound that he distrusts); Ruth seems very upset. Funny, he wouldn't have thought her the sort of woman to have pets.

It is pitch black by the time he reaches the Saltmarsh, and though the rain has stopped it is still blowing a gale. The car door is almost ripped out of his hand and, as he walks up the path, he can feel the full force of the wind in the small of his back, pushing him forwards. Jesus, what a place to live. Nelson's home is a modern, four-bedroomed house outside King's Lynn; it is all very civilised, with speed bumps and security lights and double garages. You'd hardly know you were in Norfolk at all. Ruth's cottage seems little better than a hovel and it's so isolated, stuck out here on the edge of nowhere with only the twitchers for company. Why on earth does she live here? She must earn a fair wage at the university, surely?

Ruth opens the door immediately as if she were waiting for him.

'Thanks for coming,' she sniffs.

The door opens straight into a sitting room which, to Nelson's eyes, looks a complete mess. There are books and papers everywhere, a half-drunk cup of coffee sits on the table, along with the remains of a meal, crumbs and olive stones. But then he stops noticing anything because, on the sofa, lies what must be the mutilated corpse of a small cat. Ruth has covered the body with a pink, fluffy blanket which, for some reason, makes his throat close up for a second. He pulls back the blanket.

'Have you touched it? The body?'

'She. She's a girl.'

'Have you touched her?' repeats Nelson patiently.

'Only to put her on the sofa and I did ... stroke her a bit.' Ruth turns away.

Nelson reaches over as if to pat her shoulder but Ruth moves away, blowing her nose. When she turns back, her face is quite composed.

'Do you think it was him?' she asks. 'The murderer?'

'We haven't got a murder yet,' says Nelson cautiously.

Ruth shrugs this aside. 'Who would do something like this?'

'Someone pretty sick, that's for sure,' says Nelson, bending over Sparky's body. Then he straightens up. 'Does anyone know you're involved in this investigation?'

'No.'

'Are you sure?'

'Phil, my boss, knows,' says Ruth slowly, 'and maybe some other people at the university. My next-door neighbour saw me leaving in a police car that time.'

Nelson turns away from Sparky then, almost as an afterthought, he stoops and covers the little body again with the pink blanket. Then he touches Ruth's arm and says in a surprisingly gentle voice, 'Let's sit down.'

Ruth sits in a sagging armchair. She looks away from him, out towards the curtained window. The wind is still roaring outside, making the panes rattle. Nelson perches on the edge of the sofa.

'Ruth,' says Nelson, 'we know there's a dangerous man out there. He may well have murdered two girls and he may be the person who did this to your cat. In any event, you've got to be careful. Someone, for whatever reason, is trying to frighten you and I think it's safe to assume that it has something to do with this case.'

Still looking past him, Ruth asks, 'Do you need to take her, Sparky, away?'

'Yes,' says Nelson, trying to be honest and yet not too harsh, 'we need to test for fingerprints and DNA.'

'So really,' says Ruth in a high, hard voice, 'this is a bit of a breakthrough.'

'Ruth,' says Nelson, 'look at me.' She does so. Her face is swollen with crying.

'I'm sorry about your cat. About Sparky. I had a German Shepherd once called Max. I thought the world of that dog. My wife used to say she felt quite jealous sometimes. When he was run over, I was beside myself, wanted to charge the driver with dangerous driving though it wasn't his fault really. But this is a possible murder investigation and I'm afraid your cat is a valuable clue. You want to find out what has happened to Scarlet, don't you?'

'Yes,' says Ruth, 'of course I do.'

'I promise you, Ruth, that, when the lab has finished, I'll bring Sparky back and help you bury her. I'll even light a candle in church. Deal?'

Ruth manages a watery smile. 'Deal.'

Nelson picks up Sparky's body, covering it carefully with the blanket. As he moves towards the door, he turns. 'And Ruth? Make sure you lock all your doors tonight.'

When he has gone, Ruth sits on the sofa, at the opposite end to the place where there is a faint bloodstain on the faded chintz. She looks at the remains of her meal with Shona and wonders, dully, how long ago it was that they sat at this table talking about men. It seems like days but it was in fact only a few hours ago. Since then, she has found out that Nelson has a secret in his past, spoken to her ex-boyfriend and seen her beloved cat brutally murdered. She laughs, slightly hysterically. What else will the night bring? Her mother coming out as a lesbian? David the bird warden proposing marriage? She heads for the kitchen, hell-bent on finding some wine. Flint, who has been watching from a distance, comes up and rubs against her legs. She picks him up, weeping into his dusty orange fur. 'Oh Flint,' she says, 'what will we do without her?' Flint purrs hopefully. Ruth has forgotten to feed him.

Splashing Pinot Grigio into a glass, Ruth looks across to the table by the window where her laptop is still open. She presses a key and her lecture notes appear. She clicks back through her history until she is back on the page of Nelsons: the US chess champion, the professor of physics, Harry Nilsson and Henry (Harry) Nelson of the Norfolk police. He had tried to be kind about Sparky, she recognises dimly. Part of him must have been excited about the possible clue but he had tried to acknowledge her feelings. He probably despises her for getting so upset about a cat but she doesn't care. Sparky was her pet, her companion, her friend – yes, her friend, she repeats defiantly to herself. She thinks of the little black cat, so sweet, so self-contained, and the tears run down her face. Who would want to kill Sparky?

And, for the first time, Nelson's final words sink in. *Make sure you lock all your doors tonight.* The person who killed Sparky could have killed Scarlet and Lucy too. The murderer could have been on Ruth's doorstep. He could have been listening outside her window, knife sharpened. He killed Sparky. Her entire body goes cold as she realises that the dead cat was a message addressed directly to her. *Next time it could be you.*

Then she hears it. A sound outside her window. A pause, a muffled cough and then, unmistakably, footsteps, coming closer and closer. She listens, her heart thumping with such huge, irregular beats that she wonders if she is going to have a coronary, right there on the spot. The knock on the door makes her cry out with fear. It has come. The creature from the night. The beast. The terror. She thinks of *The Monkey's Paw* and the unnamed horror that waits at the door. She is shaking so much that she drops her wine glass. The knock again. A terrible, doom-laden sound, echoing through the tiny house. What is she going to do? Should she ring Nelson? Her phone is across the room, by the sofa, and the idea of moving suddenly seems impossible. Is this it? Is she going to die, here in her cottage with the wind howling outside?

'Ruth!' shouts a voice. 'Are you in there?'

Oh thanks be to the God she doesn't believe in. It is Erik.

Half-laughing, half-crying, Ruth dives to open the door. Erik Anderssen, dressed in a black raincoat and carrying a bottle of whisky, stands smiling in the doorway.

'Hello Ruthie,' he says, 'fancy a nightcap?'

CHAPTER 11

'Drowned landscapes,' says Erik, his singsong voice echoing across the wind-flattened grass, 'have a peculiar magic of their own. Think of Dunwich, the city swallowed by the sea, the church bells ringing underwater. Think of the drowned forest on this very beach, the trees buried beneath our feet. There is something deep within us which fears what is buried, what we cannot see.'

Ruth and Erik are walking along the beach, their feet crunching on the hundreds of razor clam shells brought in by the tide. Yesterday's rain has given way to a beautiful winter's day, cold and bright. The horrors of last night seem far away. It seems impossible that Sparky is dead and that Ruth herself could be in danger. And yet, thinks Ruth, trudging along beside Erik, it is true and it did happen.

Last night she had flung herself into Erik's arms, almost incoherent with crying. He had been very kind, she remembers, had sat her down and made her coffee with whisky in it. She had told him about Sparky and he had said that, when they got the body back, they should give her a Viking funeral, a burning pyre drifting out to sea. Ruth, who wanted to bury Sparky in her garden, under the apple tree, had said nothing but had been aware that Erik was paying Sparky a huge compliment, considering her a soul worthy of such an honour. She remembers her mother telling her that animals don't have souls. Another black mark against God.

Ruth hadn't wanted to be alone last night and so Erik had slept on the sofa, folding up his long limbs under Ruth's sleeping bag and not complaining when Flint woke him up at five, bringing in a dead mouse. He has been a true friend, thinks Ruth. Despite everything, it is wonderful to see him again, to be striding over the Saltmarsh with him once more.

After breakfast, Erik suggested going to look at the henge site and Ruth had agreed readily. She feels the need to be out of doors, away from the house and the dark corners where she expects, every second, to see Sparky's little face appear. No, it is better to be in the open, to be walking along the wide expanse of beach, under the high, blue sky. Mind you, she had forgotten how far it was when the tide is out. The sand stretches for miles, glittering with secret inlets, the occasional piece of driftwood black against the horizon. It looks vast and completely featureless but Erik seems to know exactly where he is going. He strides ahead, his eyes on the horizon. Ruth, wearing her trusty Wellingtons, plods along behind him.

Last night's wind has blown the sand into odd shapes and ridges. Nearer the sea it is flatter, striped with empty oyster shells and dead crabs. Little streams run across the sand to join the sea and, occasionally, there are larger expanses of water, reflecting the blue of the sky. Ruth splashes her way through one of these pools, remembering the summer of the henge dig and the way the sand had felt under her bare feet. She can almost feel the sting of the water and the exquisite pain of walking on the clam shells. At the end of the day, her feet had been a mass of tiny cuts.

'Do you still think we should have left the henge where it was?' she asks.

Erik raises his face to the sun, shutting his eyes. 'Yes,' he says. 'It belonged here. It marked a boundary. We should have respected that.'

'Boundaries were important to prehistoric people, weren't they?'

'Yes indeed.' Erik steps delicately over a fast-flowing stream; he isn't wearing Wellingtons. 'Which is why they marked them with burial mounds, religious shrines, offerings to the ancestors.'

'Do you think that my Iron Age body marks a boundary?' Over breakfast, Ruth had told him more about her find, about the girl with her head shaved and branches twisted around her arms and legs, about the torques and the coins and the tantalising location of the body.

Erik hesitates. He uses his professional voice; measured, calm. 'Yes, I do,' he says at last. 'Boundaries in the ancient landscape were sometimes marked by isolated burials. Think of the bodies at Jutland, for example.'

Ruth thinks of the Jutland discoveries: oak coffins found in water, containing Bronze Age bodies. One had been that of a young woman and what Ruth remembers chiefly were her clothes, a surprisingly trendy outfit of braided miniskirt and crop top.

'What does gadget boy think?' asks Erik.

'Oh, he thinks it's all chance. No link between the Iron Age body and the henge.'

Erik snorts. 'How that boy ever became an archaeologist! Doesn't he understand that if the area was sacred to the Neolithic and Bronze Age people it was sacred to the Iron Age people? That the landscape *itself* is important. This is a liminal zone, between land and water, of course it's special.'

'It isn't that special to us though.'

'Isn't it? It's National Trust land, a nature reserve. Isn't that our way of saying that it is sacred?'

Ruth thinks of the National Trust, sensible women in quilted coats selling souvenirs at castle gates. It isn't her idea of sacred. Then she thinks of David and the way he spoke about the migrating birds. He is someone, she realises, who does think that the place is special.

Erik stops abruptly. He is looking at the sand, which has suddenly become dark and silty. He traces a line with his smart shoe. Underneath, the sand is quite startlingly blue. 'Burnt matter,' he says. 'The roots of ancient trees. We're getting near.'

Looking back, Ruth sees a clump of trees to the left and the spire of a church away in the distance. She remembers the view perfectly; they are very near the henge circle. But the sand, grey in the winter sun, gives nothing away. *What the Sand gets, the Sand keeps forever.*

Ruth remembers how the henge had looked that summer evening ten years ago, the ring of gnarled wooden posts sinister and otherworldly as if it had risen out of the sea. She remembers Erik kneeling before the posts in an attitude almost of prayer. She remembers, when she first entered the circle, a shiver running through her whole body.

'It's here,' says Erik.

There is nothing to see, just a slightly raised circle, darker than the surrounding sand, but Erik acts as if he has entered a church. He stands completely still, his eyes closed, and then touches the ground, as if for luck.

'Sacred ground,' he says.

'That's what Cathbad would say.'

'Cathbad! Have you seen him?'

'Yes ... Erik?'

'What?'

'Why didn't you tell me that you knew Cathbad quite well, that he'd been a student of yours?'

Erik is silent for a moment, looking at her. She can't read his cool, blue stare. Guilt? Amusement? Anger?

'Does it matter?'

'Of course it matters!' Ruth explodes. 'He's a suspect in a murder investigation.'

'Is he?'

Ruth hesitates. She knows that Nelson suspects and distrusts Cathbad but is that enough to make him a suspect? Probably. Aloud she says, 'I don't know. The police think he's hiding something.'

'The police! What do they know? Hoi polloi. Barbarians. Do you remember when they removed the protesters from the site? The unnecessary violence they used?'

'Yes.' The police had been heavy-handed when they removed the protesters. Erik and the other archaeologists had been distressed. They had lodged a complaint, which the police had ignored.

'Did you put Cathbad up to it?' asks Ruth. 'The protest?'

Erik smiles. 'No, the local pagans were up in arms already. There are a lot of pagans in Norfolk, you know. Let's just say that I encouraged him a bit.'

'Did you get him the job at the university too?'

'I gave him a reference.'

'Why didn't you tell me he was working there?'

'You didn't ask.'

Ruth turns away, stomping her way over the wet sand. Erik catches her up, puts his arm round her.

'Don't be angry Ruth. Didn't I always tell you, it's the questions that matter, not the answers?'

Ruth looks at Erik's familiar, weather-beaten face. He has grown older, his hair is whiter and there are more lines around his eyes, but he is still the same. He is smiling, his blue eyes sparkling. Reluctantly, Ruth smiles back.

'Come on,' says Erik, 'let's see if we can find that causeway of yours.'

They set off, walking inland across the dunes. A couple of waders are feeding on the mudflats. Ruth thinks of David's description of the Saltmarsh as nature's service station. The birds look up as they pass and then continue their frenzied digging. In the distance, a heron watches them, standing meditatively on one leg.

Ruth has David's map, showing the buried posts. Silently she unfurls it and hands it to Erik. He makes a hissing noise of satisfaction. 'So ... Now we have it.' He examines the map for a long time in silence. Ruth watches him with admiration. No one is better at reading a map or a landscape than Erik. For him, hills and streams and villages are signposts pointing directly to the past. She remembers him saying to her when she first started his postgraduate course, 'If you wanted to make a map of your sitting room for archaeologists of the future, what would be the most important thing?'

'Er ... making sure I have a full inventory of objects.'

He had laughed. 'No, no. Inventories are all very well in their place but they do not tell us how people *lived*, what was important to them, what they worshipped. No, the most important thing would be the *direction*. The way your chairs were facing. That would show archaeologists of the future that the most important object in the twenty-first century home was the large grey rectangle in the corner.'

Now Erik looks up from the map, sniffs the air and smiles. 'This way, I think.' They set off at a brisk walk. The wind is behind them now, blowing the coarse grass flat against the ground. They pass the tidal reed beds, the shallow water dark and mysterious. Above them a bird calls, hoarse and angry.

'Here.' Erik stops and bends down. Ruth squats beside him. There, half-buried in the peaty ground between the reeds and the mudflats, is a post. It extends about ten centimetres above the soil.

'Bog oak,' says Erik. Ruth looks more closely. The wood is dark, almost black, its surface dotted with little holes, like woodworm.

'Molluscs,' says Erik laconically. 'They eat away at the wood.'

'How old is it?' asks Ruth.

'Don't know for sure. But it looks old.'

'As old as the henge?'

'Possibly later.'

Ruth reaches out to touch the post. It feels soft, like black toffee. She has to resist the temptation to gouge in her fingernail.

'Come on,' says Erik. 'Let's find the next one.'

The next post is about two metres away. This one is harder to see, almost submerged by water. Erik paces between the posts.

'Incredible. The land between the two is completely dry, although it's marshland on either side. It must be a shingle spit, incredible that it hasn't moved over the years.'

Ruth can sense his excitement. 'So it could be a pathway through the marsh?'

'Yes, a crossing place. It was as important as marking a boundary, marking a crossing place over sacred ground. One step the wrong way and you're dead, straight to hell. Keep on the path and it will lead you to heaven.'

He is smiling but Ruth shivers, remembering the letters. *Look to the sky, the stars, the crossing places. Look at what is silhouetted against the sky. You will find her where the earth meets the sky.* Did the letter writer know about the pathway? He spoke about causeways and cursuses. Had he brought Lucy here, to this desolate landscape?

They find a total of twelve posts, leading them back almost to the car park and the place where Ruth found the Iron Age body. Erik takes pictures and makes notes. He seems completely absorbed. Ruth finds herself feeling restless, abstracted. With Nelson, she had been the expert. Now she feels relegated to the position of student.

'How will you get the wood dated?' she asks.

'I'll ask Bob Bullmore.' Bob is a member of Ruth's department, an experienced forensic anthropologist, an expert on the decomposition of flora and fauna. Ruth likes Bob; involving him is a good idea but, again, she has the sensation of being sidelined. This was my discovery, she wants to yell, you wouldn't be here if it wasn't for me.

Aloud she says, 'Shall we tell Phil?'

'Not yet.'

'Bob might tell him.'

'Not if I ask him not to.'

'Do you think we have found a link between my Iron Age body and the henge?'

Erik looks at her quizzically. '*Your* Iron Age body?'

'I found it,' says Ruth defiantly.

'We own nothing in this life,' says Erik.

'You sound like Cathbad.'

Erik looks at her for a minute, consideringly, like a lecturer assessing a new student. Then he says, 'Come and meet him.'

'Who?'

'Cathbad. Come and meet him properly.'

'Now?'

'Yes. I thought I'd look him up.'

Ruth hesitates. Part of her, the amateur detective part, wants to see Cathbad again, to assess him without Nelson's sceptical presence clouding her judgement. But she is still slightly angry with Erik for not telling her that he had been Cathbad's tutor. She considers, stuck in a liminal zone of her own between curiosity and resentment.

As she is thinking, watched quizzically by Erik, her phone rings, the noise sounding shockingly twenty-first century.

'Excuse me.' Ruth turns away.

'Ruth. It's Nelson.'

'Oh … hello.'

'Are you busy? Can you come to Spenwell? Now.'

'Why?'

'I'm at Scarlet Henderson's house. We've found some human bones in the garden.'

CHAPTER 12

Spenwell is a tiny village, hardly worthy of the name. One street of houses, a phone box and a shop that is only open for two hours in the afternoon. Scarlet's family live in a big modern bungalow built of ugly brown brick slightly redeemed by ivy. Ruth parks behind Nelson's Mercedes and two police vans. The police presence has not gone unnoticed in the small community. A group of children watch, wide-eyed, from the other side of the road, and up and down the street faces appear in windows. Their expressions are hard to read: curious, frightened, gleeful.

As Ruth approaches, Nelson appears around the side of the house. The front garden has been reduced to mud by police boots. Someone has put down planks, presumably for a wheelbarrow.

'Ruth,' Nelson greets her, 'how are you this morning?'

Ruth feels slightly embarrassed. Today she is the professional, the expert once more, she doesn't want to be reminded that last night she was sobbing over a dead cat.

'Better,' she says. 'Erik ... you know, my ex-tutor, he came round after you left.'

Nelson looks at her slightly quizzically. But all he says is, 'Good.'

'Where are the bones?' asks Ruth. She wants to bring the conversation back to business.

'Round the back. The dogs found the place.'

The back garden is long and untidy, littered with old sofas, broken bicycles and a half-constructed climbing frame built, it appears, out of reclaimed timber. The scene-of-crime officers, clad in white jumpsuits, are clustered round a large hole. The sniffer dogs are straining at their leads, tails wagging madly. With a shock, Ruth realises that the Hendersons are here too. Scarlet's father and mother, standing silently by the back door. The mother is youngish, pale and pretty with long dark hair and a waifish look. She is wearing a purple velvet skirt and is barefoot, despite the cold. The father is older and has a slightly rat-like face, thin with watery eyes. In the garden three of their children are playing on the half-finished climbing frame, apparently unconcerned.

'This is Doctor Ruth Galloway,' says Nelson to one of the jump-suited men. 'She's an expert on buried bones.' Like a dog, thinks Ruth.

Ruth looks at the hole, which seems to run along the dividing line between the Hendersons' garden and the garden next door. Nearer the house, there is a timber fence but, here, at the end of the garden, there is only flint and rubble. A boundary, thinks Ruth. She hears Erik's voice in her head. *It marked a boundary. We should have respected that.*

'Did there used to be a wall here?' she asks. She addressed the nearest white suit but Scarlet's father must have heard because he steps forward.

'There used to be an old flint wall here. I took the flints about five years ago, to make a kiln.'

If there was a wall here, thinks Ruth, then the bones can

hardly be new. She knows that she does not want the bones to be Scarlet's. She does not want the parents to be the killers; she wants Scarlet to be alive.

The white suits step back and Ruth, carrying her excavation kit in her backpack, moves forward. She kneels on the edge of the hole, takes out her small trowel and gently scrapes away at the sides. The digging is clean, she can see the marks of the shovels, and the soil is arranged in neat layers, like a terrine. A thin layer of topsoil, then the characteristic peaty soil of the area, then a line of flint. At the bottom, about a metre down, Ruth sees the yellow-white of the bones.

'Have you moved anything?' she asks.

The white-suited man answers. 'No. DCI Nelson told us not to.'

'Good.'

Wearing gloves, Ruth lifts a bone and holds it up to the light. She is aware of a collective intake of breath behind her.

Nelson leans forward and speaks into Ruth's ear. She smells cigarettes and aftershave.

'Are they human?'

'I think so, yes. But ...'

'But what?'

'They weren't buried.'

Nelson squats down beside her. 'What do you mean?'

'A burial is a disturbance. It disturbs the layers. Everything would be churned up. Look at this.' She gestures to the sides of the hole. 'Here's the grave cut. Under all these layers. These bones were laid on the ground and, over the centuries, the earth has covered them.'

'Over the centuries?'

'I think they're Iron Age. Like the other ones.'

'Why?'

'There is some pottery there. It looks Iron Age.'

Nelson looks at her for a long moment before straightening up and calling out to the hovering scene-of-crime men.

'Right, that's it, boys. Excitement over.'

'What is it, Boss?' asks one. *Boss!* Ruth can hardly believe her ears.

'The good news is it's a dead body. The bad news is it's been dead about two thousand years. Come on. Let's get out of here.'

An hour later, Ruth has bagged up the bones and sent them to the university lab for dating. Even so, she is sure they are Iron Age, but what does that mean? Because it wasn't buried in peat, this body has not been preserved, only the bones remain. Could these bones be linked to that other body, found on the edge of the Saltmarsh? And is there another link between bones, body, causeway and henge? Her mind is buzzing but she tries to concentrate on drinking herbal tea and talking to Scarlet's parents, Delilah and Alan as she has been instructed to call them.

She is not quite sure how she ended up here, in the Hendersons' chaotic kitchen, sitting on a rickety stool, balancing an earthenware mug in her hand. All she knows is that Nelson seemed very keen to accept the invitation on her behalf.

'We'd love to,' he had said. 'Thanks very much Mrs Henderson.'

'Delilah,' corrected Mrs Henderson wearily.

So now they are in the Henderson kitchen listening to Alan Henderson talking about dowsing and to the Hendersons' youngest (Ocean) fussing in her high chair.

'She misses Scarlet,' says Delilah with a resignation that Ruth finds hard to bear.

'I'm sure she does,' mumbles Ruth, 'How old is ... er ... Ocean?'

'She's two, Scarlet's four, Euan and Tobias are seven, Maddie's sixteen.'

'You don't look old enough to have a sixteen-year-old child.'

Delilah smiles, briefly illuminating her pale face with its heavy fringe of hair. 'I was only sixteen when I had her. She's not Alan's, of course.'

Ruth glances briefly at Alan who is now lecturing Nelson on ley lines. Nelson looks up and catches Ruth's eye.

'Do you have children?' Delilah asks Ruth.

'No.'

'What I'm afraid of,' says Delilah suddenly in a high, strained voice, 'is that one day someone asks me how many children I have and I say four, not five. Because then I'll know that it's over, that she's dead.' She is crying, but silently, the tears flowing down her cheeks.

Ruth doesn't know what to say. 'I'm sorry,' is all she manages.

Delilah ignores her. 'She's so little, so defenceless. Her wrist is so tiny she can still wear her christening bracelet. Who would want to hurt her?'

Ruth thinks of Sparky, also little and defenceless and yet brutally murdered. She tries to imagine her own grief magnified by a thousand.

'I don't know, Delilah,' says Ruth hoarsely. 'But DCI Nelson is doing all he can, I promise you.'

'He's a good man,' says Delilah, brushing a hand over her eyes. 'He's got a strong aura. He must have a good spirit guide.'

'I'm sure he has.'

Ruth is conscious of Nelson's eyes upon her. Alan has briefly stopped talking. He rolls a cigarette, hands shaking. Delilah gives a rice cake to Ocean who throws it on the floor.

Two dark-haired boys race into the room. To Ruth's surprise they head straight for Nelson.

'Harry! Did you bring your handcuffs?'

'Can I try them on?'

'It's my turn!'

Solemnly, Nelson pulls a pair of handcuffs from his pocket and fits them round one of the boy's hands. It makes Ruth feel slightly squeamish to see his bony wrists protruding from the restraining metal but there is no doubt that the boys are enjoying every minute.

'My turn! Let me!'

'I've only had a second. *Less* than a second.'

Ruth turns back to Delilah and sees, to her amazement, that she is now breast-feeding Ocean. Although Ruth has often signed petitions in favour of a woman's right to breast-feed in public, in practice she finds it deeply embarrassing. Especially as Ocean seems big enough to run to the corner shop for a packet of crisps.

Trying to avert her eyes, her gaze falls on a cork board over the kitchen table. It is covered in multi-coloured bits of paper: party invitations, torn-off special offers, children's drawings, photographs. She sees a picture of Scarlet holding baby Ocean and another of the twins holding a football trophy. Then she sees another photo. It is a faded snapshot of Delilah and Alan next to a standing stone, probably Stonehenge or possibly Avebury. But it is not the stone that catches Ruth's attention; it is the other person in the picture. Wearing jeans and a T-shirt and with normal-length hair it is nonetheless definitely Cathbad.

CHAPTER 13

'Are you sure it was him?'

'Certain. He had short hair and ordinary clothes but it was him without a doubt.'

'Bastard! I knew he was hiding something.'

'It could be quite innocent.'

'Then why didn't he mention it when I interviewed him? He acted as if he'd hardly heard the name Henderson.'

Ruth and Nelson are in a pub near the harbour having a late lunch. Ruth had been surprised when Nelson suggested lunch, not least because it was three o'clock when they finally left the Hendersons' house. But it seems that no landlord will refuse to serve a policeman complete with warrant card and now they are sitting in an almost empty bar looking out onto the quayside. The tide is high and swans glide silently past their window, oddly sinister in the fading light.

Ruth, slightly ashamed of being so hungry, tucks into a ploughman's lunch. Nelson eats sausages and mash like someone refuelling, not noticing what he puts into his mouth. He has insisted on paying. Ruth drinks diet Coke – she doesn't want to be caught drink-driving after all – and Nelson chooses the full-fat variety.

'My wife keeps nagging me to drink diet drinks,' he says. 'She says I'm overweight.'

'Really,' says Ruth drily. She has noticed before that you never see a thin person drinking a diet Coke.

Nelson chews meditatively for a few minutes and then asks, 'How long ago do you think the picture was taken?'

'Hard to tell. Cathbad's hair was dark and it's quite grey now.'

'More than ten years ago? Before you first met him?'

'Maybe. His hair was long ten years ago but he could always have cut it in the meantime. Delilah looked young.'

'She dresses like a teenager now.'

'She's very beautiful.'

Nelson grunts but says nothing.

'She thinks you have a strong aura,' says Ruth mischievously.

Nelson's lips form the word 'bollocks' but he doesn't say it aloud. Instead he says, 'What did you think of Alan? Bit of an unlikely partner for her, wouldn't you say? With her being so beautiful and all.'

Ruth thinks of Alan Henderson, with his sharp, rodent's face and darting eyes. He does seem an unlikely husband for Delilah who, even in her distress, seemed somehow exotic. But then they have four children together so presumably the marriage works. 'The eldest child, Maddie, isn't his,' she says. 'Maybe she married him on the rebound.'

'How the hell do you know that?'

'She told me.'

Nelson smiles. 'I thought she'd talk to you.'

'Is that why you made us have tea with them?'

'I didn't. They offered.'

'And you accepted. For both of us.'

Nelson grins. 'I'm sorry. I just thought we might need to build bridges with them. After all, we'd been there all morning digging their garden up, all the neighbours watching. They must have felt like suspects. I thought they might appreciate a nice friendly chat. And I thought Delilah might open up to you.'

'Open up? About what?'

'Oh, I don't know,' says Nelson with what sounds like studied nonchalance. 'You'd be surprised what turns out to be useful.'

Ruth wonders whether Delilah did tell her anything 'useful'. Mostly it had just seemed unbearably sad.

'It was just horrible,' she says at last, 'to see them suffering so much and not to be able to do anything about it.'

Nelson nods soberly. 'It is horrible,' he says. 'That's when I hate my job the most.'

'It was so sad, the way Delilah kept referring to Scarlet in the present tense but we don't know if she's alive or dead.'

Nelson nods again. 'It's every parent's worst nightmare. The worst, the very worst. When you have children, suddenly the world seems such a terrifying place. Every stick and stone, every car, every animal, Christ, every person, is suddenly a terrible threat. You realise you'd do anything, *anything*, to keep them safe: steal, lie, kill, you name it. But sometimes there just isn't anything you can do. And that's the hardest thing.'

He stops and takes a swig of Coke, maybe embarrassed at saying so much. Ruth watches him with something like wonder. She thought she could understand what Delilah Henderson felt, losing a beautiful child like

Scarlet, but the thought that Nelson should feel like that about the two stroppy adolescents she had seen him with at the shopping centre seems almost unbelievable. Yet, looking at his face as he stares into his glass, she does believe it.

Back home, trying half-heartedly to prepare her first lecture for next week, Ruth thinks about children. 'Do you have children?' Delilah had asked her. The implication was, if you don't, you won't understand. Nelson had understood. He might be an unreconstructed Northern policeman but he had children and that had given him access into the inner sanctum. He understood the terrible power of a parent's love.

Ruth doesn't have children and she has never been pregnant. Now that she is nearly forty and thinking that she might never have a child, it all seems such a waste. All that machinery chugging away inside her, making her bleed each month, making her moody and bloated and desperate for chocolate. All that internal plumbing, all those pipes gurgling away, all for nothing. At least Shona has been pregnant twice – and had two tearful abortions – at least she knows it all works. Ruth has no evidence at all that she can get pregnant. Maybe she can't and all those years of agonising over contraception were in vain. She remembers once with Peter when their condom broke and, in the sweaty heat of the moment, they had decided to carry on. She remembers how, the morning after, she had woken up thinking, perhaps this is it. Perhaps I'm pregnant, and the sheer power of that thought, its ability to throw everything else into acute relief. To know that you are carrying something secretly inside you. How can anything stay the same after that? But, of course, it hadn't been it. She wasn't pregnant and now she probably never will be.

Peter has a child. He will know the feelings described by Nelson. Would Peter kill for his son? Erik has three children, all now grown up. Ruth remembers him once saying that the greatest gift you can give a child is to set them free. Erik's children, scattered in London, New York and Tokyo, are certainly free, but are Erik and Magda free of them? Once you have had a child, can you ever go back to being the person you were?

Ruth gets up to make herself tea. She feels twitchy and ill at ease. She told Erik she would be fine in the house on her own but she can't help thinking about Sparky and her brutal, horrible death. Iron Age man left dead bodies as messages to the Gods. Did Sparky's killer leave her body as a message to Ruth? Did the cat's body also mark a boundary? Come no further or I'll kill you, as I've killed Scarlet and Lucy. She shivers.

Flint squeezes in through the cat flap and Ruth picks him up and cuddles him. Flint endures her embrace whilst all the time looking hopefully at the floor. Child substitute, she thinks. Well, at least she has one.

Abandoning her work, she settles in front of the TV. *Have I Got News For You* is on but she can't lose herself in Ian Hislop's wit or Paul Merton's surreal brilliance. She keeps thinking about Scarlet Henderson's parents, waiting for her in that messy family house. Delilah aching to hold her daughter one more time, perhaps wishing she could have her back inside her body, where at least she had been safe.

When she puts her hand to her face, she realises that she is crying.

Now there is a new noise at night. It comes again and again. Three cries, one after the other, very low and echoey. The third cry always lasts the longest and is the most frightening. She's used to the other sounds at night, the snufflings and rustlings, the wind that has a voice of its own, a roaring angry shout. Sometimes it feels as if the wind is going to roar in through the trapdoor and snatch her up with its cold, angry breath. She imagines herself caught up, thrown high into the air, sailing through the clouds, looking down on all the houses and the people. Funny, she knows exactly what she will see. There's a little white house, very square, with a swing in the back garden. Sometimes there's a girl on the swing, going to and fro, laughing as she flies into the air. If she closes her eyes, she can still see the house and it's hard to believe that she hasn't actually floated there on top of the clouds, looking down on the girl and the swing and the neat rows of bright flowers.

Once she saw a face at the window. A monster's face. Grey-white with black stripes on either side. She kept very still, waiting for the monster to see her and gobble her up. But it hadn't. It had sort of sniffed at the bars with its wet black nose like those shoes that she had once had for best. Then it had gone away, clattering horribly over the glass. She has never seen it again.

The new sound is very close sometimes. It happens when the night is very dark and very cold. It wakes her up and she shivers, wrapping her blanket around her. It comes once, twice, three times. She doesn't know why but she thinks it might be calling to her. Once she calls back, 'I'm here! Let me out!' and the sound of her own voice is the scariest thing of all.

CHAPTER 14

In the morning, Nelson brings Sparky's body back. He stands on the doorstep, holding the ominous-looking cardboard box, looking like a salesman who is uncertain of his welcome.

Ruth, still bleary-eyed before her first coffee, squints at him.

'I did promise.' Nelson indicates the box.

'Yes. Thank you. Come in. I'll make us some coffee.'

'Coffee would be grand.'

He puts the box carefully on the floor by the sofa. They both avoid looking at it. Ruth busies herself with the coffee and Nelson stands in the sitting room, looking around with a slight frown. Ruth is reminded of the first time she saw him, in the corridor at the university, and the impression she had of him being too big for the room. That is certainly the case here. Nelson, looming in his heavy black jacket, makes the tiny cottage seem even smaller. Erik is tall but he had seemed able to fold himself up into the space. Nelson looks as if he might, at any second, knock something over or bash his head against the ceiling.

'Lots of books,' he says, when Ruth comes in with coffee and biscuits on a tray.

'Yes, I love reading.'

Nelson grunts. 'The wife belongs to a book club. All

they do is moan about their husbands. They never talk about the bloody books at all.'

'How do you know?'

'I've listened when they meet at our place.'

'Maybe they talk about the books when you're not listening.'

Nelson acknowledges this with a slight smile.

'Did you find anything?' asks Ruth. 'From ... from Sparky?'

Nelson takes a gulp of coffee and shakes his head. 'We won't know until tomorrow at the earliest. I've had the letters tested again as well. We're checking the prints and DNA results against known offenders.'

Ruth wonders what has prompted this course of action. Nelson sounds very much as if he has a 'known offender' in mind. Before she can ask, Nelson puts down his coffee cup and looks at his watch.

'Have you got a spade?' he asks briskly.

Now the moment has come, Ruth feels curiously reluctant to go out into the garden and bury Sparky. She wants to stay inside drinking coffee and pretending that nothing bad has happened. But she knows it can't be put off and so she gets her coat and shows Nelson to the tool shed.

Ruth's garden is a tiny square of wind-blown grass. When she first moved in she had tried to plant things but they were always the wrong things and nothing ever seemed to grow except thistles and wild lavender. Next door, the weekenders have a smart deck which, in summer, they adorn with terracotta pots. Today, though, it looks as forlorn and empty as Ruth's garden. David's garden is even more overgrown though it does contain an elaborate bird table complete with a device to repel cats (Ruth fears it doesn't work).

There is a dwarf apple tree at the end of the garden and it is here that Ruth asks Nelson to dig the grave. It is odd watching someone else dig. He does it all wrong, bending his back rather than his legs, but he does the job quickly enough. Ruth looks into the neat hole and automatically checks out the layers: topsoil, alluvial clay, chalk. Flint watches them from the apple tree, tail flicking. Nelson hands Ruth the box. It feels pathetically light. Ruth wants to look inside but she knows that this would not be a good idea. Instead, she drops a kiss on the cardboard lid – 'Goodbye Sparky' – and then she places the box in the grave.

Ruth gets another spade and helps Nelson fill in the hole and, for a few minutes, the only sound in the garden is their breathing as they shovel in the heavy earth. Nelson has taken off his jacket and hung it on the apple tree. Flint has disappeared.

When the hole is filled in, Nelson and Ruth look at each other. Ruth feels as if she understands now why burials are therapeutic. Earth to earth. She has buried Sparky but her cat will always be there, part of the garden, part of her life. Then she remembers the Lucy letters. *Lucy lies deep below the ground but she will rise again.* She shakes her head, trying to rid herself of the words.

'What about the candle?' she asks Nelson.

'I'll do it on Sunday. A decade of the rosary too.'

'Only a decade?'

'Two decades and a Glory Be for luck.'

They look at each other over the newly dug grave and

smile. Ruth feels that she ought to say something but, somehow, silence feels right just then. Geese call, high overhead, and a light rain starts to fall.

'I'd better be going,' says Nelson, but he doesn't move.

Ruth looks at him, the rain falling softly on her hair. Nelson smiles, an oddly gentle smile. Ruth opens her mouth to speak but the silence is broken by a voice that seems to come from another world, another existence.

'Ruth! What are you doing out here?'

It is Peter.

When Nelson drives away, gruff and professional once more, Ruth makes more coffee and sits at the table with Peter.

He looks good, thinks Ruth. His gingery blond hair is shorter, he is about fifteen pounds lighter and he even has a tan, something so unusual (Peter has typical redhead's skin) that it makes him look almost shockingly different.

'You're looking well,' says Peter.

'I'm not,' says Ruth bluntly, aware that she is wearing no make-up and that her hair has gone crinkly from the rain.

There is a short silence.

'Who was that man again?' asks Peter.

'It's a long story,' says Ruth.

Peter is a good audience. He is satisfyingly shocked at the death of Sparky – he did love the cats, she remembers – and properly fascinated by the Iron Age bodies and the causeway. She tells him a little about the police investigations, but not about the letters, and he says that he has read about the Scarlet Henderson case.

'Poor little girl. Terrible for the parents. Do the police

really think that the murderer might have killed Sparky as a sort of warning to you?'

'It's a possibility, they think.'

'God, Ruth. You do live, don't you?'

Ruth doesn't reply. She thinks she detects a tinge of envy in Peter's voice for her supposedly exciting life. She wants to tell him that, far from being excited, she actually feels lonely and rather scared. She looks at him, wondering how honest she wants to be.

It is odd to see Peter in the cottage again. He and Ruth had lived here together for a year. Ruth bought the cottage a few years after the henge dig, still drawn to the Saltmarsh and its eerie, desolate beauty. By that time she and Peter had been living together for two years and there was some talk of their buying the place together. Ruth had resisted, at the time she wasn't even sure why, and Peter had given in. The little cottage was hers alone, and she remembers that when Peter moved out, the house didn't even seem to notice. There were a few gaps on the walls and in her bookshelves but, on the whole, the house seemed to close in on her, satisfied. At last they were alone.

'I've missed this place,' says Peter, looking out of the window.

'Have you?'

'Yes, living in London you never get to see the sky. There's so much sky here.'

Ruth looks out at the expanse of stormy, gunmetal sky where the lowering clouds are chasing each other over the marshes.

'Lots of sky,' she agrees. 'But not much else.'

'I like it,' says Peter, 'I like the loneliness.'

'So do I,' says Ruth.

Peter is looking sadly into his coffee cup. 'Poor little Sparky,' he says. 'I remember when we first brought her home. She was no bigger than that squeaky mouse toy we bought her.'

Ruth can't take much more of this. 'Come on,' she says. 'Let's go for a walk. I'll show you the causeway.'

The wind has grown stronger and, as they walk, they have to lower their heads to stop the sand blowing into their eyes. Ruth would be happy to stomp along in silence but Peter seems keen to chat. He tells her about his work, his recent skiing trip (hence the tan) and his views on the government, which had just been elected that heady summer ten years ago. He doesn't, once, mention Victoria or Daniel. Ruth tells him about her work, her family and the Iron Age bodies.

'What does Erik think?' asks Peter. He is walking fast, striding over the uneven ground. Ruth almost has to jog to keep up with him.

'He thinks they're all connected.'

'Oh yes.' Peter adopts a thick Norwegian accent. 'The sacred site, the power of the landscape, the gateway between life and death.'

Ruth laughs. 'Exactly. Phil, on the other hand, thinks it's all coincidence pending geophysics reports and radiocarbon dating.'

'What do *you* think?'

Ruth pauses. She realises that Erik never once asked her this question.

'I think they're connected,' she says at last. 'The first

Iron Age body marks the beginning of the marsh, the causeway leads almost straight to the henge which marks the point where the marsh became tidal. I don't know about the Spenwell bones but they must mark a boundary of some sort. Boundaries are important. Even now, look how important it is that we keep things in their proper place. "Keep your distance," people say. I think prehistoric people knew how to keep their distance.'

'You were always keen on your own space,' says Peter, slightly bitterly.

Ruth looks at him. 'This isn't about me.'

'Isn't it?'

They have reached the first buried post.

Peter pats the oak stump meditatively. 'Will you have to uproot the posts?'

'Erik doesn't want to.'

'I remember all that fuss when we dug up the henge. The druids tying themselves to the posts and the police dragging them away.'

'Yes.' Ruth remembers it too. Vividly. 'The only thing is ... we did find out a hell of a lot about the henge by excavating. The type of axe used to chop the wood down, for example. We even found some of the rope used to tow it.'

'Honeysuckle rope, wasn't it?'

'You've got a good memory.'

'I remember everything about that summer.'

Seeing Peter looking at her intently, Ruth avoids his gaze. She stares at the sea, where the waves are breaking a long way out, white against the grey. A stone skims past her, jumping once, twice, three times.

Ruth turns to look at Peter who grins, flexing his arm.

'You were always good at that,' says Ruth.

'It's a man thing.'

They are silent for a moment, watching the waves come closer and closer to their feet. There is always the temptation, thinks Ruth, to stay just a little bit too long, to stand on the water's edge until the spray actually gets you. And it's not always the wave you expect, the spectacular breakers hurling themselves against the shore. Sometimes it's the sneaky waves, the ones that come from nowhere, sucking the sand away from your feet; sometimes it's these waves that take you by surprise.

'Peter,' says Ruth at last, 'why are you here?'

'I told you, to research my book.'

Ruth continues to look at him. The wind is whipping the sand up into a storm. It flies in their faces, like a fine gritty rain. Ruth rubs her eyes, tasting salt in the air. Peter, too, brushes sand out of his eyes. When he looks back at Ruth, his eyes are red.

'Victoria and I, we've split up. I suppose I ... I just wanted to come back.'

Ruth takes a deep breath that is almost a sigh. Somehow, she thinks, she had known this all along. 'I'm sorry,' she says. 'Why didn't you tell me before?'

'I don't know.' Peter speaks into the wind so it is hard for her to catch his words. 'I suppose I wanted everything to be like it was before.'

After a few minutes, they turn round and walk back towards the house.

*

Halfway back, it starts to rain; sharp, horizontal rain that seems to sting their faces. Ruth has her head down and doesn't realise that they have drifted right, northwards, until she sees the hide in front of her. She has never seen this hide before, although she remembers it from the map. It is on a shingle spit, almost at the tide mark. You would need to be an extremely determined bird-watcher, she thinks, to venture this far across the marsh.

'Ruth!'

Blinded by rain, Ruth looks up to see David standing by the hide holding a plastic bag which looks as though it contains litter. She remembers Nelson shouting at his subordinate to bag up the litter from another hide, the first time she met him.

'Hallo,' says Ruth. 'Clearing up?'

'Yes.' David's face is dark. 'They never learn. There are notices everywhere and still they leave their crap all over the place.'

Ruth tuts sympathetically and introduces Peter, who comes forward to shake hands.

'David is the warden of the bird sanctuary,' she says though she does not explain who Peter is.

'Must be an interesting job,' says Peter.

'It is,' says David with sudden animation. 'This is a wonderful place for birds, especially in winter.'

'I came here years ago, for a dig,' says Peter, 'but I've never really got it out of my system. It's so lonely and so peaceful.'

David looks curiously from Ruth to Peter and then he says, 'I saw a police car outside your house, Ruth.'

'Yes,' Ruth sighs. 'You know I'm helping the police with an investigation, with the forensic side.'

'Ruth's cat was killed,' Peter cuts in, to Ruth's annoyance. 'The police think it might be significant.'

Now David looks really shocked. 'Your cat was killed? How?'

Frowning at Peter, Ruth says shortly, 'Her throat was cut. They think it could be linked to the investigation.'

'My God. How awful!' David makes a gesture as if to touch Ruth's arm but doesn't quite make contact.

'Yes, well, I was upset. I was ... fond of her.'

'Of course you were. She was company.' He says it like he knows the importance of company.

'Yes, she was.'

They stand there awkwardly for a few minutes, in the rain, and then Ruth says, 'We'd better be getting back.'

'Yes,' says David, squinting towards the horizon. 'The tide's coming in.'

'I nearly drowned once on these mudflats,' says Peter chattily. 'Got cut off by the tide.'

'Easy to do,' says David. 'The tide comes in faster than a galloping horse, they say.'

'Let's gallop off then,' says Ruth. She is fed up with both of them.

As they trudge away, Peter says, 'Funny chap. Do you know him well?'

'Not really. I've only really spoken to him in the last few months. Which is why' – she glares at Peter – 'I don't want him to know all my business.'

Peter laughs. 'I was only being friendly. Remember that, Ruth? Friendly?'

Ruth is about to retort when her phone rings. For some reason she knows it will be Nelson.

It is a text, short and to the point.

Have arrested Malone. His prints on letters. HN.

CHAPTER 15

'We've got to do something,' says Erik. 'The police haven't got a suspect so they're trying to frame Cathbad. We can't let them get away with it.'

'Apparently his fingerprints were on the letters,' says Ruth cautiously.

'Fingerprints, huh! You think they can't fake evidence? You think they aren't capable of that?'

Ruth says nothing and Erik gets up to pace angrily around the tiny office. They are at the university. Term has started and Ruth has a student consultation in ten minutes. However, Erik, who has been ranting against the police for the last half hour, shows no sign of leaving.

'What have the letters got to do with anything, anyway? Writing a letter doesn't make him a murderer. There's nothing that links him to that little girl. Nothing.'

Ruth thinks back to the photo in the Hendersons' kitchen. She now knows that there *is* something that links Cathbad to the Hendersons, something definitely tangible. Does this make him a murderer? His fingerprints were on the letters. Does this make him the author? Ruth thinks about the letters. Cathbad knows about mythology, he knows about archaeology, he is fanatically interested in the Saltmarsh. She has to admit he is a likely candidate. But why would he do it? Is he really capable of killing a little girl and taunting the police with clues? And Lucy Downey? Could he have killed her too?

'I don't know,' she says, 'I don't know any more than you.'

This isn't quite true. After receiving his text, Ruth rang Nelson. His phone was switched off but he rang her later that evening. Peter had finally gone home and she was once again trying to work.

Nelson sounded excited, almost jubilant. 'Turned out we had his prints on file. He'd been arrested a few times before, demonstrations, that sort of thing. That's why I tested again. We got a match an hour ago. And we've got a link to Scarlet.'

'Does he admit anything?'

'No.' A harsh laugh. 'Says it's all a set-up, wicked police state and all that. But he can't deny he knows the Hendersons: turns out he's the father of the eldest girl.'

'*What?*'

'Yes. He knew Delilah Henderson when she was still at school. He was a student at Manchester, she lived nearby. They had an affair and the result was Madeleine. Apparently they lived together for a bit but then she left him for another bloke.'

'Alan Henderson?'

'No, someone else. He came later. Anyway, she left Malone and he claims he hasn't seen her to this day. Had no idea she was living nearby.'

'He must have seen her on the TV. When Scarlet first went missing.'

'Hasn't got a TV. Harmful rays, apparently, polluting the atmosphere. Hasn't got a mobile phone because of the radiation. Nutcase.'

'Do you think he is mad?'

'Don't you believe it. Cunning as a nest of snakes.'

'How long can you hold him?'

'Twenty-four hours. But I'll apply for an extension.'

'Will you tell the press?'

'Not if I can help it.'

But someone did tell them, because that night on the nine o'clock radio news Ruth heard that 'a local man has been arrested in connection with the disappearance of four-year-old Scarlet Henderson.' She had switched on the TV news and, immediately, Nelson's face, dark and forbidding, had filled the screen. 'Detective Chief Inspector Harry Nelson,' intoned the newsreader, 'who, up to now, has had to admit no progress in the case of little Scarlet Henderson, was tonight unavailable for comment.' As if to prove this, Nelson swept past the hovering reporters and bounded up the steps to the police station. Ruth watched fascinated, feeling slightly smug despite herself that she knew what the inside of the station looked like, could imagine Nelson in his ungainly slice of room examining the evidence, shouting impatiently for coffee, looking again at the laughing face of Scarlet Henderson on the wall.

'The man is believed to be forty-two-year-old Michael Malone, a lab technician at North Norfolk University.'

Jesus, thought Ruth, they know his name. Now all hell will break loose.

And it had. This morning, Ruth had been stopped at the university gates and asked to show her ID. Nodding her through, the policeman had told her to avoid the chemistry wing. Naturally this had aroused her curiosity and she had driven straight round to find the entrance to the chemistry department completely blocked by cars, trailers, even a portaloo. TV camera crews jostled to and fro, waving giant fluffy microphones. Anyone entering the building was greeted by a hysterical babble of questions, 'Do you know Michael Malone? Who is he? What sort of ...' Ruth heard French, Italian, even, she thought, an American accent. Hastily she backed away to the relative calm of the archaeology block.

Erik had arrived an hour later, eyes blazing, white hair flying.

'Have you heard? Have you heard?'

'Yes.'

'What are you going to do about it?'

'Me? What can I do?'

'You're friendly with this policeman, this Neanderthal, aren't you?'

'Not exactly friendly ...'

Erik had looked at her narrowly. 'That's not what Cathbad said. He said you and this Nelson turned up together to interview him. Very cosy. He said there was a definite chemistry between you.'

'Bollocks.' Unthinkingly, Ruth employs Nelson's favourite word.

Erik didn't seem to have heard her. 'It is obvious that this Nelson is using Cathbad as a scapegoat and you, Ruth, you delivered Cathbad to him. On a plate.'

The sheer unfairness of this made Ruth gasp. 'I didn't! I asked *you* if you remembered his name. *You* told me.'

'And you told Nelson.'

'He would have found him anyway.'

'Would he? He seems a complete incompetent to me. No, he used you to deliver Cathbad. He used you, Ruth.'

'What if Cathbad did do it?' Ruth countered angrily. 'Don't you want the murderer to be found?'

Erik smiled pityingly. 'Ruth, Ruth. He really has got to you, hasn't he? You're even thinking like a policeman.'

That had been an hour ago and Ruth and Erik are still circling the topic furiously. Ruth is angry that Erik thinks her a patsy, a fool who has been used by the cynical Nelson in his attempt to pin the crime on Cathbad. But, secretly, she does feel slightly guilty. She suggested Cathbad to Nelson. She pointed him in the direction of the henge and the dig ten years ago. If Cathbad didn't do it, his life could be ruined by this notoriety. He could even go to prison for a crime he didn't commit. But what if he did do it?

'I don't know what's going on,' she says again.

Erik looks at her, his blue eyes cold. 'Then find out, Ruthie.'

Then, just as Ruth thinks it can't get any worse, Phil puts his head round the door.

'I couldn't help overhearing. It's a teeny bit loud in here. How are you, Erik?' He puts out his hand. After a second's pause, Erik takes it.

'Fine, apart from an innocent man being under arrest.'

'Oh that poor soul from the chemistry department. Do you know him?'

'Yes. A former student of mine.'

'No!' Phil's eyes are round with interest. 'Is he an archaeologist then?'

'He did a postgraduate degree at Manchester.'

'How did he end up here?'

Erik gestures towards Ruth, who is sitting behind her desk, as if for protection. 'Ask Ruth, she knows.'

'Ruth, are you involved in all this?'

'You knew I was helping with the case.'

'Just with the bones, I thought.'

This, Ruth realises, is how Phil sees her. Only concerned with bones, a dull specialisation, useful but ultimately marginal. She is not a heroine type like Shona, she does not belong centre stage.

'Ruth gave Cathbad's name to the police,' says Erik spitefully.

'Cathbad?' Phil looks confused.

'Erik knows Michael Malone as Cathbad,' Ruth shoots back. 'They're old friends.'

Phil glances from Ruth to Erik, enthralled. 'Are you?' he asks. 'Old friends?'

'Yes,' hisses Erik, 'and I'm going to clear my old friend's name.'

And he sweeps out, colliding in the doorway with Ruth's student, a polite Chinese man called Mr Tan, who is most surprised to find himself at the receiving end of a stream of Norwegian invective.

'I'll leave you to it, Ruth,' says Phil. 'Let's catch up later.'

Not if I can help it, thinks Ruth. She turns to Mr Tan. 'I'm so sorry. We were going to talk about your dissertation. What was it about again?'

'Decomposition,' says Mr Tan.

Ruth has to battle past the reporters again on her way home. The news reports gave no further developments in the case. 'Police have been granted another twenty-four hours to question the suspect, believed to be forty-two-year-old Michael Malone from Blakeney.'

Ruth switches off the radio. She still feels uneasy about Cathbad's arrest. Although she doesn't, like Erik, think that Cathbad is simply a scapegoat, equally it is hard to think of him as a murderer. Yet he *could* conceivably be the author of those letters. Erik hasn't read them. He can't hear the erudite, sinister, taunting voice. *She lies where the earth meets the sky. Where the roots of the great tree Yggdrasil reach down into the next life ... She has become the perfect sacrifice. Blood on stone. Scarlet on white.* Thinking of Cathbad in his wizard's chair, the dream-catchers glittering around him, Ruth can imagine him writing these lines. But abducting and killing a little girl? He is the father of Scarlet's half-sister, how could he possibly have done this to Scarlet? To Delilah, whom presumably he had once loved?

And what about Lucy Downey, all those years ago? Ruth thinks of Cathbad in his prime, purple cloak fluttering, exhorting his followers to stand firm against the police and the archaeologists. She has a vision of him standing within the timber circle, arms aloft, as the seawater swirls around his feet and the other druids clamber to safety. She had thought at the time that if conviction could stop the tide the sea would surely turn in its tracks. But of course it hadn't, and ten minutes later Cathbad too was scrambling for the higher ground, holding his sodden robe above his knees. Could this man – ridiculous, impressive, passionate – really be a killer? Is it possible that a few months after that stand at the henge Cathbad had kidnapped Lucy Downey and killed her?

When she reaches the Saltmarsh, the tide is out and the birds are coming in to feed, their white feathers catching the last of the setting sun. Watching them, Ruth thinks of David, his face transformed as he talked about the migrating birds; and of Peter, saying sadly that he just wanted to come back.

Going back. When Ruth met Peter she was not yet thirty. She had been newly appointed to the job at North Norfolk University and was full of energy and enthusiasm. Peter, a history research fellow at the University of East Anglia, had heard on the academic grapevine about the dig. He had simply turned up one morning with his backpack and bedroll and asked if they wanted help. They had teased him for being a city boy – though he was actually from Wiltshire and had spent five years in the Australian outback. They laughed at the straw hat that he wore to keep the sun off his pale skin, at his lack of knowledge of archaeological terms. He had always referred to the Pleistocene as the plastocine and could never remember which came first, Bronze Age or Iron Age. Yet he was obsessed with the henge and listened enthralled to Erik's tales of ritual and sacrifice. It was he who had found the first oak stump, exposed when a summer storm had blown the sand away from its base. Peter had been frantically digging around the stump when he had been caught by the tide and eventually rescued by Erik.

It was that evening that she realised she loved him, Ruth remembers. They had always got on well together, teaming up on the dig, laughing at the same things. Erik's wife, Magda, had noticed, and often seemed to contrive to leave the two of them together. Once she had read Ruth's palm and told her that a tall red-haired stranger was about to come into her life. Once Ruth had cut herself and Peter had helped her put on the Band-Aid; the touch of his hand had made her tremble. And as they sat by the campfire on the evening of his near-drowning, Ruth had looked at Peter and thought: now, it has to be now. He could have drowned today, we mustn't waste any more time. And she remembers smiling to herself because it seemed such a momentous, and yet such a joyful, thought. Peter had looked up and met her eyes. He had got up and suggested a walk to collect samphire. Magda had discouraged anyone else from accompanying them. They had walked to the water's edge, the sound of the sea rustling in the dark and, smiling, had walked into each other's arms.

And now, as Ruth lets herself into her cottage, she wonders if she really wants Peter back in her life. After the walk on Sunday, he has called twice but she hasn't seen him again. He is staying nearby, she could call him tonight, suggest going out for a drink, but she knows she won't. She is not sure what Peter means by 'coming back'. Does he mean coming back to *her*? And, if so, is that what she wants? Having ended the relationship, with so much heart-searching, does she really want them to get together again? And why does the new slightly bitter Peter seem more attractive than the adoring Peter of five years ago?

Inside the cottage a clock ticks lugubriously and the seabirds are calling from the marshes. Otherwise, all is silent. Flint, who is obviously nervous without Sparky, leaps down from the sofa back, making Ruth jump. There is something ominous in the silence, she realises, as if the house is waiting for something. Her footsteps, as she goes to the kitchen to feed Flint, echo on the floorboards. The radio is no help – the reception is so bad that all she can hear are muffled crackles, as if the announcer has been gagged and is struggling for freedom. This is so disconcerting that she switches it off and the silence returns, heavier than ever.

Ruth makes herself some tea and sits at her computer, meaning to do some work. But the silence is still at her back, making the hairs on her neck rise. She swings round. Flint is lying on the sofa again but he is not asleep. He is watchful, alert, looking beyond her, towards the window and the twilight. Is there something out there? Summoning up all her courage, Ruth goes to the door and opens it noisily. Nothing. Only the birds wheeling and calling as they fly inland. A long way off, she can hear the sea. The tide is turning.

Ruth slams the door shut and, as an afterthought, puts on the security chain. Then she pulls the curtains and sits down to work.

But the Lucy letters insist on running through her mind. The same phrases, over and over again. *You are looking for Lucy but you are looking in the wrong places ... Look where the land lies. Look at the cursuses and the causeways.*

Ruth rubs her eyes. Flint jumps onto the table and rubs his head against her hand. Mechanically, she strokes him. She is missing something, she knows it. It is as if she has all the evidence from a dig, all the pottery sherds and flakes of flint, all the soil samples, and she can't put it together to make a proper picture. What did Erik say? *The most important thing is the direction.*

Ruth gets out her map of North Norfolk. She traces a line from Spenwell, where the bones were found in the Hendersons' garden, to the bones at the edge of the Saltmarsh. She catches her breath. The line, cutting through Spenwell village and the dual carriageway, is almost exactly straight. Trembling slightly, she continues the line along the route marked by the causeway. It leads where she always thought it would: the line points, as straight as an arrow, to the centre of the henge circle. To the sacred ground.

She looks down at her page of notes. Under the heading 'Cursuses' she has written: 'Can be seen as lines pointing to sacred places. Longest cursus in Britain = 10 km. Sight lines – tell you where to look.'

The house is still waiting; it is dark outside now and even the birds are silent. With a shaking hand Ruth reaches for her phone.

'Nelson? I think I know where Scarlet is buried.'

CHAPTER 16

They wait for the tide and set off at first light. When they return from the henge circle, with Scarlet's body zipped into a police body bag, Ruth is driven back to her house. She left Nelson in the car park where they first found the bones. He is waiting for a policewoman to arrive so they can break the news to Scarlet's parents. Ruth doesn't offer to accompany them. She knows it is pure cowardice, but right at this moment she would rather run into the sea and drown herself than face Delilah Henderson. Nelson presumably feels the same but he still has to do it. He doesn't speak to Ruth, or to the scene-of-crime officers who arrive promptly in their white jumpsuits. He stands apart, looking so forbidding that no one dares approach him.

On the way home Ruth asks the driver to stop so she can be sick. She is sick again, back in the cottage, listening to the radio news. 'Police searching for four-year-old Scarlet Henderson have found a body believed to be that of the missing child. Police sources are refusing to confirm ...' The missing child. How can those few words convey the horrific pathos of the little arm encircled by the silver bracelet? The little girl taken from the people who loved her: murdered, buried in the sand, covered by the sea. When had he buried her? At night? If she had looked would Ruth have seen lights, like will o'the wisps, guiding her to the dead child?

She calls Phil and tells him that she won't be coming in. He is agog but remembers to feel sorry for Scarlet's parents: 'Poor people, it doesn't bear thinking about.' But Ruth has to think about it, all day long. Ten minutes later, Peter phones. Does Ruth want him to come over? She says no, she is fine. She doesn't want to see Peter; she doesn't want to see anyone.

By midday, the Saltmarsh is seething with people. It has started to rain again but still she can see little figures crawling over the sands and, in the distance, the lights of police boats out to sea. A new gaggle of journalists swarms past, screeching and cackling like flocks of feeding birds. Ruth sees David standing outside his house, binoculars in hand, looking thunderous. He must hate the Saltmarsh being invaded like this. The birds have been frightened away and the skies are low and dark. Thank God Sammy and Ed have gone back to London so Ruth doesn't have to bear their curiosity and concern. She pulls the curtains. Thank God too that the press haven't caught up with her yet.

Erik rings. He is conciliatory, concerned. Ruth wishes she didn't think that he is as much concerned with the archaeological site as with Scarlet's fate. The police are digging madly in the very centre of the henge circle. For Erik, as for David, the site will be contaminated forever. He can hardly say this, though, and after a few platitudes he rings off.

Despite everything, she is still shocked when she switches on the TV news and sees the Saltmarsh, rain-washed and grey, filling the screen. 'It was at this desolate spot,' intones the newsreader, 'that police made the tragic discovery, early this morning ...' No mention of Ruth. Thank you, God.

The phone rings. Ruth's mother. Not such good work, God.

'Ruth! It's on TV. That awful place where you live.'

'I know Mum.'

'They've found her, that poor little girl. Our Bible study group has been praying for her every night.'

'I know.'

'Daddy said he saw your house on TV.'

'I'm sure he did.'

'Isn't it terrible? Daddy says be sure to lock your windows and doors.'

'I will.'

'That poor little girl. Such a pretty little thing. Did you see her picture on the news?'

Should Ruth tell her mother that she was the one who found the body? Who lifted up the little arm, miraculously preserved by the peat, and looked at the silver bracelet, decorated with entwined hearts? Should she tell her mother that she saw an identical bracelet on Delilah Henderson's wrist as they sat chatting in her kitchen? Should she tell her that she watched as the little body was lifted from its grave and the hand dangled down, as if in farewell? Should she tell her mother that she knows the murderer, even if she does not know his name, that she hears his voice in her dreams? Should she tell her about Sparky, left bleeding on her doorstep as a threat, or a warning?

No, she won't tell her any of these things. Instead she promises to lock her doors and to ring tomorrow. She feels too tired even to argue when her mother says she hopes the child was baptised and so can go to heaven.

'Who wants to go to heaven with all those Christians?' has always been Ruth's response. Now she thinks about Alan and Delilah Henderson. Do they think they will see Scarlet again, that they will be reunited in a better place? She hopes so. She really hopes so.

The rain continues to fall, somewhat thwarting the journalists who tramp back along New Road, their mobile phones subdued. Ruth, who hasn't eaten all day, pours herself a glass of wine and switches on the radio. 'What does the death of little Scarlet Henderson tell us about our society …' She switches it off again. She doesn't want to hear people, people who have never seen Scarlet, talk about lessons learnt or the decline of morals or why children are no longer safe to play. Scarlet wasn't safe; she was snatched from her garden while she played on the makeshift climbing frame with her twin brothers. Neither of them had seen anything. One minute Scarlet was there, the next she wasn't. Delilah, inside the house with a fretful Ocean, had not even known that her daughter was missing until she called her in for tea, two hours later. Forensics will have to prove when Scarlet was actually killed. Ruth prays it was soon, while she was still happy from the game with her brothers, before she knew too much.

It is dark outside now. Ruth pours herself another glass of wine. The phone rings. Ruth picks it up wearily. Peter? Erik? Her mother?

'Doctor Ruth Galloway?' An unfamiliar voice, slightly breathless.

'Yes.'

'I'm from *The Chronicle.*' The local paper. 'I hear you were involved with the discovery of Scarlet Henderson's body?'

'I've got nothing to say.' Ruth slams down the phone, hands shaking. Immediately it rings again and she takes it off the hook.

Flint crashes in through the cat flap, making Ruth jump sky high. She feeds him and tries to get him to sit on her lap but he too is twitchy, prowling round the room with his head low and whiskers quivering.

It is nine o'clock. Ruth, who has been up since four, is exhausted but feels too strung up to go to bed. Neither, for some reason, can she read or watch TV. She just sits there, in the dark, watching Flint circling the room and listening to the rain drumming against the windows.

Ten o'clock and a heavy knock on the door sends Flint running upstairs. Though she doesn't quite know why, Ruth is trembling from head to foot. She switches on a light and edges towards the door. Though the rational archaeologist in her tells her that it is probably only Peter or Erik or Shona (who surprisingly hasn't rung yet), the irrational side, which has been taking hold all day, tells her that something dreadful lurks outside the door. Something terrible arisen from the mud and the sand. *What the Sand gets, the Sand keeps forever.*

'Who is it?' she calls out, trying to keep her voice steady.

'Me. Nelson,' comes the reply.

Ruth opens the door.

Nelson looks terrible, unshaven, red-eyed, his clothes soaking. He steps wordlessly into the sitting room and sits down on the sofa. It seems, at that moment, completely right that he should be there.

'Do you want anything to drink?' she asks. 'Tea? Coffee? Wine?'

'Coffee please.'

When she comes back with the coffee, Nelson is leaning forward on the sofa, his head in his hands. Ruth notices the amount of grey in his thick, dark hair. Surely he can't have aged in just a few months?

Ruth puts the coffee on the table beside him. 'Was it terrible?' she asks timidly.

Nelson groans, rubbing his hands over his face. 'Terrible,' he says at last, 'Delilah just ... just crumpled up like someone had squeezed all the life out of her. She just collapsed and lay there, curled up in a ball, crying, calling out for Scarlet. Nothing any of us could say was any good. How could it be? Her husband tried to hold her but she fought him off. Judy, the DC, was very good, but what could anyone say? Jesus. I've broken bad news before in my time but never anything like this. If I go to hell tomorrow, it can't be worse than this.'

He is silent again for a few moments, frowning into his coffee mug. Ruth puts her hand on his arm but says nothing: what can anyone say?

Eventually Nelson says, 'I hadn't really understood how much she believed that Scarlet was still alive. I think we all thought ... after two months ... she must be dead. Like with Lucy, you gradually stop hoping. But Delilah, poor cow, really believed that her little girl was going to walk back in through the front door one day. At first she kept saying, "She can't be dead, she can't be dead." I had to tell her, "I've seen her," and then, Christ, I had to ask them to identify the body.'

'Did they both go?'

'I wanted Alan to go on his own but Delilah insisted on coming too. I think, right up to the moment that she saw the body, she was still hoping it wasn't Scarlet. When she saw the body, that's when she collapsed.'

'Do they know how long ... how long she'd been dead?'

'No. We'll have to wait for the forensic report.' He sighs, rubbing his eyes. Then, speaking for the first time in his business-like, policeman's voice, 'She didn't look like she'd been dead long, did she?'

'That was the peat,' says Ruth, 'it's a natural preservative.'

They are silent again for a moment, deep in their own thoughts. Ruth thinks of the peat, preserving the timbers of the henge and now guarding its new secret. If they had never found her would Scarlet, like the Iron Age bodies, have been left there for hundreds, thousands of years? Would she have been found by archaeologists, puzzled over as an academic curiosity, her real history forever unknown?

'I've had another letter,' Nelson says, breaking the silence.

'What?'

In answer, Nelson brings a crumpled piece of paper out of his pocket. 'It's a copy,' he explains. 'Original's with forensics.'

Ruth leans forward to read:

Nelson,

You seek but you do not find. You find bones where you hope to find flesh. All flesh is grass. I have told you this before. I grow tired of your foolishness, your inability to see. Do I have to draw a map for you? Point a line to Lucy and to Scarlet?

The nearer the bone, the sweeter the flesh. Do not forget the bones.

In sorrow.

Ruth looks at Nelson. 'When did you get this?'

'Today. In the post. It was sent yesterday.'

'So, when Cathbad was in custody?'

'Yes.' Nelson looks up. 'Doesn't mean he couldn't have arranged to have it sent though.'

'Do you think that's what he did?'

'Maybe. Or this letter could be from a different person.'

'It reads like the others,' says Ruth, examining the typewritten paper. 'Biblical quotation, the tone, the reference to sight. It even says "I have told you this before."'

'Yes. That struck me too. Almost as if he was trying too hard to tie it to the other letters.'

Ruth looks at the words, *Point a line to Lucy and to Scarlet*. She remembers last night tracing the path on the map from the Spenwell bones to the marsh bones to the henge circle. She shivers. It is almost as if the writer was at her shoulder, watching her as she drew the line that led to Scarlet. And the bones. *Do not forget the bones*. There is a lot about bones in this letter. Bones are her speciality. Is the writer sending her a message?

'The nearer the bone, the sweeter the flesh,' she reads aloud. 'That's horrible, like cannibalism.'

'It's a proverb,' says Nelson. 'I looked it up.'

'So, do you still think Cathbad did it?'

Nelson sighs, running his hands through his hair so that it stands up like a crest. 'I don't know, but I haven't got enough to charge him. No DNA, no motive, no confession. We've been over his caravan with a toothcomb, found nothing. I'll keep him until I get the forensics report. If I find a trace of his DNA on Scarlet then he's finished.'

Ruth looks at Nelson. Maybe it's the rumpled hair and the dishevelled clothes but he looks younger somehow, almost vulnerable.

'But you don't think he did it, do you?'

Nelson looks at her. 'No, I don't,' he says.

'Then who did?'

'I don't know.' Nelson lets out another sigh that is almost a groan. 'That's the terrible, shaming thing. All those hours of investigation, all that police time, all that searching and questioning and I've still got no bloody idea who killed those two little girls. No wonder the media are shouting for my head.'

'I got a call from *The Chronicle* this evening.'

'Bastards! How did they know about you? I've been so careful to keep your name out of it.'

'Well, they were bound to find out sometime.'

Who could have told them though, Ruth thinks. Erik? Shona? Peter?

'They'll make life hard for you,' warns Nelson. 'Is there anywhere you could go for a few days?'

'I could stay with my friend Shona.' Even as she says it, Ruth dreads the long cosy evenings of Shona trying to worm out information. She'll just have to work late most nights.

'Good. I've sent my wife and kids away to my mum. Just until the worst is over.'

'When *will* the worst be over?'

'I don't know.' Nelson looks at her again, his dark eyes troubled. She can hear the rain and the wind outside but somehow it seems a long way away, as if this room, this tiny circle of light, is all that is left in the world.

Nelson is still looking at her. 'I don't want to go home,' he says at last.

And Ruth reaches out to lay her hand on his. 'You don't have to,' she says.

The silence wakes Ruth. The wind and the rain have stopped and the night is still. She thinks she hears an owl hooting and, very far off, the faint sigh of the waves.

The moon shines serenely through the open curtains and illuminates the crumpled bed, the strewn clothes and the sleeping figure of DCI Harry Nelson, breathing heavily, one arm flung out across Ruth's breasts. Gently Ruth lifts the arm and gets up to put on some pyjamas. She can't believe she went to bed naked. Somehow that is even harder to believe than the fact that she went to bed with Nelson. That she laid her hand on his, that she, seconds later, reached over to touch her lips with his. She remembers his slight hesitation, a whisper of indrawn breath, before his hand reached up behind her head and he pulled her to him. They had clung to each other, kissing desperately, hungrily, as the rain battered against the windows. She remembers the roughness of his skin, the surprising softness of his lips, the feel of his body against hers.

How could this have happened? She hardly knows Harry Nelson. Two months ago she had thought him just another boorish policeman. All she does know is that last night they seemed to share something that set them apart from all the world. They had seen Scarlet's body as it rose, lifeless, from the sand. They had, in some small way, shared her family's pain. They had read the letters. They knew of the evil presence out there in the dark. They knew of Lucy Downey too, feared that the next discovery would be her body. And, at that moment, it had seemed only natural that this knowledge should draw them into each other's arms, that they should blot out the pain with the comforts of the body. They might never do it again but last night ... last night had been right.

Even so, thinks Ruth, pulling on her nicest pyjamas (she isn't about to let him see the grey ones with built-in feet), he'd better leave soon. The press knows about her. The last thing either of them wants is for the media to discover the leading policeman in the Scarlet Henderson case in bed with the bones expert. She looks down at Nelson. In sleep he looks much younger, his dark eyelashes fanned out on his cheek, his harsh mouth gentle. Ruth shivers but not from the cold.

'Nelson?' she shakes him.

He is awake immediately.

'What is it?'

'You'd better go.'

He moans. 'What time is it?'

'Almost four.'

He looks at her for a moment as if wondering who she is and then smiles. The surprisingly sweet smile that she has only seen once or twice before.

'Good morning Doctor Galloway.'

'Good morning DI Nelson,' says Ruth, 'you'd better get dressed.'

As Nelson reaches for his clothes, Ruth sees a tattoo high on his shoulder, blue writing around some kind of shield.

'What does your tattoo say?' she asks.

'Seasiders. It's a nickname for my team, Blackpool. Had it done when I was sixteen. Michelle hates it.'

There, he has said her name. Michelle, the perfect wife, who hovered between them all last night, is suddenly there in the room. Nelson, pulling on his trousers, seems unconscious of what he has said. Perhaps he does this all the time, thinks Ruth.

Dressed, he looks a different person. A policeman, a stranger. He comes over to her, sits on the bed and takes her hand.

'Thanks,' he says.

'What for?'

'Being there.'

'Just doing my duty as a citizen.'

He grins. 'You should get a medal.'

Ruth watches as he retrieves his mobile from under the bed. She feels oddly detached, as if she is watching something on television. But she doesn't really watch that sort of programme; she prefers documentaries.

'Will you go to your friend's house?' asks Nelson, shrugging on his jacket.

'Yes. I think so.'

'Well, keep in touch. Any trouble from those press bastards, give me a shout.'

'I will.'

At the doorway he turns and smiles. 'Goodbye Doctor Galloway,' he says.

And he is gone.

CHAPTER 17

Unable to get back to sleep, Ruth gets up and showers. Watching the water running off her body, she thinks of Nelson and wonders if she is symbolically cleansing herself, rubbing off any taint of his touch, his smell, his presence. That's certainly what her parents would want her to do. Be baptised, be born again. A phrase from her churchgoing past comes into her mind: washed in the blood of the lamb. She shivers. It sounds too much like the letter writer for her liking. She thinks of that last letter with its references to bones and flesh. Were those references meant for her?

She dries herself briskly and goes into her bedroom. She strips the bed (more symbolic cleansing?) and dresses quickly in trousers and fleece. Then she gets out a bag and starts to pack some clothes. She will take Nelson's advice and go to Shona's for a few days. She'll call Shona from the university.

Packing her unaesthetic grey pyjamas, she thinks of Nelson. Did he sleep with her only to blot out the horror of finding Scarlet's body? He can't possibly fancy her, not with Miss Blonde Housewife 2008 waiting for him at home. Does she fancy him? If she is honest, yes. She has been attracted to him ever since she saw him in the corridor that first time, looking too big and too grown up for his surroundings. He is an antidote to the weedy academic types around her, men like Phil and Peter, even Erik. Nelson would never sit and pore over dusty reference books; his preference is for doing things: striding over the marshes, questioning suspects, driving too fast. Sleeping with women who aren't his wife? Well, maybe. She senses it isn't the first time he has been unfaithful to the sainted Michelle. There was something practised about his demeanour this morning, gathering up his clothes, carefully not making any promises about when they would meet next. But there had been emotion too last night, something almost shy, and surprisingly tender. She remembers his sharp intake of breath when she first kissed him, the way he had murmured her name, the way he had kissed her, softly at first and then much harder, almost violently, his body pressed against hers.

Stop thinking about it, she tells herself as she lugs the bag downstairs. It was a one-off. It will never happen again. How can it? He is married, they have almost nothing in common. It was only the circumstances of last night that conjured up that particular spell. From now on they will just be policeman and expert witness, two professionals working together.

Flint purrs around her ankles and Ruth wonders what to do about him. She can't take him to Shona's. The change would upset him, especially coming so soon after Sparky's disappearance. She'll have to ask David to feed him. She remembers him saying once that he didn't like cats because they kill birds but surely he wouldn't mind just for a couple of days? Anyway, with the weekenders back in London there is no one else to ask.

It is still only six o'clock. She makes herself coffee and toast (her first meal for twenty-four hours, she'll be a size 12 before she knows it) and sits at the table to watch the sun come up. The sky is still dark but there is a faint line of gold against the horizon. The tide is out and the early morning mist lies low over the marsh. This time yesterday, she and Nelson were just setting out across the mudflats.

At seven, she goes to call on David. She is sure he gets up early, for the dawn chorus or something. It is light now and the day is cold and clear, the sky washed clean by yesterday's rain. There will be nothing to stop the journalists today. Nelson is right; she must get away.

David takes a long time to open the door but when he does he is, thankfully, fully dressed. He is wearing waterproofs and looks like he has already been outside.

'I'm sorry to call so early,' says Ruth, 'but I've got to go away for a few days. Could you possibly feed Flint, my cat?'

David looks bemused. 'Flint?' he repeats.

'My cat. Could you come in and feed him for a few days? I'd be really grateful.'

David seems to be registering her for the first time. 'Ruth,' he says. 'Were you involved in all that drama yesterday?'

Drama. The word seems wrong for what happened yesterday on the Saltmarsh. While the day had felt many things, it had never felt unreal. 'Yes,' says Ruth shortly, 'I found the body.'

'My God!' David looks really shocked. 'How awful. I can see why you'd want to get away.'

'The press were after me yesterday. I want to lie low for a bit.'

'The press.' David's face darkens. 'Vermin. Did you see them yesterday? Trampling over the reed beds, dropping litter and cigarette butts everywhere. Will they be back today, do you think?'

'I'm afraid so.'

'I'd better be on patrol.' David looks grim. Ruth thinks it might be time to remind him about Flint. She proffers her key.

'So, is it alright about the cat? His food's in the kitchen. He has one small tin every day and some biscuits. Don't let him persuade you he should have more. Otherwise, he'll just come and go. He's got a cat flap. I'll leave my contact details on the table.'

David takes the key. 'Food. Cat flap. Contact details. Fine. Yes. OK.'

Ruth hopes that he will remember.

The roads are clear and she gets to the university in record time. The car parks are empty. It seems that journalists, like academics, are not early risers. She punches in the code to open the doors and escapes to her office with a sigh of relief. Here, at least, she can be safe for a while.

Three cups of coffee and several pages of lecture notes later, there is a knock at the door.

'Come in,' says Ruth. She assumes it will be Phil, coming for his dose of vicarious excitement.

But it's Shona. Ruth is surprised; Shona hardly ever ventures over from the Arts Faculty.

'Ruth!' Shona comes over to give her a hug. 'I've just heard about yesterday. You actually found that poor little girl's body.'

'Who told you?' asks Ruth.

'Erik. I saw him in the car park.'

It will be all over campus, thinks Ruth. She realises she was stupid to imagine that she could be safe, even here.

'Yes, I found her. She was buried in the peat, right in the centre of the henge circle.'

'My God.' Shona had been on the dig ten years ago; she would know the significance of the place, the sacred ground.

'Does Erik know where she was found?' asks Shona, sitting down.

'Yes. I think he's more upset about that than anything. The police digging up the site. Contaminating the context.' Ruth surprises herself with the bitterness in her voice.

'Why are they still digging?'

'Well, they think the other girl may be buried there. Lucy Downey.'

'The one who disappeared all that time ago?'

'Ten years ago. Just after the henge dig.'

'Do the police think they were killed by the same person?'

Ruth looks at Shona. Her face is soft, concerned, but Ruth also catches a trace of the slightly shamefaced curiosity that she recognises all too well. In herself.

'I don't know,' she says. 'I don't know what the police think.'

'Are they going to charge that druid chap?'

'Cathbad? I'm sorry, Shona, I just don't know.'

'Erik says he's innocent.'

'Yes,' agrees Ruth. She wonders how much Erik has told Shona.

'What do *you* think?' persists Shona.

'I don't know,' says Ruth for what feels like the hundredth time. 'It's hard to think of him as a murderer. He always seemed a harmless old thing, into peace and nature and all that. But the police must have some evidence otherwise they wouldn't be able to hold him.'

'That Detective Nelson sounds a real hard bastard.'

Briefly Ruth thinks of Nelson. Sees, as if projected in technicolour onto the wall opposite, his face above hers. Feels his stubble against her cheek.

'I really don't know him that well,' she says. 'Look Shona, I've got a favour to ask you. Can I stay with you for a few days? You see, the press have got wind that I was involved. I think they might come round to my house and I'd just like to get away for a bit.'

'Of course,' says Shona at once. 'You're more than welcome. Tell you what, we'll have a takeaway and a few bottles tonight. Have a real girls' night in. Forget about everything and just unwind. What do you think?'

She doesn't quite know why but Ruth doesn't enjoy her girls' night in as much as she expected. For a start she is exhausted and after a few glasses of Pinot Grigio she feels her eyelids begin to droop. Then, for perhaps the first time in her adult life, she just isn't that hungry. Usually she loves takeaways: the flimsy silver cartons, the gloriously greasy food, the mystery dish that you're never sure whether you ordered. Usually, she loves it all. But, tonight, after a few mouthfuls of crispy, aromatic duck, she pushes away her plate. The smell of soy sauce is starting to make her feel sick.

'What's up?' asks Shona, her mouth full. 'Dig in. There's loads.'

'I'm sorry,' says Ruth, 'I'm not very hungry.'

'You have to eat,' intones Shona, as if Ruth were an anorexic schoolgirl rather than an overweight woman in her late thirties. 'At least have another drink.' She sloshes more wine into Ruth's glass. 'Come on, chill out.'

Shona lives in a terraced house on the outskirts of King's Lynn. It is near the centre of town, all very urban, the perfect antidote to the Saltmarsh. And at first Ruth had just stood in the tiny front garden listening to the traffic and breathing in the pungent aroma of garlic and cumin from the nearby Indian takeaway. 'Come in,' Shona said. 'Stay outside too long and your car will get clamped. Christ, the parking round here.'

Ruth had come in and installed herself in Shona's spare room (polished floor, pine bed, Egyptian cotton sheets, prints of Paris and New York). Now I can relax, she told herself. No one knows where I am. I can calm down, have a nice meal and a few glasses of wine. I'll be a new person tomorrow.

But it hasn't quite worked out like that. She feels twitchy, ill-at-ease. She keeps checking her phone though she isn't expecting anyone to call. She worries that David will forget to feed Flint. She misses her cottage and the desolate, doomed view over the Saltmarsh. She feels almost sick with tiredness but she knows she won't be able to sleep tonight. As soon as she shuts her eyes the whole thing will play again, like some X-rated movie on a continuous loop: the early-morning trek over the mudflats, the discovery of Scarlet's body, the little arm hanging down, Nelson at her door, red-eyed and unshaven, Nelson's body moving against hers ...

Everything reminds her. Shona's ambient music playing softly in the background reminds her of the rain and the voices of the birds, suddenly stilled. The soft candlelight makes her think of the will o'the wisps with their treacherous flickering lights, leading unwary travellers to their deaths. When she looks at Shona's bookshelves and sees T.S. Eliot nestling next to Shakespeare she thinks of the Lucy Downey letters. *We who were living are now dying.*

'So do you think he will?' asks Shona, pouring more wine into Ruth's glass.

'What?' Ruth has completely lost track of the conversation.

'Leave Anne. Do you think Liam will leave Anne?'

Not in a million years, thinks Ruth. Just as Nelson will never leave Michelle.

'Maybe. I don't know. Are you sure you want him to?'

'I don't know. If you'd asked me six months ago I would have said yes, but now? I think I would be terrified, to be honest. There's something safe about going out with a married man.'

'Is there?'

'Yes, you always think, if it wasn't for his wife, he'd be with me. You don't have to face up to anything else that might be wrong with the relationship. And it stays exciting. You don't have a chance to get bored.'

'Have you done this before then?' As far as Ruth knows, Liam is Shona's first married lover but she is talking like a veteran of extra-marital affairs. Like Nelson, she thinks cynically.

Shona's face suddenly takes on a closed, watchful

expression. She fills up her own glass, splashing wine onto the trendy rush-matting rug.

'Oh, once or twice,' she says, with what sounds like deliberate casualness. 'Before I met you. Now, for heaven's sake drink up, Ruth. You're way behind.'

Ruth was right about not being able to sleep. She tries to immerse herself in Rebus but Rebus and Siobhan become, embarrassingly and explicitly, herself and Nelson. She even opens her laptop and starts to work but, although way behind Shona, she has drunk too much to be interested in Mesolithic burial sites. Tombs, burials, bodies, bones, she thinks blurrily – why is archaeology so concerned with death?

She drinks some water, turns over her pillow and determinedly shuts her eyes. A hundred, ninety-nine, ninety-eight, ninety-seven, how many flint mines in Norfolk, hope David remembers Flint, hope Flint doesn't kill any rare marsh birds ... Sparky's body in its flimsy cardboard coffin ... Scarlet's arm hanging down below the tarpaulin ... ninety-six, ninety-five ... *We who were living are now dying* ... ninety-four, ninety-three ... He'll never leave his wife ... Why has Peter come back, why can't Shona forget about Liam, does Cathbad still love Delilah, why are the Iron Age bodies in a line, why did the line point to Scarlet ... ninety-two, ninety-one ...

The bleeping of her phone is a welcome relief. She snatches it up gratefully. A text message. The little screen gleams green in the dark. Caller unknown.

I know where you are.

The sky is full of noises. Thumping noises, crackling noises like very large birds hooting and calling. She knows it is daytime because the window is closed. She can't see anything, only hear the noises. She is scared and huddles in the corner of the room, under the blanket.

For a long time he doesn't come and she is hungry and more scared than ever. She finishes her water and looks in the dark for the piece of bread she thinks she dropped a few days ago. She wonders if she will die if he doesn't come to feed her. Maybe he is dead.

He doesn't come for a long time and her mouth is dry and the bucket in the corner starts to smell.

She edges her way around the room, looking for the bread. She can see lights through the sides of the trapdoor and she wants to call out but is afraid to. The stone walls are damp and mossy, smooth when she runs her hands over them. She can reach higher now, almost to the dry bits at the top where the stones are all crumbly like bread-crumbs. Why can she reach higher? Is she getting bigger? He says so. Too big, he says. What does that mean? Too big for what?

She reaches as high as she can and pulls at one of the stones. It comes away in her hands, surprising her, making her fall backwards. She sits on the floor and feels the edge of the stone with her thumb. It is sharp, it cuts her. She licks the blood; it tastes like the metal cup she drinks from but it's also salty, odd-tasting, strong. She licks until the blood has gone.

She takes the stone to the corner of the room where there is soil, not floor. She digs a hole and, very carefully, she places the stone in the hole and covers it with earth. Then she stamps on the soil until it is all smooth again and no one but her would know that something is buried there.

It is the first time she has had a secret. It tastes good.

CHAPTER 18

Exhaustion finally sends Ruth to sleep at two a.m. For several hours she had just sat there, listening to her heart pounding and looking at the text message. Those few chilling words. Who could have sent it? Is it *him*, the letter writer, the murderer? Who knows where she is? Who has her mobile phone number? Must it – and her stomach contracts as if she is about to be sick – must it be someone she knows?

She knows that she has to ring Nelson, but somehow, she doesn't want to call him in the middle of the night. Yesterday has blurred all the issues. She doesn't want Nelson to think she is hassling him. What is more important, she asks herself sternly, being murdered in your bed or a man getting the wrong idea about you? She wishes her subconscious was more liberated.

She falls asleep and wakes a few hours later, still upright and stiff all over. Her phone has fallen to the floor and, hand trembling, she picks it up. No new messages. Ruth sighs and burrows down inside the bed. Right now, she is so tired that death seems almost an attractive option, to go to sleep and never wake up.

When she wakes again there is proper, yellow daylight outside the window and Shona is standing by her bed holding a cup of tea.

'You have slept well,' she says brightly. 'It's past nine.'

Ruth sips the tea gratefully. It's ages since someone brought her tea in bed. In daylight, sitting in Shona's sunny, tasteful spare room, she no longer feels destined to die a violent death. She feels, in fact, ready to fight. She gets up, showers, and dresses in her toughest, most uncompromising clothes (black suit, white shirt, scary earrings). Then she goes downstairs ready to kick ass.

She is sitting in her car, ready to drive to work when her phone goes off. Despite her scary earrings, she is absolutely terrified, breathing hard, palms clammy.

'Hi Ruth. It's Nelson.'

'Oh. Nelson. Hello.' For some reason, her heart is still thumping.

'Just wanted you to know, we're releasing Malone tomorrow.'

'You are? Why?'

'Forensic reports have come back and there's none of his DNA on Scarlet. So we're charging him with writing the letters and that's all. He'll come up in court tomorrow and I expect he'll get bail.'

'Is he still a suspect?'

Nelson laughs humourlessly. 'Well, he's the only one we've got, but we've got nothing that ties him to the murder. We haven't got any reason to keep holding him.'

'What will he do?'

'Well, he can't leave the area. I suspect he'll lie low though. Might even get police protection, what with all the media interest.' Nelson sounds so scornful that, despite herself, Ruth smiles.

'What did the ... the post-mortem say?'

'Death was by asphyxiation. Looks like something was shoved in her mouth and she choked on it. Her hands were tied with some sort of plant plaited together.'

'Some sort of *plant*?'

'Yes, looks like honeysuckle and – you'll like this – mistletoe.'

Ruth thinks of the letters and their mention of mistletoe. Does this mean that the writer was the murderer? Does this mean that it was Cathbad after all? Then she thinks of the ropes that had hauled the henge timbers into place. Honeysuckle rope. As Peter had remembered.

'Body had been in the ground about six weeks,' Nelson is saying. 'Hard to tell because of the peat. No sign of sexual abuse.'

'That's something,' says Ruth hesitantly.

'Yes,' says Nelson, his voice bitter. 'That's something. And we'll be able to let the family have the body for burial. That'll mean a lot to them.' He sighs. Ruth imagines him scowling as he sits at his desk, looking through files, making lists, deliberately not looking at the photo of Scarlet Henderson.

'Any road' – Nelson's voice changes gear, rather jerkily – 'How are you? No more calls from the press, I hope.'

'No, but I had an odd message last night.' Ruth tells him about the text message. She imagines Nelson's eyes shooting heavenwards. How much more trouble is this woman going to cause me?

'I'll get someone on to it,' he says. 'Give me the number.'

She does so. 'Can you trace a mobile phone number?'

'Yes. Mobile phones have a unique number that they send out every time they make a call. It's like they check in to their local base. If we have the number, it won't be hard to trace the call. Of course, if he's clever, he'll have ditched the phone.'

'Do you think it was ... him?'

'Christ knows. But we need to get you some protection. How long are you staying with your mate?'

'I don't know.' As she says this, Ruth is assailed by a longing for her home. For her bed and her cat and her view over the ill-omened marshes.

'I'll send some men to watch her house and to keep your place under surveillance. Try not to worry too much. I don't think he'll come out into the open. He's too clever.'

'Is he?'

'Well, he's been too clever for me, hasn't he?'

'You'll catch him,' says Ruth with more conviction than she feels.

'Wish the press agreed with you. Take care, love.'

As she clicks off her phone, Ruth thinks: *love?*

At the university, the first person she sees is Peter. He's waiting outside her room and the memory comes back, unbidden, of seeing Nelson in the same place, so harsh and unyielding next to the conciliatory Phil. Unlike Nelson on that occasion, who had shown all the swagger of a professional coming into a room full of amateurs, Peter looks nervous, flattening himself apologetically against the wall every time a student goes past (which, as it is still early, is not very often).

'Ruth!' He steps forward to greet her.

'Peter. What are you doing here?'

'I wanted to see you.'

Ruth sighs inwardly. The last thing she needs this morning is Peter going on about his marriage and wanting to relive the henge dig.

'You'd better come in,' she says ungraciously.

In her office, Peter swoops on her cat doorstop. 'I remember buying you this. I can't believe you've still got it.'

'It's useful,' says Ruth shortly. She's not about to tell him that she has kept it for sentimental reasons, which wouldn't be true. Well, not entirely true.

Peter sinks down in her visitor's chair. 'Great office,' he says, looking up at Indiana Jones. Ten years ago, she hadn't been important enough for an office of her own.

'Bit small,' she says.

'You should see my office at UCL. I have to share it with an archivist with a personal freshness problem. I only get the desk Mondays and Thursdays.'

Ruth laughs. Peter could always make her laugh, she thinks grudgingly.

Peter smiles too, looking fleetingly like his old self, but then his face looks grave again.

'What a terrible business on the Saltmarsh,' he says, 'you finding that little girl's body.'

'Yes.'

'How did you know she was there?'

Ruth looks up sharply. This seems an odd question. Who was to say that it wasn't the police who discovered the location?

'It was a hunch,' she said at last. 'I was looking at the map and I saw a line leading from the Spenwell body to my Iron Age body to the henge. The posts that I showed you, the causeway, they seemed to mark the route. I thought of cursuses, underground paths that seem to point to significant things in the landscape. I suddenly realised that the causeway was a cursus.'

'And it led to the body?'

'Yes.'

'But are you saying it was deliberate? That someone buried her there knowing all about causeways and cursuswhatsits?'

'Cursuses. I don't know. The police think that maybe the murderer knows about archaeology.'

'*Do* they?' Peter is silent for a few seconds, obviously considering this. Then he looks up and says, 'That reminds me, Erik's set up a dig next week to look at the causeway.'

'Has he got police permission?'

'Apparently so. He spoke to your mate Nelson. He says it's OK as long as they don't go into the henge circle. And, obviously, they've got to show the police anything they find.'

Erik has spoken to Nelson, whom apparently he dislikes and distrusts. Nelson has given permission for the dig. Ruth's head swims in a miasma of contradictions, loyalties, memories.

'When did you see Erik?' she asks at last.

'Yesterday. We had lunch together.'

'Did you?' Ruth tries to imagine the scene. Erik always liked Peter, seemed to approve of him as a partner for Ruth, but she can't quite imagine them sitting down for a cosy pizza together.

'Where did you go?'

'Oh, some sushi place he knows.'

So, no pizza then. 'Did he say anything about Cathbad? Michael Malone?'

'Only that the police had got the wrong man. He seemed quite heated about it. Kept going on about a police state; you know what an old hippie he is.'

Yet Erik was quite prepared to go to Nelson for permission to dig, thinks Ruth. Nothing, *nothing*, comes in the way of the archaeology.

'They're releasing Cathbad,' says Ruth. 'It'll probably be on the news today.' Well, Nelson didn't tell her to keep it a secret.

'Really?' says Peter with interest. 'Releasing him without charge?'

'There may be some charges, I don't know.'

'Come off it, Ruth, you seem to know everything.'

'I don't,' snaps Ruth, unreasonably irritated.

'Sorry.' Peter looks contrite. It doesn't suit him. 'So,' he asks brightly, 'how's Shona?'

'Fine. The same. Going on about how she's going to give up men and become a nun.'

'Who is it this time?'

'A lecturer. Married.'

'Is he promising to leave his wife?'

'Naturally.'

Peter sighs. 'Poor old Shona.' Perhaps he is thinking about his own marriage because he seems to slump in his chair; even his hair seems muted. 'I always thought she'd get married and have ten children. The old Catholic upbringing coming out.'

Ruth thinks of Shona's two abortions; the defiant declarations of independence before, the endless tears afterwards. 'No,' she says, 'no children.'

'Poor Shona,' says Peter again. He sinks even further into his chair. It's going to take a rocket to shift him.

'Peter,' says Ruth, lighting the fuse, 'did you want something? I ought to be getting on.'

He looks hurt. 'Just to see how you were. I wondered if you'd like to go out for a drink tonight?'

Ruth thinks of going back to another girls' night in: Pinot Grigio, Liam, takeaway, mysterious text messages.

'OK,' she says. 'That'd be nice.'

They go to a restaurant in King's Lynn, near the pub where Ruth had lunch with Nelson. This place, though, has pretensions: lower-case menu, blonde wood floors, square plates, banks of flickering candles. Chasing a lone scallop over acres of white china, Ruth says, 'Where did you find this place?' Then she adds hastily, 'It's great.'

'Phil recommended it.' That figured.

It's early and there are only two other couples dining, two thirtysomethings who are clearly counting the minutes until they can be in bed together and an elderly couple who do not exchange one word all evening.

'Blimey, why don't they get a room?' mutters Ruth as the thirtysomething woman starts licking wine off the man's fingers.

'Probably married to other people.'

'Why do you say that?'

'If they were married to each other, they wouldn't be talking, let alone be performing sex acts on each other's fingers,' says Peter in a low voice. 'Look at the old dears over there. Fifty years of wedded bliss and not a word to say to each other.'

Ruth wants to ask if this was what his marriage was like. Say nothing, she tells herself, and he'll come out with it. Peter was never very good at silences.

Sure enough, Peter sighs and takes a gulp of over-priced red wine. 'Like me and Victoria. We just ... drifted apart. I know it's a cliché but it's true. We just ran out of things to say to each other. Woke up one morning and discovered that, apart from Daniel, we had nothing in common. Oh we still like each other, it's all very friendly, but that something, that vital something, has gone.'

But that's what happened to us, Ruth wants to say. She remembers that feeling of looking at Peter – intelligent, kind, good-looking Peter – and thinking, 'Is this it?' Is this what I have to settle for, a nice man who, when he touches me, I sometimes don't even notice?

But Peter has his rose-tinted spectacles on again. 'With us, we had so much in common,' he says dreamily, 'archaeology, history, books. Victoria's no intellectual. Her only serious reading matter is *Hello* magazine.'

'That's very patronising,' says Ruth.

'Oh, don't get me wrong,' says Peter hastily, 'Victoria's a wonderful woman. Very warm and giving.' (She's put on weight, thinks Ruth.) 'I'm very fond of her and we're both devoted to Daniel but it's not a marriage any more. We're more like flatmates, sharing childcare and housework, only talking about who's picking up Daniel the next day or when the Tesco delivery is coming.'

'Well, what did you expect to be talking about? Renaissance architecture? The early poems of Robert Browning?'

Peter grins. 'Something like that. Well, *we* talked, didn't we? Do you remember the nights around the campfire talking about whether Neolithic man was a hunter-gatherer or a farmer? You said that women would have done the hunting and you tried to creep up on that sheep to show how it could be done.'

'And fell flat on my face in sheep crap,' says Ruth drily. She leans forward. It seems very important to make this clear to Peter. 'Look Peter, the henge dig was ten years ago. That was then. This is now. We're different people. We had a relationship and that was great but it's in the past. You can't go back.'

'Can't you?' asks Peter, looking at her very intently. In the candlelight his eyes are very dark, almost black.

'No,' says Ruth gently.

Peter stares at her in silence for a minute or two, then he smiles. A different smile, sweeter and much sadder. 'Well, let's just get pissed then,' he says, leaning forward to fill up her glass.

She doesn't get pissed but she's probably slightly over the limit when she gets into her car.

'Drive carefully,' says Peter as he heads towards a new-looking Alfa Romeo. Mid-life crisis?

'I will.' Ruth is glad that she doesn't have to negotiate the treacherous New Road with the darkness of the marsh all around. It's only a few minutes' drive to Shona's, she should be alright. She drives slowly, following other, more decisive, cars. On the radio, someone is talking about Gordon Brown. 'He wants to go back to the way things were.' Don't we all, thinks Ruth, taking a left turn into Shona's road. Despite her tough words, she sympathises with Peter and his yearning for the past. There is something very tempting about the idea of going back to Peter, accepting that the mysterious perfect man is not going to turn up, that Peter is the best that she is going to get, probably a lot better than she deserves. What's stopping her? Is it the shadowy Victoria and Daniel? Is it Nelson? She knows that nothing will come of the night with Nelson – it is just that imagining herself in bed with Peter seems comforting and familiar; it does not, for one minute, seem exciting.

She finds a space by the Indian restaurant and starts to walk towards Shona's house. Out of reflex, she checks her text messages. Just one:

I know where you are.

CHAPTER 19

Scarlet Henderson's funeral takes place on a grim, rainy Friday afternoon. A line from a folk hymn comes into Ruth's head: 'I danced on a Friday when the sky turned black.' The heavens are certainly weeping for Scarlet Henderson today; the rain falls relentlessly all morning.

'It's bad luck to have a funeral on a Friday,' says Shona, looking out of her sitting-room window at the water cascading down the street.

'For Christ's sake,' explodes Ruth. 'When is it good luck to have a funeral?'

She shouldn't have snapped at Shona. She's only trying to be supportive, has even offered to come to the funeral with her, but Ruth says she should go alone. She feels somehow that she owes it to Scarlet, the little girl she knows only in death. Owes it too to Delilah and Alan. And to Nelson? Maybe. She hasn't spoken to him in days. Cathbad's release was on every newscast with Nelson, stony-faced, claiming to be following up new leads. Ruth suspects this is a lie, a suspicion shared, apparently, by most of the press.

The church, a squat modern building on the outskirts of Spenwell, is packed. Ruth finds a space at the back, wedged into the end of a pew. She can just see Nelson at the front of the church. He is wearing a dark grey suit and looking straight in front of him. He is flanked by other burly figures who she thinks must be policemen. There is a policewoman too. Ruth sees her searching in her bag for a tissue and wonders if this is Judy, who helped break the news to Scarlet's parents.

The arrival of the tiny coffin, accompanied by a shell-shocked Delilah and Alan, the chrysanthemums spelling out the name 'Scarlet', the siblings, cowed and wide-eyed in their dark clothes, the reedy singing of 'All Things Bright and Beautiful' – all seem designed to break your heart. Ruth feels the tears prickling at the back of her eyes but she does not let them fall. What right has she to cry over Scarlet?

The vicar, a nervous-looking man in white robes, makes a few anodyne remarks about angels and innocence and God's right hand. Then, to Ruth's surprise, Nelson steps forward to do a reading. He reads very badly, stumbling over the words, eyes downcast.

'"I am the resurrection and the life," says the Lord. "Those who believe in me, even though they die, will live, and everyone who lives and believes in me will never die."'

Ruth is reminded uncomfortably of the letters. The writer of the Lucy Downey letters would love this, all his old favourites are here: life, death, the certainty of the after-life and a comforting pall of mysticism thrown over the whole. Did Cathbad write those letters? And, if so, why? To frustrate the police? She knows that Cathbad dislikes the police – and archaeologists too, for that matter – but is that enough of a reason? Where is Cathbad today? Did he want to come, to comfort the woman he once loved, to comfort his daughter, Delilah's eldest, now weeping silently into her mother's hair?

At last it's over and the little white coffin passes so close that Ruth could almost touch it. She sees, again, that image of the arm hanging down, almost imagines that she can see it reaching out of the coffin, asking for her help. She shuts her eyes and the vision fades. The last hymn is playing; people are getting to their feet.

Outside, the rain has stopped and the air is cold and clammy. The coffin, followed by Scarlet's family, is driven away for a private cremation. The remaining mourners seem visibly to relax: talking, putting on coats, a couple of people lighting cigarettes.

Ruth finds herself next to the policewoman, who has a sweet, freckled face and eyes swollen with tears.

Ruth introduces herself and the policewoman's face lights up with recognition. 'Oh, I know about you. The boss has talked about you. I'm Judy Johnson, Detective Constable Judy Johnson.'

'You're the one who –' Ruth stops, not knowing if she should go on.

'Who broke the news. Yes. I've had the training, you see, and they like a woman to go, especially if there's a child involved.'

'Nelson ... DCI Nelson said you were very good.'

'That's kind of him but I'm not sure how much anyone could do.'

They are silent for a moment, looking at the undertaker's cars lining the road outside. Nelson is getting into one of the cars. He doesn't look round.

'See those people over there?' Judy indicates a grey-haired couple walking slowly away from the church. 'They're Lucy Downey's parents. You know the Lucy Downey case?'

'I've heard of it, yes. How do they know the Hendersons?'

'When Scarlet went missing, Mrs Downey contacted Delilah Henderson to offer support. They're lovely people. Makes it even worse somehow.'

Ruth watches the lovely people as they walk past the rain-sleek cars. The woman, Lucy Downey's mother, looks old, grey-haired and round-shouldered. Her husband is more robust; he has his arm around her as if he is used to protecting her. How must they feel, attending this funeral when they have never been able to say goodbye to their own daughter? Do they, in some corner of their hearts, still think she is alive?

'Can I give you a lift home?' asks Judy.

Ruth looks at her, thinking of the drive back to Shona's house; Shona's solicitude, lightly tinged with curiosity, the night in the tasteful spare room.

'No thank you,' she says. 'I've got my car. I'm going straight home.'

And she does. She drives straight back to the New Road. She knows she will have to go back to Shona's house to pick up her clothes but, at this moment, all she wants to do is go home. The marshes are grey and dreary under the lowering skies but Ruth is still unaccountably glad to be back. She parks in her usual spot beside the broken fence and lets herself in, shouting joyfully for Flint. He must have been waiting for her because he comes running in from the kitchen, looking ruffled and hard done by. Ruth picks him up, breathing in the lovely, outdoor smell of his fur.

The house is as she left it. David has obviously collected her post and put it in a neat pile. Flint seems fine so he must have remembered to feed him. The empty bottle of white wine is still on the table next to Nelson's abandoned coffee mug. The sofa cushions are on the floor. Blushing, Ruth picks them up and bashes them back into shape.

The post is mostly boring: bills, overdue library books, a flyer from a local theatre where Ruth went to see a play six years ago, charity appeals, a postcard from a friend in New York. Ruth leaves most of it unopened and goes into the kitchen to make a cup of tea. Flint jumps onto the work surface and meows loudly. He must have been getting into bad habits. Ruth puts him back on the floor whereupon he immediately jumps up again.

'Stupid cat. What are you playing at?'

'Cats aren't stupid,' says a voice behind her. 'They have highly developed mystical powers.'

Ruth starts and swings round. A man wearing a muddy cloak over jeans and an army jacket stands smiling, quite at ease, at her kitchen door.

Cathbad.

Ruth backs away. 'How did you get in?' she asks.

'I came in when that man came to feed the cat. He didn't see me. I can make myself invisible, didn't you know? I've been watching the house for a while. I knew you'd be back. This place has got quite a hold over you, hasn't it?'

The statement is disturbing on so many levels that, for a moment, Ruth can only stand and stare. Cathbad has been watching her house. He guesses, quite rightly, that the Saltmarsh has a hold over her. What else does he know?

'What are you doing here?' she says at last, trying to make her voice steady.

'I wanted to talk to you. Have you got any herbal teas?' He gestures towards her mug. 'Caffeine's a poison.'

'I'm not making you a cup of tea.' Ruth hears her voice rising. 'I want you to get out of my house.'

'It's natural for you to be upset,' says Cathbad kindly. 'Have you been to the funeral? Poor little girl. Poor, undeveloped soul. I've been sitting here sending positive thoughts to Delilah.'

'I'm sure she was very grateful.'

'Don't be angry, Ruth,' says Cathbad with a surprisingly sweet smile. 'We've got no quarrel after all. Erik says you've got a good heart.'

'Very kind of him.'

'He says you understand about the Saltmarsh, about the henge. It wasn't your fault the barbarians destroyed it. I remember you that summer, hand in hand with your boyfriend. It was a magical time for you, wasn't it?'

Ruth lowers her eyes. 'Yes,' she admits.

'It was for me, too. It was the first time I'd felt really at one with nature. Knowing that the ancients built that circle for a reason. Feeling the magic still there after all those centuries and being able to experience it, just for a short time, before it was gone forever.'

Ruth remembers something that always annoyed her about the druids, even in the old days. They felt that the henge was theirs alone, that they were the only heirs of its creators. We are all descended from them, Ruth wanted to say, it belongs to all of us. She still has no idea what Cathbad is doing here.

'What do you want?' she says.

'To talk to you,' says Cathbad again. He stoops and picks up Flint, who disgusts Ruth by purring loudly. 'This is a very wise cat,' he announces, 'an old soul.'

'He's not that bright,' says Ruth. 'My other cat was cleverer.'

'Yes. I'm sorry about what happened to her.'

'How did you know?' asks Ruth. 'How did you know about my other cat?'

'Erik told me. Why? Did you think I did it?'

Ruth doesn't know what to think. Is she trapped in the kitchen with a cat killer, or worse, a child murderer? She looks at Cathbad as he stands there, holding Flint in his arms. His face is open, slightly hurt-looking. He doesn't look like a killer but then what does a killer look like?

'I don't know what to think,' she says. 'The police have charged you with writing those letters.'

Immediately, Cathbad's face darkens. 'The police! That bastard Nelson has it in for me. I'm going to sue him for wrongful arrest.'

'*Did* you write them?'

Cathbad smiles and puts Flint gently back on the floor. 'I think you know I didn't,' he says. 'You've read them, after all.'

'How did you...?'

'Nelson's not as clever as he thinks he is. He gave it away. Yakking on about archaeology terms. There's only one person who could have told him all that. You're very friendly, you two, aren't you? There's definite energy between you.'

Ruth says nothing. Cathbad may not, as Erik claims, be magic but there is no denying that some of his shots hit the mark.

'I know you, Ruth,' says Cathbad chattily, hitching himself up to sit on the work surface. 'I watched you fall in love with that red-haired fellow all those years ago. I know what you're like when you're in love. You were in love with Erik too, weren't you?'

'Of course not!'

'Oh yes you were. I felt sorry for you because you didn't get a look-in, what with his wife and girlfriend both on the dig.'

'Girlfriend? What do you mean?'

'That beautiful girl with all the hair. Looks like a Renaissance picture. *Primavera* or something. Teaches at the university. She was sympathetic to us, I remember. Joined in the protests. Well, until it started to get serious.'

'Shona?' Ruth whispers. 'That's not true.'

'No?' Cathbad looks at her, head on one side, while Ruth shuffles quickly through her memories. Shona and Erik always liked each other. Erik called her The Lady of Shalott after the Waterhouse portrait. An image comes to her, clear as a film flashback, of Shona plaiting Erik's grey ponytail. 'Like a horse,' she is saying, 'a Viking carthorse,' and her hand rests lightly on his cheek.

Cathbad smiles, satisfied. 'I need you to clear my name, Ruth,' he says.

'I thought the police didn't press charges.'

'Oh no, they didn't charge me with the murders, but if they never find the killer, it'll always be me, don't you see? Everyone will always think I did it, that I killed those two little girls.'

'And did you?' asks Ruth, greatly daring.

Cathbad's eyes never leave her face. 'No,' he says. 'And I want you to find out who did.'

He has come back. When she sees him climbing in through the trapdoor she doesn't know if she is pleased or sorry. She is hungry though. She tears at the food he has brought – crisps, sandwiches, an apple – stuffing another mouthful in her mouth before she has finished the first.

'Steady,' he says, 'you'll make yourself sick.'

She doesn't answer. She hardly ever speaks to him. She saves talking for when she is alone, which, after all, is most of the time, when she can chat to the friendly voices in her head, the ones that tell her it is darkest before dawn.

He gives her a drink in a funny orange bottle. It tastes odd but she gulps it down. Briefly she wonders if it is poison like the apple the wicked witch gave Snow White, but she is so thirsty she doesn't care.

'I'm sorry I couldn't come before,' he says. She ignores him, chewing up the last of the apple, including the pips and core.

'I'm sorry,' he says again. He often says this but she doesn't really know what it means. 'Sorry' is a word from long ago, like 'love' and 'goodnight'. What does it mean now? She isn't sure. One thing she knows, if he says it, it can't be a good word. He isn't good, she is sure of it now. At first she was confused; he brought her food and drink and a blanket at night and sometimes he talked to her. Those were good things, she thought. But now she thinks

that he keeps her locked in, which isn't good. After all, if he can climb through the trapdoor, up into the sky, why can't she? Now she is taller she has tried to jump up to the door and the barred window but she never manages it. Maybe one day, if she keeps getting taller and taller, as tall as ... what was it called? As tall as a tree, that's it. She'll push her branches through the hole and carry on, up, up to where she hears the birds singing.

When he has gone she digs up her sharp stone and runs the edge of it against her cheek.

CHAPTER 20

Ruth is awoken from confused dreams by a furious knocking at the door. She staggers downstairs, groggy with sleep, to find Erik, dressed in army surplus and a bright yellow sou'wester, standing on the doorstep.

'Good morning, good morning,' he says brightly, like some crazed holiday rep. 'Any chance of a cup of coffee?'

Ruth leans against the door frame. Is he mad or is she? 'Erik,' she says weakly, 'what are you doing here?'

Erik looks at her incredulously. 'The dig,' he says. 'It starts today.'

Of course. Erik's dig. The one approved by Nelson. The dig that aims to answer the riddle of the Iron Age body and the buried causeway. To find out whether the Saltmarsh has any more secrets.

'I didn't know it was today,' says Ruth, backing into the house. Erik follows, rubbing his hands together. He has probably been up for hours. Ruth remembers that one of his traditions on a dig was to see the sun rise on the first day and set on the last.

'Yes,' Erik is saying casually. 'Nelson said it had to be after the funeral and that was yesterday, I believe.'

'It was. I was there.'

'Were you?' Erik looks at her in surprise. 'Why ever did you go?'

'I don't know,' says Ruth, putting on the kettle. 'I felt involved somehow.'

'Well, you aren't involved,' says Erik shortly, removing his sou'wester. 'High time you stopped all this detective nonsense and concentrated on archaeology. That's what you're good at. Very good. One of my very best students, in fact.'

Ruth, who bridles with indignation at the start of this speech, softens somewhat by the end. Even so, she isn't about to let Erik get away with this.

'Archaeologists *are* detectives,' she says. 'That's what you've always said.'

Erik dismisses this with a shrug. 'This is different, Ruthie. You must see that. You've given the police the benefit of your professional advice. Now leave it at that. There's no need to become obsessed.'

'I'm not obsessed.'

'No?' Erik smiles in an irritating, knowing way that reminds Ruth of Cathbad. Have they been discussing her?

'No,' says Ruth shortly, turning away to pour the coffee. She also puts some bread in the toaster. No way is she going to dig on an empty stomach.

'The poor girl is dead,' says Erik gently, his accent like a lullaby. 'She is buried, she is at peace. Leave it at that.'

Ruth looks at him. Erik is sitting by the window, smiling at her. The sun gleams on his snowy hair. He looks utterly benign.

'I'm going to get dressed,' says Ruth. 'Help yourself to coffee.'

The dig is already well underway by the time Ruth arrives. Three trenches have been marked out with string and pegs:

one by the original Iron Age body, the other two along the path of the causeway. Archaeologists and volunteers are very gently lifting off the turf in one-inch squares; they will aim to put the grass and soil back at the end of the dig.

Ruth remembers from the henge excavation that digging on this marshy land is a tricky business. The furthest trench, which is beyond the tide mark, will fill with water every night. This means it will, in effect, have to be dug afresh every day. And the tide can take you by surprise. Ruth remembers that Erik always used to have one person on 'tide watch'; sometimes the tide comes in slowly, creeping silently over the flat landscape. At other times the earth becomes water before you have time to catch your breath. These fast tides, called rip tides, could cut you off from land in the blink of an eye.

Even the trenches near to dry land have their problems. Although Erik has already mapped the area, the land can shift overnight, nothing remains certain. Archaeologists tend to become twitchy if they can't rely on their co-ordinates.

Ruth finds Erik leaning over the furthest trench. Because of the shifting ground, the trench is narrow and reinforced with sandbags. Two men are standing in the trench, looking nervously at Erik. Ruth recognises one of them as Bob Bullmore, the forensic anthropologist.

Ruth kneels beside Erik, who is examining one of the posts.

'Are you going to take it out?' asks Ruth.

Erik shakes his head. 'No, I want to keep it in place but I'm worried the waves will loosen it if we dig too far down.'

'Don't you need to see the base?'

'Yes, if possible. Look at this wood though. It looks as if it has been sawn in half.'

Ruth looks at the post. The other, softer wood has been worn away by the constant movement of the tides. What's left is the hard centre of the wood, ragged and somehow menacing-looking.

'It looks like the same wood that was used for the henge posts,' says Ruth.

Erik looks at her. 'Yes, it does. We'll have to see what the dendrochronology says.'

Tree-dating, or dendrochronology, can be amazingly exact. A tree lays down a growth ring each year: more in wet years, fewer in dry years. By looking at a graph showing growth patterns, archaeologists can chart the growth fluctuations. This process is called 'wiggle watching' (Peter always used to find this hilarious). Wiggle watching, combined with radiocarbon dating, can tell you the actual year and the actual season when a tree was felled.

Ruth goes to help with the trench where the Iron Age body was discovered. She still has a fellow feeling with this girl who was fed mistletoe and tied down to die. She sees her as somehow linked to Lucy and Scarlet. She can't help thinking that if she solves the riddle of the Iron Age girl she might just throw some light on the deaths of the other two girls.

More than anything though it is wonderful to be digging again. Like the day when she helped Nelson fill in Sparky's grave, it is a relief to forget the heartache and terror and excitement in uncomplicated physical labour. Ruth settles down to trowelling, getting into a rhythm, ignoring the twinges in her back and concentrating on moving the soil in neat cross-sections. After yesterday's rain the ground is sticky and sodden.

Cathbad eventually left last night after Ruth promised to help clear his name. She would have promised almost anything to get him out of the house; he was giving her the creeps sitting there in his wizard's cloak with his knowing grin. But, despite herself, as she digs, she can't stop his words running on a continuous loop in her head.

I felt sorry for you because you didn't get a look-in, what with his wife and girlfriend both on the dig ...

Did Erik and Shona have an affair on the henge dig? Shona is very gorgeous and Ruth knows that no man is impervious to beauty (look at Nelson with Michelle). But Erik has a beautiful wife of his own, and one, moreover, who seems to share his interests and enthusiasms. Ruth thinks of Magda, whom she has always liked and admired. Magda has almost been a surrogate mother, one who won't say threateningly that she is praying for her or buy her an Oxfam goat for Christmas. Magda, with her sea-blue eyes and ash-blonde hair, her voluptuous figure in fisherman's jumpers and faded jeans, her gleam of Nordic jewellery at the neck and wrists. Ruth remembers once reading about the goddess Freya, the patroness of hunters and musicians, with her sacred necklace and persuasive powers and thinking – that's Magda. Easy to imagine Magda, both youthful and ageless, holding the sacred distaff of life, the power of life and death. How could Erik have risked all this for an affair with Shona?

Is she jealous, Ruth asks herself as she trowels and sifts?

Not sexually jealous. She has always known that Erik could never be interested in her, but she had thought that she was special to him. Hadn't he written on the title page of *The Shivering Sand*, 'To Ruth, my favourite pupil'? But it turns out that she hadn't been his favourite after all. Ruth digs her trowel into the soil with unnecessary venom, causing a mini landslide and earning her a shocked look from the dreadlocked girl next to her.

'Ruth!'

Eager to be distracted from her buzzing, unpleasant thoughts, Ruth looks up. Standing in the trench, she sees the newcomer from the bottom up: walking boots, waterproof trousers, mud-coloured jacket. David.

David kneels down on the edge of the trench.

'What's going on?' he asks.

Ruth pushes a lock of sweaty hair out of her eyes. 'It's an archaeological dig,' she says. 'We're excavating the Iron Age grave and the causeway.'

'Causeway?'

'Those buried posts you showed me. We think it's a Bronze Age causeway. A kind of pathway possibly leading to the henge.' Ruth looks down, hoping David won't realise that it was she who told the archaeologists about the posts.

But David has other things on his mind. 'Well, mind you don't go near the hide. The furthest one. There's a rare Long Eared Owl nesting there.'

The Long Eared Owl sounds made up but Ruth can see that David is genuinely worried. 'I'm sure we won't go near the hide,' she says soothingly. 'The trenches are all over to the south.'

David stands up, still looking anxious. 'By the way,' Ruth calls after him, 'thanks for looking after Flint. My cat.' She had meant to get him a box of chocolates or something.

His face is transformed by a sudden smile. 'That's OK,' he says. 'Any time.'

David is looking over towards the car park. Following his gaze, Ruth sees a familiar dirty Mercedes coming to a halt by the bird sanctuary notice board. Nelson, wearing jeans and a battered Barbour jacket, gets out and strides towards the trench. Unconsciously, Ruth rubs her muddy hands on her trousers and tries to smooth her hair.

'Hello Ruth.' Ruth is fed up with looking up at people. She heaves herself out of the trench.

'Hello.'

'Bit of a circus, isn't it?' says Nelson, looking round disapprovingly at the archaeologists swarming over the site. The dreadlocked girl chooses this moment to start singing a high-pitched folk song. Nelson winces.

'It's all very organised,' says Ruth. 'Anyway, you gave permission for the dig.'

'Yes, well, I need all the help I can get.'

'Did you find anything at the henge circle?'

'Not a thing.' Nelson is silent, looking out, past the pegged-out trenches and the neat mounds of soil, towards the sea. He is thinking, she is sure, of the morning when they found Scarlet's body.

'I saw you yesterday,' says Nelson, 'at the funeral.'

'Yes,' says Ruth.

'Good of you to go.'

'I wanted to.'

Nelson looks as if he is going to say something else, but at that moment a familiar lilting voice cuts in. 'Ah, Chief Inspector ...' It is Erik.

As far as Ruth knows, this is a promotion for Nelson, but he doesn't offer a correction. He greets Erik fairly cordially, and after a few words with Ruth the two men walk away talking intently. Ruth feels unaccountably irritated.

By lunchtime she is tired and fed up. She is considering sneaking off back to her cottage for a cup of tea and a hot bath when two slim hands wrap themselves over her eyes.

'Guess who?'

Ruth breaks free. She has recognised the perfume anyhow. Shona.

Shona flops down on the grass next to Ruth. 'Well?' she asks, smiling. 'Found anything interesting?'

As usual Shona looks stunning despite (because of?) looking as if she hasn't tried. Her long hair is caught up in a messy bun and she is wearing jeans that make her legs look like pipe-cleaners and a puffy silver jacket which only emphasises her slimness. I'd look like a walking duvet wearing that, thinks Ruth.

'Just some more coins,' she says. 'Nothing much.'

'Where's Erik?' asks Shona, slightly too casually Ruth thinks.

'Talking to Nelson.'

'Really?' Shona raises her eyebrows at Ruth. 'I thought they couldn't stand each other.'

'So did I but they seem matey enough now.'

'Men,' says Shona lightly, pulling her jacket more tightly

round her. 'It's bloody freezing. How long are you going to stay?'

'I was just thinking of going back to the house for a cup of tea.'

'What are we waiting for then?'

CHAPTER 21

On the way back to the house, Ruth wrestles with her conscience. Shona has really been very kind to her, letting her stay with her at a moment's notice. Ruth hasn't even thanked her properly, just disappeared yesterday leaving a brief answerphone message. She needs to go back and pick up her things. Shona has been a good friend to her over the years. When Ruth split up with Peter, she provided a shoulder to cry on plus several vats of white wine. They have spent countless evenings together, laughing, talking, crying. They even went on holiday together, to Italy, Greece and Turkey. Is Ruth really going to let Cathbad's spiteful rumours get in the way of this friendship?

'I'm sorry about taking off like that,' she says at last. 'For some reason after the funeral I just wanted to be at home.'

They have reached that home now. Ruth opens the door for Shona.

'That's OK,' says Shona. 'I completely understand. Was it awful, the funeral?'

'Yes,' says Ruth, putting on the kettle. 'It was terrible. The parents were just shattered. And the little coffin ... it was all too heart-breaking.'

'I can imagine,' says Shona, sitting down and taking off

the silver jacket. 'There can't be anything worse than losing a child.'

Everyone says that, thinks Ruth, maybe because it's true. It's difficult to imagine anything worse than burying your child, a complete inversion of the natural order of things. Briefly, she thinks of Lucy Downey's parents walking away from the funeral, arm-in-arm. Was that worse? To lose your daughter and not be able to say goodbye?

She makes tea and sandwiches and they sit there companionably in silence. Outside it has started to rain, which strengthens Ruth's resolve not to go back to the dig.

Eventually Ruth says, 'I saw Cathbad yesterday.'

'Who?'

'Michael Malone. You know, the one they questioned about Scarlet's murder.'

'Jesus! Where did you see him?'

'Here. He came to talk to me.'

'Bloody hell, Ruth.' Shona shivers. 'I'd have been terrified.'

'Why?' asks Ruth, even though she had been so scared that she had slept last night with a kitchen knife by her bed. 'He wasn't charged with the murder, you know.'

'I know, but even so. What did he want?'

'Said he wanted me to clear his name.'

'What a cheek.'

'Yes, I suppose so,' says Ruth, who has been obscurely flattered.

'What's he like, this Cathbad?'

Ruth looks at her. 'Don't you remember him? He remembers you.'

'What?' Shona has taken out her combs and shaken out her hair. She stares at Ruth, apparently bewildered.

'Don't you remember him from the henge dig? He was the leader of the druids. Always wore this big purple cloak. He remembers you were sympathetic to them, joined in the protests.'

Shona smiles. 'Cathbad ... Now I remember. Well, he was quite a gentle soul as I recall.'

'Erik says he has magic powers.'

Now Shona laughs aloud. 'Dear old Erik.'

'Cathbad says you had an affair with Erik.'

'What?'

'Cathbad. He says you and Erik had an affair on the henge dig, ten years ago.'

'Cathbad! What does he know?'

'Did you?'

Instead of answering, Shona twists her hair into a tight knot and puts the combs back in, their little teeth digging viciously into her skull. She doesn't look at Ruth, but Ruth knows the answer now.

'How could you do it, Shona?' she asks. 'What about Magda?'

She is shocked at the virulence with which Shona turns on her.

'What do you care about Magda, all of a sudden? You don't know anything about it, sitting there, judging me. What about you and Peter? He's married now, didn't you know?'

'Peter and I aren't ...' stammers Ruth. 'We're just friends,' she finishes lamely. Inside, though, she knows that Shona is right. She is a hypocrite. What did she care about Michelle when she invited Nelson into her bed?

'Oh yeah?' sneers Shona. 'You think you're so perfect, Ruth, so above all those human feelings like love and hate and loneliness. Well, it's not as simple as that. I was in love with Erik,' she adds, in a slightly different tone.

'Were you?'

Shona flares up again. 'Yes, I bloody well was! *You* remember what he was like. I'd never met anyone like him. I thought he was so wise, so charismatic, I would have done anything for him. When he told me that he was in love with me, it was the most wonderful moment of my life.'

'He told you that he was in love with you?'

'Yes! Does that surprise you? Did you think he had the perfect marriage with Magda? Jesus, Ruth, they both have affairs all the time. Did you know about Magda's toyboy, back home in Sweden?'

'I don't believe you.'

'Ruth, you're such an innocent! Magda has a twenty-year-old lover called Lars. He fixes her sauna and then hops into bed with her. And he's one of many. In return, Erik does what he likes.'

To rid her mind of the image of Magda with her twenty-year-old handyman lover, Ruth turns to the window. The Saltmarsh has almost disappeared beneath the slanting, grey rain.

'Did you think I was the first?' asks Shona bitterly. 'There are graduate students all over England who can say they went to bed with the great Erik Anderssen. It's almost an essential part of your education.'

But not of my education, thinks Ruth. Erik treated me as a friend, a colleague, a promising student. He never once said a single word that could be construed as a sexual invitation.

'If you knew he was like that,' she asks at last, 'why did you go to bed with him?'

Shona sighs. All the anger seems to seep out of her, leaving her limp, like her silver jacket lying collapsed on the floor.

'I thought I was different, of course. Like all the other silly little cows, I thought I was the one he really loved. He said he'd never felt like that before, he said he'd leave Magda, that we'd get married, have children …' She stops, biting her lip.

And then Ruth remembers Shona's first abortion, just a few months after the henge dig.

'The baby …' she begins.

'Was Erik's,' says Shona wearily. 'Yes. I think it was then that I realised he didn't mean any of it. When I told him I was pregnant, he just went mad, started pressuring me to have an abortion. Do you know, I actually thought he'd be pleased.'

Ruth says nothing. She thinks of Erik talking about his grown-up children: 'You have to set them free.' Well, he hadn't wanted this one set free. As a fervent believer in a woman's right to choose, Ruth doesn't condemn Shona for having an abortion. But she does condemn Erik for his deceit, his hypocrisy, his …

'Poor Ruth,' says Shona, looking at her with a strange, dispassionate smile. 'All this is worse for you. You always admired him so much.'

'Yes,' says Ruth hoarsely. 'Yes I did.'

'He's still a great archaeologist,' says Shona. 'I'm still

friends with him. And with Magda,' she adds with a slight laugh. 'I guess it's just the way he is.'

'I guess so,' says Ruth tightly.

Shona rises, picking up her silver jacket. At the door she turns. 'Don't blame either of us too much, Ruth,' she says.

When Shona has gone, Ruth sits down at the table. She is amazed to find that she is shaking. What is so surprising about finding out that two grown-up people have had an affair? Alright, Erik was married, but these things happen as she knows all too well. Why does she feel let down, angry, *betrayed*?

She supposes that she must really have been in love with Erik all these years. She remembers when she first met him, as a graduate student in Southampton; the way that he seemed to take her mind apart, shuffle it and put it back together a different shape. He changed her view of everything: archaeology, landscape, nature, art, relationships. She remembers him saying, 'The human desire is to live, to cheat death, to live forever. It is the same over all the ages. It is why we build monuments to death – so that they live on after we die.' Did Erik's desire to live simply mean that he could do whatever he wanted?

And when she met Magda she had been so pleased. She had thought nobody could be good enough for Erik but Magda was. She had loved their relationship, that affectionate companionship, so different from her parents' stilted formality. She could never imagine Erik and Magda calling each other Mummy and Daddy or driving to a garden centre on a Sunday afternoon. They lived the perfect life, climbing mountains, sailing, spending the winters writing and researching and the summers digging. She remembers the log cabin by the lake in Norway, the meals eaten on the deck, the hot tub, the evenings eating, drinking and talking. Talking. That's what she remembers most about Erik and Magda. They had always talked, argued sometimes, but always they had listened to each other's views. Ruth remembers many times listening to Erik and Magda as, glasses of wine in their hands and the Northern lights shining above them, they had fitted their differing theories together so that they came up with something new, better, more complete. Not for them the moment described by Peter: 'We just ran out of things to say to each other.'

Ruth is not stupid. She knows that she created idealised parents in Magda and Erik and that is why she feels so let down now. And if she was also secretly in love with Erik, well that just makes a perfect Freudian hole-in-one. What upsets her most, she thinks, looking out over the rain-sodden marshland, is that she had thought she was special. Even if Erik had not fancied her, he had thought her an especially talented student. On the henge dig he had continually deferred to her. 'Ruth will understand this even if the rest of you don't' implied that he and she shared a special understanding. Ruth, he had said, had 'an archaeologist's sense', a quality which, apparently, cannot be taught. Erik's approval has carried Ruth through many difficult years, insulated her against Phil's patronising indifference, comforted her when she never quite seemed able to get that book proposal down on paper.

She knows it is childish, but Ruth feels that she needs to be reminded of Erik's good opinion, so she takes down her copy of his book *The Shivering Sand*. She opens it at the title page. There it is, in black and white. *To Ruth, my favourite pupil.*

Ruth looks at the words for a long moment. It is as if she has suddenly seen a gross misshapen shadow on the wall – the horns and the tail and the cloven hoofs. Blindly, almost staggering, she gets up and goes to the desk where she keeps her copies of the Lucy Downey letters. Hands shaking, she leafs through the letters until she gets to the two that are handwritten.

She lays them on the table next to Erik's dedication. The handwriting is the same.

CHAPTER 22

For what seems like hours, she just stands there, unable to move. Almost unable to breathe. An icy paralysis seems to have taken over her whole body. Think, Ruth, think. Breathe. Can Erik really have written these letters? Is it possible that Erik, as well as being a hypocrite and a serial seducer, is also a murderer?

The worst thing is that she can almost believe it. Erik knows about archaeology. He knows about Norse legends and Neolithic ritual and the power of the landscape. She can hear his voice, that beloved singsong voice, telling campfire stories of water spirits and shape-changers and the creatures of the dark. With a sudden, fresh chill she remembers his words that very morning: *The poor girl is dead. She is buried, she is at peace.* Almost an exact echo of one of the letters.

Can it possibly be true? Erik was still living in England when Lucy Downey vanished. It was just after the henge dig. He could have sent those early letters. He didn't go back to Norway until eight years later. But could he have sent the recent letters about Scarlet Henderson? He has only been back in England since January. Nelson showed her a letter dated last November. 'He hasn't forgotten,' said Nelson. Could Erik have sent that letter? Or arranged to have someone else send it?

It's crazy, Ruth tells herself, moving stiffly to stroke Flint who is purring round her ankles. Erik would not be capable of writing those evil, taunting, *warped* letters. He is a humanitarian, the first to support striking miners or victims of natural disasters. He is kind and thoughtful; comforting Ruth in the shock of Peter's marriage, grieving with Shona when her father died. But he is also, thinks Ruth, the man who speaks approvingly of human sacrifice ('Isn't the same thing happening in Christian Holy Communion?'), who advised Ruth to forget Peter with another lover ('It's the easiest way') and who, presumably, was sleeping with Shona and encouraging her to abort their child whilst weeping with her about her father. Erik is amoral, he is somehow outside normal human rules; that is one of the most attractive things about him. But is it also something that makes him capable of unimaginable evil?

If he wrote the letters, did he kill the two little girls? Mechanically feeding Flint, Ruth realises that she has poured the cat food right over the sides of the bowl. Flint pushes furrily past her to get at the food. She remembers a conversation she had with him about her Iron Age body. 'How could anyone do that?' she had asked. 'Kill a child for some religious ritual?' 'Look at it this way,' Erik had said calmly. 'Maybe it's a good way to go. Saves the child the disillusionment of growing up.' He had smiled as he said it but Ruth remembers feeling chilled. Could Erik have killed the two girls to save them the disillusionment of growing up?

She can't bear it any more. Grabbing her coat and bag, she rushes out into the rain. She is going to speak to Shona.

*

Shona is still out when she arrives. Ruth slumps down on the doorstep, too exhausted to remember that she has a key. She just sits there, looking at the people going in and out of the Tesco Express and wondering what it must be like to have no more to worry about than whether to have chops or sausages for supper and whether you've got enough potatoes for chips. Her own life seems to have become dark and grim, like the sort of film she would avoid watching late at night. When did this happen? When they dug down into the peat and found the body of Scarlet Henderson? When she first saw Nelson, standing in the university corridor? When she first looked down at her student introductory pack and saw the words, Personal Tutor: Erik Anderssen?

When Shona eventually appears, swinging down the road carrying a Thresher's bag and a rented DVD, she looks so blameless, so innocent, with her long legs and silver jacket, that Ruth thinks that she must be mistaken. No way can Shona be mixed up in any of this. She is Ruth's dear friend, her crazy, lovable, scatty friend. But, then, Shona sees Ruth, and a curious trapped look comes over her face, like a fox cornered in a suburban garden. Almost instantly though, charm breaks out again and she smiles, proffering the bag and the DVD.

'Girls' night in,' she says. 'Want to join me?'

'I've got to talk to you.'

Now Shona looks positively terrified. 'OK,' she says, opening the door. 'You'd better come in.'

Ruth doesn't even give Shona time to take off her coat.

'Did Erik write those letters?'

'What letters?' asks Shona nervously.

Ruth looks around the room, at the sanded floor and the trendy rugs, at the photos in decorated frames – almost all of Shona herself, she notices now – at the patchwork throw over the sofa, at the new novels stacked on the table, at the bookshelves with their battered copies of the classics, from T.S. Eliot to Shakespeare. Then she looks back at Shona.

'Jesus,' she says, 'you helped him, didn't you?'

Shona seems to look around for a means of escape, the trapped fox again, but then, as if finally surrendering, she collapses onto the sofa and covers her face.

Ruth comes nearer. 'You helped him, didn't you?' she says. 'Of course, he'd never have thought of all that T.S. Eliot stuff by himself, would he? You're the literature expert. Your Catholic background probably helped too. He supplied the archaeology and the mythology, you did the rest. Quite the perfect little team.'

'It wasn't like that,' says Shona dully.

'No? What was it like?'

Shona looks up. Her hair has come down and her eyes are wet, yet Ruth is beyond being moved by her appearance. So Shona is beautiful and she's upset. So what? She's played that trick too many times before.

'It was him. Nelson,' says Shona.

'*What?*'

'Erik hates him,' says Shona, rubbing her eyes with the back of her hand. 'That's why he wrote the letters, to get at Nelson. To distract him. To stop him solving the case. To punish him.'

'What for?' whispers Ruth.

'James Agar,' says Shona. 'He was Erik's student. At Manchester. It was during the poll tax riots. Apparently a group of students attacked a policeman and he was killed. James Agar was only on the outskirts of the group. He didn't do anything but Nelson framed him.'

'Who told you this? Erik?'

'It was common knowledge. Everyone knew it. Even the police. Nelson wanted a scapegoat so he picked on James.'

'He wouldn't do that,' says Ruth. Wouldn't he? She thinks.

'Oh, I know you like him. Erik says you've been totally taken in by him.'

'Does he?' Despite everything, the bitchiness of this still stings. 'And you weren't taken in by Erik, I suppose?'

'Oh, I was,' says Shona wearily. 'I was obsessed with him. I would have done anything for him.'

'Even helped to write those letters?'

Shona looks up, her face defiant. 'Yes,' she says. 'Even that.'

'But why, Shona? This was a murder investigation. You were probably helping the murderer get away.'

'Nelson's a murderer,' snaps Shona. 'James Agar died in prison, a year after Nelson framed him. He killed himself.'

Ruth thinks of Cathbad's poem 'In Praise of James Agar'. She thinks of Nelson's face as he looked down at the scrawled lines. She thinks of the locked cabinet in Cathbad's caravan.

'Cathbad,' she says at last. 'Where does he come into this?'

Shona laughs, slightly hysterically. 'Didn't you know?' she says. 'He was the postman.'

CHAPTER 23

Nelson has had a tough day. But then again, he almost can't remember a time when his life didn't consist of defending himself against people who wanted him sacked, trying to motivate an increasingly depressed team and ignoring Michelle's demands to come home while at the same time trying to catch a murderer. He had thought that Scarlet's funeral yesterday must be the lowest point. Jesus, that little white coffin, Scarlet's brothers and sisters looking so shocked and vulnerable in their new black clothes, seeing Lucy Downey's parents again and feeling how he had let them down. And then having to stand up and spout all that stuff about the resurrection and the life. He had caught sight of Ruth in the congregation and wondered if she was thinking what he was thinking: the letter writer would love this.

And then there is Ruth. He knows he shouldn't have gone to bed with her. It was totally unprofessional as well as wrong. He has betrayed Michelle, whom he loves. He has, in fact, been unfaithful on two other occasions but he comforts himself that these were brief flings which didn't mean anything. Did Ruth mean something then? She's not really his type. But, that night, he has to admit, was something else. At that moment, Ruth seemed to understand him totally, in a way that Michelle has never done. She seemed to understand, to forgive him and offer herself to him in a way that even now threatens to bring tears to his eyes. Why had she done it? What does she see in him? He's not intellectual enough for her. She likes poncy professors with theories about Iron Age pottery, not uneducated Northern policemen.

So why had Ruth slept with him? She made the first move, he tells himself for the hundredth time. It wasn't all his fault. He can only suppose that she, like him, was caught up in the horror of it all, finding Scarlet's body, telling the parents. The only escape was in simple, straightforward sex. Some of the best sex, he has to admit, that he has ever had.

He doesn't know where he stands with her now. She's not the sort who will go all soppy, declaring undying love and begging him to leave Michelle. He has spoken to her on the phone a few times and she has always seemed fine, professional and calm, despite having some scary stuff to cope with. He admires that. Ruth is tough, like him. When he saw her yesterday at the dig, she had been very cool. He'd watched her as he approached, she was totally absorbed in her work, he was sure she had no idea that he was there. He doesn't know why, but suddenly he wanted her to look up, to wave, smile, even to rush over and fling her arms round him. Of course, she hadn't done any of these things. She had simply carried on with her job, just as he was carrying on with his. It was the sensible, adult way to behave.

He had quite a good chat with that Erik Anderssen bloke at the dig. Of course he's an old hippie, way too old to have his hair in a ponytail and wear all those leather bracelets. But still, he had told Nelson some interesting things. Turns out there's a prehistoric forest buried underneath the Saltmarsh. That's why you sometimes find odd-looking stumps of trees and bits of timber. They even found some wood that had come all the way from North America. Anderssen had also talked about ritual. 'Think of a burial,' he'd said. 'From the body to the wood of the coffin to the stone of the graveyard.' Nelson had shivered, remembering Scarlet's coffin, that little wooden box, on its final journey.

He'd come back from the dig to be met by his boss. Superintendent Whitcliffe is a career policeman, a graduate who favours linen suits and slip-on shoes. Just standing near him makes Nelson feel shop-soiled and more than usually untidy. He has the sensation, which he remembers from school, of his hands and feet being several sizes larger than they ought to be. Still, Nelson is not about to let Whitcliffe push him around. He's a good cop; he knows it and Whitcliffe knows it. He's not going to be the scapegoat on this case.

'Ah, Harry,' Whitcliffe had said, managing to convey the message that Nelson should have been there to meet him, though he had not said he was coming. 'Been out and about?'

'Following up leads.' He was damned if he was going to add 'sir'.

'We need to talk, Harry,' Whitcliffe had said, sitting down behind Nelson's desk and neatly establishing superiority. 'We need another statement.'

'We've got nothing to say.'

'That's just it, Harry,' sighed Whitcliffe, 'we need to

have something to say. The press are after our blood. You arrest Malone and then release him –'

'On bail.'

'Yes, on bail,' said Whitcliffe tetchily. 'That doesn't change the fact that you've got no evidence to charge him with the murders. And without him you've got no suspects. With all the coverage of the little girl's funeral, we need to be seen to be doing something.'

The little girl's funeral. Whitcliffe had been there, in neat black tie, saying caring, compassionate things to Scarlet's parents. But for him it was just another job, an exercise in damage limitation. He had not, like Nelson, gone home and puked his guts out.

'I am *doing something*,' said Nelson. 'I've been working flat out for months. We've searched every inch of the Saltmarsh ...'

'I hear you've let the archaeologists loose there today.'

'Have you seen how they work?' demanded Nelson. 'They really examine every inch of ground. It's all planned; nothing missed, nothing overlooked. Our forensic teams could never match it. If there's anything to find, they'll find it.'

Whitcliffe smiled. A humorous, understanding smile that made Nelson want to smack him. 'You sound quite a fan of archaeology, Harry.'

Nelson grunted. 'Lots of it's bollocks, of course, but you can't deny they know their stuff. And I like the way they do things. It's organised. I like organisation.'

'What about this Ruth Galloway? She seems to have become quite involved in the case.'

Nelson looked up warily. 'Doctor Galloway's been a great help.'

'She found the body.'

'She had a theory. I thought it was worth testing.'

'Has she any other theories?' Whitcliffe was smiling again.

'We've all got theories,' said Nelson, standing up. 'Theories are cheap. What we haven't got is any evidence.'

All the same, he knows he can't stall Whitcliffe forever. He will have to give a statement to the press and what the hell can he say? Malone was the only suspect, and for a while he had seemed quite promising. He fitted what Whitcliffe would call 'the offender profile'. He had links with the Henderson family, he was a drifter and he was full of all that New Age crap, just like the writer of the letters. But then they had found Scarlet's body and there was DNA all over it. The only problem was that none of it matched Malone's. Without the DNA link, Nelson was stuffed. He'd had to let Malone go, only charging him with wasting police time.

Scarlet had been tied up, gagged and strangled. Then someone had carried her body right out to the peat beds and buried her where that henge thing used to be. Does this mean the murderer had to know about the henge? Ruth said that there is a path, a causeway or something, leading right to the place where Scarlet was buried. Were the police meant to find her, then? Has the murderer been watching them all the time, laughing at them? He knows that the killer is often someone known to the family, someone close. How close? Was it the killer who left those messages on Ruth's phone? Is he watching her too? Despite himself, Nelson shivers. It's late now and the incident rooms are deserted.

He knows he'll be blamed if they don't find Scarlet's

killer. He knows too that it won't be long before the press makes the link with Lucy Downey. They don't know about the letters of course, and he'll be crucified if that gets out, but in some ways none of that bothers him. He's got no time for the press – one reason why, despite Michelle's fantasies, he'll never make chief constable – and he knows he's done his best. No. He wants to find the killer for the sake of Lucy's and Scarlet's families. He wants to put the bastard away forever. It won't bring Lucy and Scarlet back but it will, at least, mean that justice has been done. The words have a cold, biblical ring that surprises him, but when you come down to it that is what police work is all about. Protecting the innocent and punishing the guilty. Saint Harry the Avenger.

A sound downstairs makes him sit up. He hears the desk sergeant's voice. It sounds as if he is remonstrating with someone. Maybe he ought to investigate. Nelson gets up and starts towards the door. And finds himself colliding with his expert witness, Doctor Ruth Galloway.

'Jesus,' says Nelson, putting out both hands to steady her.

'I'm OK.' Ruth leaps away as if he is infectious. For a second they stare awkwardly at each other. Ruth looks a mess, her hair wild, her coat on inside out. Christ, thinks Nelson, maybe she is a bunny boiler after all.

'I'm sorry,' she is saying, taking off her dripping coat, 'but I had to come.'

'What's the matter?' asks Nelson neutrally, retreating behind his desk.

In answer, Ruth slams a book and a piece of paper down on his desk. He recognises the paper instantly as a copy of one of the letters. The book means nothing to him though Ruth has opened it and is pointing at some writing on the first page.

'Look!' she is saying urgently.

To humour her, he looks. Then he looks again.

'Who wrote this?' he asks quietly.

'Erik. Erik Anderssen.'

'Are you sure?'

'Of course I'm sure. And his girlfriend confirms it. He wrote the letters.'

'His girlfriend?'

'Shona. My ... my colleague at the university. She's his girlfriend. Well, ex-girlfriend, if you like. Anyway, she admits he wrote the letters and she helped him.'

'Jesus. Why?'

'Because he hates you. Because of James Agar.'

'James Agar?'

'You know, the student who was accused of murdering that policeman.'

Whatever he expected it wasn't this. James Agar. The poll tax riots, police bussed in from five forces, the streets full of tear gas and placards, trying to hold the line, students spitting in his face, the alley where Stephen Naylor's body had been found. Naylor, a new recruit, only twenty-two, stabbed to death with a kitchen knife. James Agar, coming towards him, eyes unfocused, carrying the bloody knife as if it didn't belong to him.

'James Agar was guilty,' says Nelson flatly.

'He committed suicide in prison,' says Ruth. 'Erik blames you. James Agar was his student. He says you framed him.'

'Bollocks. There were a dozen witnesses. Agar was guilty alright. Do you mean to tell me that Anderssen wrote all these letters, all this ... *crap* ... because of some student?'

'That's what Shona says. She says Erik hated you and wanted to stop you solving the Lucy Downey case. He thought the letters would distract you, like the Jack-the-Ripper tapes distracted the police in Yorkshire.'

'He wanted the murderer to go free?'

'He sees you as a murderer.'

Ruth says this without emphasis, giving no clue what she actually thinks. Suddenly Nelson feels angry, thinking of Ruth and Erik and this Shona, all academics together, siding, as bleeding-heart lefties always do, with the villains rather than the police.

'I'm sure you agree with him,' he says bitterly.

'I don't know anything about it,' says Ruth wearily. She does look tired, Nelson realises, her face white, her hands shaking. He relents slightly.

'What about Malone?' he asks. 'He wrote a poem about James Agar. Do you remember? He even offered it as an example of his handwriting.'

'Cathbad was James Agar's friend,' says Ruth. 'They were students together at Manchester.'

'Was he involved in writing the letters?'

'He posted them,' says Ruth. 'Erik wrote the letters, with Shona's help, and Cathbad posted them from different places. Remember, he told us he was a postman?'

'What about the recent letters? I thought Anderssen had been out of the country.'

'Erik emailed them to Cathbad. He printed them out and posted them.'

'Have you spoken to Anderssen?'

'No.' Ruth looks down. 'I went to see Shona and then I came to you.'

'Why not go direct to Anderssen?'

Ruth looks up, meeting Nelson's gaze steadily. 'Because I'm scared of him,' she says.

Nelson leans forward and puts his hand on hers. 'Ruth, do you think Anderssen killed Lucy and Scarlet?'

And Ruth answers, so quietly he can hardly hear her. 'Yes.'

There are the sounds again but this time she is ready for them. She crouches, holding her stone, prepared to spring if the trapdoor opens. When he comes down with her food, she watches the back of his head as he puts the plates on the floor. Where would be the right place? On top, where the hair is going all straggly? At the back of his neck, horribly red and raw-looking? He turns to look at her and she wonders if this isn't the best way, right in the face, between the eyes, in his awful, gaping mouth, across his horrid, gulpy neck.

He examines her, which she hates. Looks into her mouth, feels her arm muscles, makes her turn round and lift up her feet, one after the other.

'You're growing,' he says. 'You need some new clothes.'

Clothes. The word reminds her of something. A smell, that's it. A soft, comforting smell. Something held against her face, silky, smooth, rubbing between her thumb and forefinger. But he is talking about what's on her body: a long, scratchy, top thing and trousers that seem suddenly to be too short. She can see quite a bit of her legs sticking out at the bottom. They look white, like the inside of a twig. They look like they can't possibly work, but they do. She has been practising running, round and round this little room, on the spot, up and down. She knows that soon she will have to run for real.

He cuts her nails with a funny red knife he keeps in his pocket. She'd like a knife like that. If she had one she'd ... but her head gets all red and buzzy and she has to stop thinking.

'Don't worry about the noises outside,' he says. 'It's just ... animals.'

Animals. Pony, dog, cat, rabbit, incey wincey spider climbing the water spout. She says nothing, feeling the stone in her pocket. She likes it when it cuts her, just a little bit.

He looks at her. 'Are you alright?' he says.

She doesn't answer. Instead she hangs her head down so she can't see him. Her hair is long, it smells of dust. Sometimes he cuts her hair with the little knife. She remembers a story where someone escapes by climbing on hair. Does she have enough hair to make a ladder? It doesn't sound possible; it's one of those things that only happens in stories. Escape. Does that only happen in stories too?

So she says nothing. And, when he goes, the quiet fills the room, beating against the sides. Making her head ache.

CHAPTER 24

Ruth sits in Nelson's office, a cup of undrinkable coffee in front of her. It is cold in the high-ceilinged room. She is still wearing her digging trousers, baggy army-surplus, but stupidly had taken off her thick jumper back at her house. It seems like days ago. Her coat is still dripping and is anyway far too thin. She wishes she had worn her sou'wester or an anorak. She wraps her hands around the plastic cup. At least it is hot.

Nelson has disappeared to round up some officers to arrest Erik. *Arrest Erik*. The words have an impossible sound; that Erik should be a suspect in a murder case, that Ruth should be the one to direct the police to his door. It seems crazy, like a nightmare. It seems that one minute she was sitting in her little house by the Saltmarsh, preparing her lectures, grumbling about her mother and listening to Radio 4, and now she is in the middle of this drama of murder and betrayal. It is as if she has pressed the wrong button on her TV remote control and, just at this instant, she would give anything to switch back to the boring programme about crop rotation.

Nelson crashes back into the room accompanied by Judy, the policewoman Ruth met at the funeral.

'Right,' he says, grabbing his jacket, 'let's go. I'll go in the first car with Cloughie. Ruth, you follow behind with

Judy. On no account are you to get out of the car. Do you understand?'

'Yes,' says Ruth, rather sulkily. She wants to remind Nelson that she is not one of his officers.

The cars set off through the night. It is still raining, a slow, steady drizzle sparkling in the headlights. The cars head out of King's Lynn and along the coast road, past deserted caravan parks and boarded-up family hotels. Ruth leans her head against the cold window and thinks about her first view of Norfolk, arriving that summer with her tent and bedroll, driving from Norwich station with Erik and Magda, seeing the Saltmarsh in all its evening splendour, the sand stretching for miles, the sea a faint line of blue against the horizon. Could she have imagined then that this is how it would end? In a speeding police car on the way to accuse her former mentor of murder ...

Nelson's car comes to a halt in front of the blameless-looking seaside guest house. The Sandringham, it's called, though any resemblance to the Queen's house must exist only in the owner's fevered imagination. The look, Ruth notes, is traditional seaside kitsch: net curtains, gnomes in the garden, stained glass over the front door. Nelson and Sergeant Clough climb the crazy-paving steps and Clough leans heavily on the doorbell. *The Sandringham Guest House*, reads the sign, *Bed and Breakfast, En-suite rooms, colour TV, home cooking. Vacancies.*

Ruth cringes inside the second car. What will Erik say when he looks in the car and sees Ruth sitting there? Will he know she has betrayed him? Because, despite everything, she still thinks of it as a betrayal. She has delivered Erik into Nelson's hands. She feels like Judas.

It is nearly ten o'clock and there is only one light on inside the guest house. It's upstairs, directly above the door. Ruth remembers Erik telling her that he was the only guest – February is, after all, hardly the holiday season. Is that his light then? Is he inside, calmly working on some scholarly article about Bronze Age Field Systems?

Ruth sees the front door open. Nelson leans forward, speaking to the unseen opener. Ruth imagines him waving his warrant card like they do in films, before barging his way inside yelling, 'Police! Freeze!' But she is disappointed. The door shuts and Nelson and Clough make their way slowly back to the car.

Nelson leans in through the window. His forearm rests on the window frame a few inches away from Ruth. She has to fight an insane desire to touch it.

'He's gone,' says Nelson.

'Gone for good?' asks Judy, twisting round in the front seat.

'Looks like it. His room's empty. He left a cheque to pay his tab.'

For a second, Ruth feels absurdly pleased that Erik hasn't run off without paying. Then she thinks, he could be a murderer, isn't that a bit worse than not paying a hotel bill?

'What now?' asks Judy.

Nelson looks at Ruth. 'Any ideas, Doctor Galloway?'

Ruth doesn't meet his eye. 'He could be with Shona, I suppose.'

Shona's house is in darkness. At first Ruth thinks that she must be out (with Erik?) but, after a few minutes, she appears at the door wearing a dressing gown. She looks rumpled and, even at this distance, slightly drunk.

Judy has gone to the door this time. Maybe this, like bereavement, is another moment when they send for a woman officer. The police, like the Neanderthals, don't seem a very enlightened society.

Shona steps back to allow Judy to enter. Alone in the car, Ruth starts to shiver. She jumps when the passenger door opens. Nelson leans in.

'Are you OK?'

'Fine,' she says, setting her jaw to stop her teeth chattering.

'You're freezing. Hang on.'

He pulls off his heavy police jacket and hands it to her. 'Put this on.'

'But it's yours.'

He shrugs. 'I'm not cold. Keep it.'

Ruth pulls on the jacket gratefully. It smells of garages and, very faintly, of Nelson's aftershave. Nelson, in his shirtsleeves, certainly does not seem cold. He jogs slightly on the balls of his feet, impatient for Judy to come back. Ruth is reminded of the first time that she saw him and the way he had almost run up the hill towards the buried bones.

At last Judy is coming out of the house. Nelson goes to meet her. They confer quickly and then Judy gets back in the car.

'He's not there,' she tells Ruth. 'She says she hasn't seen him. I'm putting out a call to all units. The boss says I've got to take you to a safe house.'

Ruth watches Nelson getting into the other car. He gave me his jacket, she thinks, but he can't be bothered to say goodbye. Suddenly, she feels incredibly tired.

'Is there anyone you could stay with?' asks Judy.

Ruth looks back at Shona's house. The lights are off. No more girls' nights in for her there.

'A friend?' prompts Judy. 'Family?'

'There is someone,' says Ruth.

The house is one of a row of fisherman's cottages on the seafront near Burnham Ovary. Squat, whitewashed, used to withstanding the wind and rain from the sea. Ruth stands irresolute on the doorstep, listening to the waves crashing against the sea wall. What if he isn't there? Will she have to sleep under her desk at the university, to be woken at nine by Mr Tan and her other students? At the moment, it seems quite an attractive proposition.

Ruth looks back at the police car, which is discreetly waiting in the street. She wonders if the neighbours are watching behind their curtains.

'Ruth!' She swings round to see Peter silhouetted in a rectangle of light. Ruth opens her mouth to tell him about Erik and Shona and to ask him for a place to sleep but, to her intense embarrassment, she starts to cry. Huge, gulping, unromantic sobs.

Peter reaches out and draws her inside. 'It's OK,' he says. 'It's OK.'

And he shuts the door behind them.

CHAPTER 25

'I'm sorry,' says Ruth, sitting down on Peter's sofa. As in all rented houses, the furniture looks the wrong shape for the room. The sofa is mysteriously uncomfortable.

'What's going on?' asks Peter, still stranded in the doorway.

'You'd better sit down,' says Ruth.

She tells him about the letters, about Shona and Erik and, finally, about the match with Erik's handwriting.

'Jesus.' Peter lets out a long sigh. 'Are you sure?'

'Yes,' says Ruth, 'and Shona admits it. They wrote the letters because they wanted to disrupt the investigation.'

'Why would they want to do that?'

'Because one of Erik's students was accused of murdering a policeman. He was found guilty and committed suicide in jail. He blames Nelson, the policeman in charge of the Scarlet Henderson case.'

'Why?'

'Nelson gave evidence against the student. James Agar, his name was.'

'And the police are now after Erik?'

'Yes, but he seems to have disappeared.'

'What about Shona?'

'She says she doesn't know where he is.'

Peter is silent for a moment and then he looks at Ruth,

his face troubled. 'Do they ... do the police think that Erik could have murdered the little girl?'

'They think it's a possibility.'

'And what do you think?'

Ruth hesitates before answering. If she is honest, she no longer knows what she thinks. She believed that Erik was omnipotent and that Shona was her friend. Now neither of those things seems to be true.

'I don't know,' she says at last, 'but I think it must be a possibility. The letter writer seemed to leave clues about where Scarlet's body was buried.'

'Could that just be a coincidence?'

Ruth thinks of the cryptic, teasing tone of the letters. 'It could be. The letters hint at all sorts of things. It's easy to read things into them.'

'Why would Erik want to kill her?'

Ruth sighs. 'Who knows? Maybe he thought he needed to make a sacrifice to the Gods.'

'You don't believe that, surely?'

'No I don't. But maybe Erik did.'

Peter is silent once more.

Peter makes omelettes and opens a bottle of red. Ruth eats hungrily. Lunch with Shona seems centuries ago. They both drink a good deal, keen to blot out the evening's revelations.

'You know,' Peter keeps saying, 'I just can't believe it of Erik. He always seemed a real New Ager to me. Into peace and love and free dope for all. I just can't imagine that he would kill a little girl.'

'But what if he really believed all that stuff – about

sacrifices and offerings to the Gods? Maybe he felt he needed to make an offering to appease the Gods for taking the henge away.'

'You're saying that he's mad.'

Ruth is silent, swirling the red wine round in her glass. 'Who are we to say what is mad and what is sane?'

'You're quoting Erik!'

'Yes.' Ruth tucks her feet under her on the sofa. Despite everything, she is beginning to feel very sleepy.

'You loved him didn't you?' says Peter in a different voice.

'What?'

'You loved him. All the time I thought it was me but it was Erik. He was the one you really loved.'

'No,' protests Ruth. 'I did love him, but as a friend. As a teacher, I suppose. I loved Magda too. It was different with you.'

'Was it?' Peter crosses the room and kneels in front of her. 'Was it, Ruth?'

'Yes.'

Peter kisses her and, for a second, she feels herself dissolving into his arms. Would this be so wrong, she asks herself? He is separated from his wife, she is single. Who would they be hurting?

'God, Ruth,' Peter murmurs into her neck, 'I've missed you so much. I love you.'

That does it. Ruth sits up, pushing Peter away. 'No.'

'What?' Peter is beside her on the sofa now, his arms around her.

'You don't love me.'

'I do. It was a mistake, marrying Victoria. You and I were always meant to be together.'

'No, we weren't.'

'Why not?'

Ruth takes a deep breath. It seems very important to get this right. To have one thing that is clear and straight and unambiguous. 'I don't love you,' she says. 'Is it OK if I sleep on the sofa?'

She wakes in the morning to find herself covered with Nelson's jacket and with a duvet. Grey light is streaming in through the thin curtains. The time on her mobile is 07:15. No new messages. Ruth sits up; her head hurts and her eyes feel gritty. How much did she have to drink last night? Two empty bottles lie on the floor. Not much by undergraduate standards perhaps but more than she has drunk for years. She can't even remember going to sleep. She remembers Peter slamming out of the room after she told him that she didn't love him. He must have come back, though, to put the duvet over her. God, she feels sick.

She gets up, intending to find a loo and a shower, but when she opens the door she comes face-to-face with Peter, carrying a cup of tea.

'Thank you,' she says, taking the cup. 'I feel terrible.'

Peter smiles. 'So do I. We're not young anymore, Ruth. Bathroom's upstairs, by the way. First on the left. Towels in the airing cupboard next door.'

'Thanks,' says Ruth. Perhaps it's not going to be so bad after all.

It's horrible, putting her old clothes on after her shower, but at least she is clean. Wrapping her hair in a towel, she goes downstairs. Peter is making toast in the tiny kitchen.

Ruth sits down, trying to think of a subject that will clear the air: something light and non-controversial. Should they talk about the weather, the dig, what's happening in *The Archers*? She needs something that reminds Peter of his real life, away from Norfolk, of his wife and child.

'Have you got a picture of your little boy?' asks Ruth at last. 'I haven't seen him since he was a baby.'

Peter looks surprised but he gets out his phone, a sleek, black affair, and pushes it across the table to Ruth. 'In there,' he says. 'Under PICTURES.'

Ruth scrolls down, with difficulty. She hates these tiny phones. They make her feel like a giantess. The first picture is of a smiling, red-headed boy.

'Do you think he looks like me?' asks Peter.

'Yes,' says Ruth, though the photo is so small it's hard to see.

'It's the red hair. In the face he looks more like Victoria.'

Ruth clicks down, trying to find more pictures. All the pictures seem to be of Daniel though she does see one of the Saltmarsh, a tiny grey rectangle. There are no pictures of Victoria.

'What are you going to do now?' asks Peter, putting toast in front of her.

'Go into work, tidy things up there. Then maybe go away for a bit. See my parents.'

As she says this, she has a sudden vision of the M11 stretching out in front of her, grey and featureless. Her mother will be sure to ask about Peter.

'Blimey. Things must be desperate.'

Ruth smiles, but when she looks at Peter his face is suddenly dark. He looks, for a second, like a stranger.

'Remember Ruth,' he says. 'I know where you are.'

*

'Is Erik really a suspect?' asks Phil, shutting his office door behind her. 'What's going on, Ruth?'

'I'm not sure,' lies Ruth. 'I just know the police want to talk to him.'

All the way to the university, she has been thinking about Peter's words. *I know where you are.* Could Peter have sent her those messages? She has never given him her mobile number but it would have been easy enough for him to get it. He could have asked anyone. Erik, Shona, even Phil. But why would Peter want to scare her like that? It doesn't make sense, but one thing is clear – she can trust no one.

'What's going on?' repeats Phil, obviously trying to keep the excitement out of his voice. 'The police have been here looking for Erik. We had your friend Shona from the English department here earlier. She was very distraught.'

Ruth can just imagine Shona sobbing picturesquely on Phil's shoulder. Maybe he's next on her married lecturers list.

'They surely can't' – Phil lowers his voice dramatically – '*suspect* him?'

'I don't know,' says Ruth wearily. 'Look Phil, I've got a favour to ask you. The police think I should get away for a few days and I was thinking of going to my parents in London. Is it OK if I have a few days off? I've only got one lecture and a tutorial this week.'

But Phil is still staring at her, wide-eyed. 'Do they think you're in danger? From Erik?'

'I'm sorry, Phil,' says Ruth, 'I can't say any more. Is it OK if I have the time off?'

'Of course,' says Phil. Then, 'Can I ask you something, Ruth?'

'Yes,' says Ruth warily.

'Why are you wearing a policeman's jacket?'

She had meant to leave early but it's getting dark by the time she reaches the Saltmarsh. All at once there seemed to be so many things to do: cancelling her lecture, arranging for Phil to take her tutorial on Animal Remains in Wetland Archaeology, ringing her parents to warn them of her arrival, avoiding Shona's increasingly desperate messages. Then, in the middle of it all, Nelson had rung.

'Ruth. You OK?'

'Fine.'

'Judy said she took you to a friend's house last night. I don't want you to do that again. I want you in a safe house.'

'I'm going to my parents. In London.'

A pause.

'Good. That's good.' He sounded distracted; she could almost hear him shuffling through papers as he talked.

'Have you found Erik yet?' she asked.

'No. He seems to have vanished off the face of the earth. But we'll get him. We've got people watching the guest house, his girlfriend's house, the university. There's an alert at all the airports.'

'What about Cathbad's place?'

'Oh, we've thought of that. I paid a visit to friend Malone this morning. Says he hasn't seen Anderssen for days but we're watching him too.'

'Must be expensive, all this surveillance.'

And Nelson had laughed hollowly. 'It'll be worth it if we catch him.'

Ruth had taken a taxi to the police station to pick up her car but she hadn't seen Nelson. The desk sergeant had told her that he was out 'following up on information received.' She wondered if that meant he had found Erik. She had almost left Nelson's jacket for him at the police station but something made her keep it with her. The jacket reminded her of Nelson and, in some strange way, made her feel braver. Besides, it was very warm.

As she turns into New Road it is four o'clock. Ominous grey clouds are gathering over the sea. A storm is on its way. The wind has suddenly dropped and the air is heavy with expectancy. There is a livid yellow line on the horizon and even the birds are still.

As she lets herself into her house, Flint greets her hysterically. God, she had forgotten him last night. In the kitchen he has tipped over his biscuits and torn a hole in the cardboard. He looks at her balefully as she fills up his bowl. She'll have to take him with her to her parents. She can't face asking David again and she doesn't know how long she'll be away. She goes up to the attic to get his travelling basket and, as she does so, she hears the first distant rumble of thunder.

She packs quickly, throwing in tops and trousers and jumpers. No point in worrying about what to take, her mother will criticise it all anyway. Ruth is still wearing the jacket. She'll tell her mother that policeman chic is all the rage in Norfolk. She adds a detective novel and her laptop. She might as well try to get some work done. She drags her suitcase onto the landing, knocking over the cardboard cut-out of Bones as she does so. Beam me up, Scotty. Pushing Bones aside, she hurries downstairs. Five o'clock.

Damn, it will be midnight before she gets to London at this rate. And the roads will be hell. She looks out of the window. It is pitch black now and the wind has started up again. Her gate is swinging wildly to and fro as if an invisible child is playing on it. Hastily, she grabs Flint and shoves him (protesting) into the cat basket. She must hurry up.

And yet, despite everything, she finds herself going to her desk for one last look at the Iron Age torque which started the whole thing. She doesn't know why she does this. She should have given the torque to Phil to put with the other finds but, for some reason, she can't bear to let it go.

It gleams dully in her hand, the twisted metal somehow both sinister and beautiful. Why was it put into the grave? To show the status of the dead girl or as an offering to the Gods of the underworld and of the crossing places – the Gods who guard the entry onto the marshlands?

For a full minute, Ruth stands there, weighing the heavy gold object in her hand.

Then a voice says informatively, 'Around seventy BC, I think. The time of the Iceni.'

It is Erik.

CHAPTER 26

Ruth swings round, heart hammering. At the same moment a particularly violent blast of wind throws itself against the house. The storm has arrived.

'A rough night,' says Erik in a conversational voice. He is wearing a black raincoat and is carrying an umbrella which has obviously just blown inside out. He throws the umbrella aside and steps forward, smiling.

'Erik,' she says stupidly.

'Hello Ruth,' says Erik. 'Did you think I would leave without saying goodbye?'

Erik takes a step closer. He's still smiling but his blue eyes are cold. As cold as the North Sea.

'The police are looking for you,' says Ruth.

'I know,' he smiles. 'But they won't look here.'

Why hadn't Nelson thought to guard this house, thinks Ruth in despair. But he thinks she is safely on her way to her parents. There's no one to help her. She starts to back towards the door.

'What's wrong, Ruthie? Don't you trust me?'

'No.'

'I didn't kill them, you know.' He picks up the torque and examines it closely. 'I didn't kill those little girls. I'm not a Nix. I'm not an evil sea spirit. I'm just Erik.'

His voice is as hypnotic as ever. Ruth shakes her head to clear it. She mustn't be taken in.

'You wrote the letters. The letters told me where to find Scarlet.'

'Rubbish,' says Erik. 'You twisted the facts to suit your theory just as all academics do.'

'Aren't you an academic?'

'Me?' Erik smiles. 'No. I am a teller of tales. A weaver of mysteries.'

He is, she understands suddenly, quite mad.

Slowly, she moves towards the door. Her hand is touching the handle. Then Flint, realising that he is about to be left behind in his cat basket, sets up an unearthly yowl. Erik starts and jumps towards Ruth. What he means to do she doesn't know, but one look at his eyes decides her. She throws herself through the door and out into the night.

The wind is so strong that she can hardly stay upright. It is coming directly from the sea, racing across the marshes, flattening everything in its path. Rain beats against her face, trying to force her back to Erik, but she stumbles on. At last she reaches her car. Her trusty, rusty Renault. Madly, she scrabbles at the door.

'Looking for these?' She looks round and there is Erik holding up her car keys. He is still smiling. With his white hair flattened by the rain, he looks like a wizard. Not a comfortable Harry Potter wizard but a creature from the wind and the rain. An elemental.

Ruth runs. She darts across New Road, jumps over the ditch – already full of rushing water – that leads to the marshes and sets out into the dark.

'Ruth!' She can hear Erik behind her. He too is across the ditch and she can hear him stumbling over the coarse grass and low bushes. Ruth stumbles too, falling heavily on the muddy ground, grazing her hands on loose stones. But she keeps going, panting, gasping, weaving through the stunted trees, with no idea where she's going except that she must escape from Erik. He will kill her, she knows. He'll kill her just as he killed those two little girls. For no reason. For the reason that he is mad.

She can hear him behind her. Despite his age, he's fit, much fitter than her. But desperation drives her on. She falls into a shallow stream and knows she must be getting near the tidal salt marshes. The wind is even louder now and the rain stings her face. She stops. Where is Erik? She can't hear anything now except the wind.

Exhausted, she sinks down on the ground. It is soft and reed stalks brush against her face. Where is the sea? She mustn't wander onto the mudflats or that will be the end of her. The tide comes in like a galloping horse, David said. It is easy to imagine wildly galloping hooves in the noise of the wind, the white horses of the waves storming in across the marshes. She crouches amongst the reeds, trying to gather her wits about her. She must ring Nelson, get help, but, as she scrambles for her mobile, she realises that she has packed it in her bag. The wind screams around her and in the background she hears another, even more sinister, noise. A roaring, rushing, relentless sound.

She is lost on the Saltmarsh and the tide is coming in.

CHAPTER 27

Nelson's mood is dark as he drives back to the station. The so-called 'information received' has turned out to be a load of bollocks. A man answering Erik Anderssen's description had been spotted at a King's Lynn pub. But when Nelson arrived at the pub it turned out to be folk music night, which meant that every man in the place answered to Erik Anderssen's description, grey ponytail, smug expression and all.

He glowers out at the rain as he edges through the Sunday night traffic. Then he thinks, sod it, and puts on his siren. The traffic parts for him in a way that he never ceases to find satisfying as he heads back to the station.

Christ, he hopes Ruth is OK. Still, she should be safely on her way to London now. Not that he thinks Erik will try to contact her. Privately, he's sure that he has already left the country, leapt on a late flight last night and is happily on the way to ... where's a place in Norway? Oslo, that's it. He'll be sitting in a café in Oslo now, drinking whatever Norwegians drink and laughing his bearded head off.

The desk sergeant tells him that Ruth collected her car an hour ago. Nelson frowns. That's too late for his liking. Whatever was she doing, hanging about all day? He'd spoken to her at lunchtime, she should have left straight away.

At his office door he is stopped by a constable. He doesn't know her name but he composes his face into something like a smile. She is young (they get younger all the time) and looks nervous.

'Er ... there's someone to see you, Detective Chief Inspector.'

'Yes?' he says encouragingly.

'He's in your office. He wouldn't leave a name.'

Why the hell hadn't he been stopped downstairs, thinks Nelson irritably. He pushes open the door and the first thing he sees is a swirl of purple cloak. He shuts the door behind him, very quickly indeed.

Cathbad is sitting, quite at his ease, on Nelson's side of the desk. He had his feet, encased in muddy trainers, actually on the desk. Nelson can see mud on one of his beautiful clean 'to do' lists.

'Get your feet off my desk!' he bellows.

'You really must watch that anger, Detective Chief Inspector,' says Cathbad. 'I'm sure you must have Aries rising.' But he takes his feet off the desk.

'Now get out of my chair,' says Nelson, breathing heavily.

'We own nothing in this world,' counters Cathbad, getting up fairly quickly all the same.

'Did you just come here to spout New Age rubbish at me?'

'No,' says Cathbad calmly. 'I've come to give you some information about Erik Anderssen. I thought I would bring the news in person so I slipped out when your two ... er ... guards were otherwise occupied.'

Nelson's hands clench into fists as he thinks of the

officers sent to watch Cathbad. They've made a fine job of surveillance. What the hell were they doing? Sheltering in their car probably, unwilling to face a cold night on the beach in Blakeney. Goons!

'What information? If you've come to tell me he's at a folk music gig you're wasting your breath.'

Cathbad ignores this. 'Erik telephoned me an hour ago. He told me that he was on his way to see Ruth Galloway.'

Nelson's heart starts to beat faster but he forces himself to speak calmly. 'Why are you so keen to help the police all of a sudden?'

'I dislike the police,' says Cathbad loftily, 'but I abhor all forms of violence. Erik sounded distinctly violent to me. I think your friend Doctor Galloway could be in danger.'

Ruth lies in the reed bed, listening to the roar of the tide and the howling of the wind and thinks, what the hell am I going to do now? She can't go back to the house and every moment that she stays on the Saltmarsh adds to the danger. Soon the tide will come in and she has no idea if she is already on the tidal mudflats. But Ruth has no intention of cowering in the mud, waiting to die. She has to find a way out; at any rate she may as well run as lie here waiting for Erik to catch her. She starts to zigzag through the reeds, head down against the wind.

A mighty crack of thunder almost throws her off her feet. It's a deafening, industrial sound, like two express trains colliding. Immediately, another lightning blast turns the sky white. Christ, the storm must be right overhead. Is she going to be struck by lightning? Another explosion of thunder sends her, instinctively, down amongst the reeds with her arms over her head. She is lying in a shallow stream. This is dangerous. Water conducts electricity, doesn't it? She can't even remember if she is wearing rubber soles. She edges forward on her stomach. This is how she imagines the First World War: face down in the mud while mortar shells explode into the sky. And this is no man's land alright. Hand over hand, she crawls slowly forward.

Jaw clenched, Nelson drives like a maniac towards the Saltmarsh. Next to him, humming softly, sits Cathbad. There is no one whose company Nelson desires less, but there are two important reasons why Cathbad is currently occupying the passenger seat of Nelson's Mercedes. One, he claims to know the Saltmarsh 'like the back of his hand', and two, Nelson does not trust him to be out of his sight for a second.

Clough and Judy are following in a marked police car. Both cars have their sirens blaring but there is little traffic as they scorch through the country lanes. The storm, raging unnoticed above them, has driven everyone inside.

At New Road, Nelson recognises Ruth's car and his breathing eases a little. Then he sees the open door swinging in the wind and he feels his heart contract. When he enters the sitting room, however, his heart almost jumps out of his chest. Because the room is filled with a terrible, unearthly wailing. He stops dead and Cathbad cannons into the back of him.

To Nelson's eternal shame it is Cathbad who notices the cat basket and goes to rescue Flint.

'Go free, little cat,' he murmurs vaguely. Flint doesn't

need telling twice. Tail fluffed up in outrage, he disappears through the open front door. Nelson hopes that he hasn't gone forever. He doesn't want another of Ruth's cats meeting a sticky end.

By the time Clough and Judy arrive, Nelson has already searched the tiny cottage. There is no sign of Erik or Ruth though a packed suitcase sits by the door and a broken umbrella, like a prehistoric bird, has been thrown onto the floor. Cathbad is examining a crumbled piece of metal which was lying on the table.

'What's that?' asks Nelson.

'Looks like an Iron Age torque,' replies Cathbad. 'Full of magic.'

Nelson loses interest immediately. 'They can't have gone far,' he says. 'Johnson, Clough, go and ask the neighbours if they heard anything. Radio for some dogs and an armed response team. You and me' – he grasps Cathbad's arm – 'we're going for a little walk on the Saltmarsh.'

Bent double, Ruth is running across the Saltmarsh. Falling headlong into muddy streams, clawing herself out, tasting blood in her mouth, getting up again and falling again, this time into a pond about a foot deep. Spluttering, she staggers to her feet. The marsh is full of water like this, some stretches several feet wide. She retraces her steps, finds some firmer ground and starts running again.

On she runs; she has lost a shoe and her trousers are ripped to pieces. Thank God though for the police jacket, which has, at least, kept her top half dry. She must keep going, she owes it to Nelson if no one else. It really would finish his career if another body was found on the marshes.

She pulls the coat more tightly round her and, as she does so, she feels a faint, a very faint, glow of courage, as if it is being transferred to her via the coat. Nelson wouldn't be scared by a bit of wind and rain, now would he?

But where is Nelson? And, more to the point, where is Erik? She stops, tries to listen, but she can hear only the wind and the rain and the thunder. *What the thunder said.* Isn't that T.S. Eliot? For a second she thinks of the letters, of Erik and Shona quoting T.S. Eliot to taunt Nelson. She can believe this, though it makes her sad, but does she really believe that Erik killed Scarlet Henderson? Does she really believe that he would kill her? Trust no one, she tells herself, staggering onwards over the uneven ground. Trust no one but yourself.

Then she hears a sound which makes her heart stop. A voice like no human voice she has ever heard. It is as if the dead themselves are calling her. Three calls, low and even, the last shuddering away into silence. What the hell was that?

The call comes again, this time from very close by. For no reason that she knows, she starts to move towards it and suddenly finds herself facing a solid wall.

She can't believe it at first. But it is, unmistakably, a wall. Gingerly, she puts out a hand to touch it. No, it isn't a mirage. It is a solid wall, wood, made of rough boards nailed together.

Of course, it's the hide! She has reached the hide. She almost laughs out loud in her relief. This must be the furthest hide, the one where she and Peter met David that day. But that hide, she remembers, is above the tidal mark. She is safe. She can shelter inside until the storm passes. Oh, thank God for bird watchers.

Half-drunk with relief, she staggers into the hut. It's open on one side so it doesn't offer brilliant shelter but it's a great deal better than nothing. It is wonderful to be out of the wind and the rain. Her face aches as if she has been repeatedly slapped and her ears are still ringing. She rests her head against the rough wood wall and closes her eyes. It's crazy but she could almost go to sleep.

Outside the storm is still raging but she has almost become used to it. Now the wind sounds like children's voices calling. How sad they sound, like the cries of sailors lost at sea, like the will o'the wisps searching the world for comfort and warmth. Ruth shivers. She mustn't get spooked now and start thinking about Erik's fireside tales. About the long green fingers reaching up out of the water, about the undead creatures roaming the night, about the drowned cities, the church bells ringing deep below the sea ...

She jumps. She has heard a cry coming from beneath her feet. She listens again. For a moment, the storm is still and she hears it again. Unmistakably a human voice. 'Help me! Help me!'

Stupidly Ruth looks at the wooden floor of the hide. It is covered by a carpet of rush matting. She tears at the carpet. It is obviously pinned down but comes away after the third or fourth tug. Below are floorboards and a trap-door. Why on earth would there be a trapdoor in a bird-watching hide? And there is the voice again. Calling from beneath the floor.

Hardly knowing what she is doing, Ruth bends down and puts her face to the trapdoor.

'Who's there?' she calls.

There is a silence and then a voice answers, 'It's me.'

The simplicity of this response strikes Ruth to the heart. It presupposes that Ruth knows the owner of the voice. And, almost at once, she feels as if she does.

'Don't worry,' she shouts, 'I'm coming.'

There is a bolt on the trapdoor. It slides back easily as if it is used regularly. Ruth opens the door and peers down in the darkness. At the same time a flash of lightning illuminates the surroundings.

A face looks back up at her. A girl, a teenager perhaps, painfully thin with long, matted hair. She's wearing a man's jumper and tattered trousers and has a blanket round her shoulders.

'What are you doing here?' asks Ruth stupidly.

The girl just shakes her head. Her eyes are huge, her skin grey with pallor.

'What's your name?' asks Ruth.

But, all of a sudden, she knows.

'Lucy,' she says gently. 'You're Lucy, aren't you?'

CHAPTER 28

Judy and Clough report that there is no response from either of Ruth's neighbours.

'Houses look shut up, Sir.' Nelson tells them to stay and wait for the dog handlers. He will search on the Saltmarsh.

'In this?' says Clough, gesturing towards the dark expanse of the marsh, where the trees are almost blown flat by the wind. 'You'll never find them.'

'There's quicksand,' says Judy, as a particularly savage blast almost knocks her off her feet. 'And the tide comes in really quickly. I used to live around here. It's not safe.'

'I know a way,' says Cathbad.

They all look at him. His cloak is flying out in the wind, his eyes are bright. Somehow he doesn't look quite as ridiculous as usual.

'There's a hidden way,' Cathbad goes on. 'I discovered it ten years ago. It's a sort of shingle spit. It leads from the lowest hide right up to the henge circle. Solid ground all the way.'

That must have been the path Ruth took to find Scarlet's body, thinks Nelson. 'Can you find it in the dark?' he asks.

'Trust me,' says Cathbad.

Which none of them finds very reassuring.

*

The sound of her name seems to have a devastating effect on the girl. She starts to cry loudly. A child crying rather than a teenage girl.

'Let me out!' she sobs. 'Oh please, let me out.'

'I will,' says Ruth grimly.

She reaches down and grabs the girl's arm. It feels brittle, as if it might snap. Then she hauls, but she is not strong enough to take the girl's weight, skinny as she is. Oh, why hadn't she kept going to the gym?

'I'm coming down,' she says at last. 'Then I'll give you a leg up.'

The girl backs away but Ruth is determined. She jumps in through the trapdoor and falls heavily onto the concrete floor below. The girl is standing against the opposite wall, her teeth bared like an animal at bay. In her hand she holds a stone. A flint, decides Ruth, giving it a sharp, professional look. A sharp one.

Ruth tries a smile. 'Hello,' she says. 'Hello Lucy. I'm Ruth.'

The girl lets out a small, frightened sound but doesn't move.

Ruth looks around. She is in a small, square, underground dungeon. Looking up, she sees the trapdoor in the ceiling, and a barred window which also has a wooden cover. The room is empty apart from a low bed, a bucket and a plastic box which seems to contain a baby's toys. The walls and the floor are all concrete, rough in places, and there is moisture running down the walls. The whole place smells of damp and urine and fear.

My God, thinks Ruth in horror, has Erik really kept her a prisoner all this time? What about when he was in

Norway? Cathbad, that must be the answer. This is the link between Erik and Cathbad. Cathbad is his jailer.

And now they must escape. Ruth turns to the girl, who is still cowering against the wall.

'Come on.' She holds out her hand again. 'I'm going to help you get out of here.'

But the girl, Lucy, just whimpers and shakes her head.

'Come on, Lucy,' says Ruth, trying to keep her voice as calm and gentle as possible. Trying to make it sound as if they have all the time in the world and there isn't a madman on their trail and a raging tempest outside. 'Come on. I'll take you home. You'd like to go home, wouldn't you, Lucy? See your mum and dad?'

She'd expected Lucy to react to the words mum and dad but the girl is still looking terrified. Ruth edges slowly towards her, dredging her mind for every soothing platitude she can think of.

'There, there. It's OK. Don't worry. It'll be alright.'

What were some of the meaningless things her mother used to say to her? Annoying little catchphrases but nevertheless as soothing as a cup of cocoa when you can't sleep. Ruth has never had children so it is her own childhood she must conjure up. Remember the days when her mother was not just someone who annoyed her on the phone, but the most important person in the world. The litany of motherhood.

'Don't worry. No use crying over spilt milk. Never get well if you pick it. Tears before bedtime. Tomorrow's another day. All's well that ends well. It's just a phase. Don't cry. It's darkest before dawn.'

And, as if the last words are the magic spell that releases

the princess from the tower, Lucy throws herself into Ruth's arms.

Nelson drives Cathbad to the car park in silence. The only sounds are the overloaded windscreen wipers swishing to and fro and Nelson's fingers drumming impatiently on the steering wheel. Perhaps fortunately for his continued well-being, Cathbad does not comment on this typically Scorpio impatience.

The trees around the car park are blown into a frenzy. The boarded-up kiosk looms eerily out of the dark, promising ghostly Cornettos and Calippo Shots. Grimly, Nelson gets a rope and a heavy-duty flashlight out of the trunk. Cathbad hums serenely.

They walk up the gravel track to the first hide. Nelson is in the lead, shining the flashlight in front of him. He doesn't think of himself as imaginative, but the noise of the wind howling across the marshes is starting to give him the creeps. The thunder rumbling overhead just adds to the clichéd horror film atmosphere. Behind him Cathbad sighs with what sounds like happiness.

They pass the first hide and Cathbad pushes in front.

'The path,' he says calmly. 'It's near here.'

Nelson hands him the flashlight. If they get lost he will kill Cathbad first and arrest him afterwards.

After a few yards, Cathbad veers off the gravel track and starts to head out over the marsh. Despite the flashlight, it's pitch black. Here and there, Nelson can see glimpses of water, dark and dangerous. It's like walking into the unknown, like one of those ridiculous trust exercises they make you do on police training courses. Except that

Nelson doesn't trust Cathbad, not one little bit. Following Ruth across the marshes, even in the daylight, had been difficult enough. It takes all his self-control now not to elbow Cathbad out of the way and insist on turning back to the track.

Suddenly Cathbad stops. 'Here it is,' he murmurs. Nelson sees him shine the flashlight onto the ground. A bolt of lightning turns the sky white. Cathbad grins at him. 'Follow me,' he says.

About a mile away, across the black marshland, Ruth holds Lucy in her arms. It feels strange, cuddling this thin, vulnerable body. Ruth doesn't know many teenagers and those she does know are hardly likely to fling their arms around her and sob into her shoulder.

'There, there,' says Ruth in her mythical mother persona. 'It'll be alright. Come on, Lucy.'

But Lucy just cries and cries, her entire body shaken with the force of her sobbing.

'Come on,' Ruth is forced to say at last. 'Come on. Before *he* gets back.'

That does the trick alright. Lucy breaks away, her eyes round with fear.

'Is he coming?' she whispers.

'I don't know,' says Ruth. Who knows where Erik is? Hopefully he is lost out there on the dark marshes but, knowing Erik, he probably has a sea sprite's sixth sense that will allow him to walk unharmed through the storm and arrive just as they are trying to escape. She doesn't say this to Lucy though. Taking advantage of the girl's loosened grip, she propels her gently below the trapdoor.

'I'm going to give you a leg up. You know,' she adds desperately, 'like on a pony.' She has never ridden a pony but she is hoping that Lucy has.

'A pony,' Lucy repeats carefully.

'Yes. I'm going to push you up through that hole and then climb up myself. OK?' she finishes brightly.

Almost imperceptibly, Lucy nods.

'Put your arms up,' says Ruth. Lucy does so. Clearly she is used to obeying orders. In the event, Ruth does not give her a leg up; instead she clasps Lucy round the waist and lifts her. It is surprisingly easy. Either Lucy weighs almost nothing or Ruth has developed superhuman strength. To her amazement, Lucy grasps the edge of the trapdoor and deftly swings herself up. Then she peers down at Ruth, her lips curved in something like a smile.

'Well done, Lucy! Well done!' She is so elated that she has almost forgotten that she has still got to get herself up.

Desperately, Ruth looks around for something to climb on. She spots the plastic box of toys and pulls it over to the space below the trapdoor. She stands on top. Still not high enough. So she gets the bucket, tipping its pungent-smelling contents into the corner, and puts it upside-down on top of the box. Now she balances precariously on the bucket. Yes! She is able to grab the rim of the trapdoor. Then, using every ounce of superhuman strength, she struggles to pull herself up. Her fingers scrabble madly on the hide's wooden floor and, amazingly, she feels something else pulling determinedly at her hand. It is Lucy. Lucy trying to help her. Whether or not this makes the difference, suddenly her torso is up through the trapdoor. One final heave and her legs are up too. Ruth lies panting on the floor of the hide.

Lucy is watching her. When she leans forward, her voice is again that breathy little whisper.

'Are we going home?'

'Yes.' Ruth struggles to her feet and takes Lucy's hand. She can hear the rain drumming on the roof but the thunder seems to have stopped. She looks at Lucy's thin, shivering body. How is she ever going to get her home? Ruth takes off the policeman's jacket and wraps it around Lucy. It comes to below her knees.

'There,' she says in her bright 'mother' voice. 'Now you'll be fine.'

But Lucy is looking beyond her. Staring at the entrance to the hide. She has heard something and now Ruth hears it too. Footsteps. A man's footsteps. Coming quickly towards them.

CHAPTER 29

Purple cloak flying out behind him, Cathbad leads the way across the marshes. Occasionally he stops and shines the flashlight at the ground and then he turns slightly to the right or left. Nelson follows. He feels his jaw locked with frustration, but he has to admit that, so far, Cathbad hasn't put a foot wrong. On either side of them he can see still water and dark, treacherous marshland but their feet remain on the twisting stony path. Thunder is rolling above them, the rain beats down unmercifully. Nelson is soaked but none of this matters if they find Ruth.

It is so dark that sometimes he almost loses sight of Cathbad, though he is only a few paces in front. Then he sees a glimmer of purple and realises that the old nutter is still there. Once or twice, Cathbad turns to him, grinning manically.

'Cosmic energy,' he says.

Nelson ignores him.

Where the hell is Ruth? And Erik? Whatever possessed Ruth to go running off like that, chasing over the marshes on the worst night of the year? Nelson sighs. When he thinks of Ruth, a kind of reluctant tenderness constricts his throat. He thinks of her lists, her love for her cats, her refusal to drink station coffee, the calm way she can dig through layers of mud and come up with a priceless treasure. He thinks of the way she fed him coffee and listened, the night Scarlet was found. He thinks of her body, actually rather magnificent unclothed, white in the moonlight. He thinks of her at Scarlet's funeral, her eyes red, and of her face when she told him that Erik was the author of the letters. He sighs again, almost a groan. He's not in love with Ruth but somehow she gets to him. If anything happens to her, he will never forgive himself.

Cathbad stops again and Nelson almost bumps into him.

'What's the matter?' He has to shout to be heard above the wind.

'I've lost the path.'

'You're joking!'

Cathbad sweeps the beam of the flashlight over the ground.

'Some of the posts are submerged ...' he mutters. 'I think this is it.'

He takes a step forward and disappears. He doesn't even have time to scream. He just vanishes, swallowed up by the night. Nelson jumps forward and is just in time to catch a handful of cloak. He pulls, the cloak tears, but now he has got hold of Cathbad's arm. Cathbad is up to his neck in the mud and it takes all Nelson's strength to haul him out. Finally, with a ghastly sucking noise, the marsh relinquishes its prey. Cathbad kneels on the path, head down, panting. He is completely covered in mud, his cloak in tatters.

Nelson yanks him to his feet. 'Come on, Cathbad, you're not dead yet.' It is the first time he has called Malone by his adopted name, but neither of them notices this.

Cathbad grasps Nelson's arm; his eyes look white and wild in his blackened face. 'I am in your debt,' he says, fighting for breath. 'The spirits of the ancestors are strong, they are all about us.'

'Well, we're not about to join them yet,' Nelson tells him briskly. 'Where's that flashlight?'

Ruth and Lucy stare at each other, terrified. The footsteps are coming nearer. Ruth's mind works frantically. They are trapped, they can't leave the hide without Erik catching them. Unconsciously Ruth moves in front of Lucy. Will Erik attack them both? How can she defend herself, defend Lucy? She looks wildly around the hide but it is completely empty. If only she had a stone or a piece of wood. Where is the stone that Lucy was carrying?

The footsteps come nearer and, at the same moment, the moon slides out from the behind the clouds. A man's figure approaches, wearing a yellow rain slicker. Hang on, wasn't Erik in black? The man reaches the steps to the hide and, in the moonlight, Ruth sees his face.

It isn't Erik. It is David.

'David!' shouts Ruth. 'Thank God!' David has come to save her again. David, who knows every step of the marshes. David who, she realises, is the only person who really loves the place. She feels giddy with relief.

But, behind her, Lucy starts to scream.

Nelson hears the scream. He grabs Cathbad's arm.

'Where did that come from?'

Cathbad points over to the right. 'From over there,' he says vaguely.

'Come on.' Nelson sets out, running, staggering over the waterlogged ground.

'No!' shouts Cathbad. 'You're off the path.'

But Nelson keeps running.

Lucy screams and, in that second, Ruth understands everything.

'You!' She stares at David. 'It was you.'

David looks calmly back at her. He looks no different from the kind, diffident, slightly eccentric David she thought she knew. Christ, she had even, for a minute or two, almost fancied him.

'Yes,' he says. 'Me.'

'You killed Scarlet? You kept Lucy a prisoner here for all these years?'

David's face clouds. 'I didn't mean to kill Scarlet. I brought her as company for Lucy. Lucy was growing up. I wanted a younger one. But she struggled. I tried to make her be quiet and ... she died. I didn't mean to do it. I buried her in the sacred place. Erik told me it was the right thing to do.'

'Erik? So he knew about this?'

David shakes his head. 'He didn't know but he talked to me, all those years ago, about burial places and sacrifices. He told me that in prehistoric times they buried children on the marshland, as an offering to the Gods. So I buried Scarlet where the wooden circle used to be. But you dug her up again.' His face darkens.

'You killed my cat,' bursts out Ruth. She knows she shouldn't mention Sparky, she shouldn't be antagonising David, but she can't help herself.

'Yes. I hate cats. They kill birds.'

He takes a step closer. Ruth grabs hold of Lucy, who is shaking violently.

'Keep away from her.'

'Oh, I can't let you go now,' says David, in a sweet, reasonable voice. 'She'd never survive in the wild. She's been in captivity too long. I'll have to kill you both.'

And then Ruth sees that he is holding a knife, a very serious-looking knife. The moonlight gleams on the jagged blade.

'Run!' she yells and, dragging Lucy after her, she sprints past David and into the night.

CHAPTER 30

Holding Lucy's hand tightly, Ruth runs. She doesn't know where she is going, she doesn't give a thought to the tide or the marshes, she hardly notices the wind and the rain, all she knows is that they are running for their lives. A murderer is after them, a man who has killed once before and who is intent on silencing them. Beside her, Lucy runs surprisingly well, hardly making a sound. Ruth hangs grimly onto her hand. She mustn't let Lucy go. Alone, in the dark, on the tidal marsh, she would have no chance at all.

Ruth can hear David behind them. He is wading through the stream they have just crossed. She must change direction, head for home. But where is home? She makes a random left turn and finds herself facing a pool of water. She runs on and finds the ground getting softer and softer. Oh God, she must be on the mudflats. She has a sudden vision of Peter, ten years ago, calling for help as the tide advanced. Erik had saved him but he is not going to save Ruth.

And then she hears something. Almost as if Erik's voice is coming back to her, over the years. She stops, listening. It sounds almost like 'Police'. She must be hallucinating.

But it was a mistake to stop. With horrifying suddenness, David's face suddenly looms out of the dark. Ruth screams and Lucy breaks free.

'Lucy!' yells Ruth.

David lunges forward, grabbing Ruth's foot. She kicks out. He falls back. Ruth takes to her heels again; she must find Lucy before David does.

But David is right behind her. She can hear his ragged breathing; hear the splashing as he wades through the pool. Frantically, Ruth turns and finds herself scrambling up a sandy slope. A sand dune. She must be right near the sea but she barely has time to think this when she is falling down the other side of the dune and landing in water. Salt water. Looking ahead, she can see nothingness. Only the ink-black sea, flecked with white foam, coming relentlessly towards her. She turns and wades inland, along a narrow channel of water. Where's Lucy? She must find Lucy.

Ahead of her, she can see a square dark shape in the water. She heads for it and sees what it is. A Second World War pill box, a small brick structure about a metre high. They are dotted all over the marshes. For want of anything better to do, she climbs on top of the box. If she jumps, she can reach the higher ground, where she should be safe from the tide. She jumps and lands heavily on the opposite bank. A brief thrill of elation runs through her. She has done it! Super Ruth!

But then the elation vanishes. Standing over her, knife in hand, is David.

Nelson runs across the salt marsh. He hardly notices that he falls many times, staggering in and out of the water. Behind him he can hear Cathbad shouting something about the tide but he ignores him. Someone is screaming. Ruth is in danger.

'Police!' he yells. 'Freeze!'

He hasn't even got a gun; what's he going to do when he gets there? He doesn't think about that, just runs doggedly on.

And then he sees the solid shape of the hide, looming up out of the featureless darkness. He runs towards it.

The hide is deserted, eerie in the moonlight. Nelson climbs the steps and looks down into the dark hole left by the trap-door. Thank God he took the flashlight from Cathbad. Its bright beam illuminates the underground room.

'Jesus,' breathes Nelson.

'Sorry Ruth,' says David, again sounding quite normal, the shy helpful neighbour who had looked after her cat and to whom (Oh God!) she had given her mobile phone number.

'David ...' Ruth croaks.

'I have to kill you,' explains David, 'now you know about Lucy.'

'Why did you do it?' asks Ruth. She genuinely wants to know the truth, even though she knows it might be the last thing she hears.

'Why?' asks David, surprised. 'For company, of course.'

He moves towards her, holding out the knife. Ruth backs away, wondering what her chances are. They are standing on a raised bank; behind David is the pool she passed earlier. She has no idea how deep it is. Even if she manages to get past him, she can hardly swim across the water in the dark. Behind her are the sand dunes and the sea crashing relentlessly forwards. She is exhausted and overweight; she knows David would catch her easily. She opens her mouth to say something. To beg for mercy? She doesn't know. But, then, another noise fills the night.

Three echoing calls, harsh and even. It is the sound that she heard earlier, beside the hide. David looks at Ruth, his face is transfixed.

'Did you hear that?' he whispers.

Without waiting for an answer, he turns his back and starts walking away from her, towards the sound. It comes again. Calling, calling across the black marshes. Is it the voice of a dead child? The will o'the wisps? At this moment, Ruth will believe anything. She too starts to move towards the sound.

What happens next is like a dream. Or a nightmare. Moving as if hypnotised, David walks straight into the pool. He is waist deep but does not even seem to notice. Ruth sees his yellow jacket moving steadily through the inky water. Then, the clouds move and Ruth sees a figure on the opposite bank. A figure wearing a dark jacket that comes to below its knees. Lucy. There is something in her stance, something poised and purposeful, that is almost terrifying. Suddenly Ruth has no doubt that it is Lucy who is making the strange, unearthly call.

David, though, is beyond thought. He walks on through the water, head up, pulled as if on invisible strings. And then, so suddenly that no one has time to cry out, a huge white-edged wave comes crashing over the sandbank and into the pool. David loses his balance and disappears under the water. Another wave follows, turning the pool into a cauldron of foamy water. Ruth feels spray on her face and shuts her eyes. When she opens them again, the pool is still and David has vanished.

Now Ruth screams but she knows no one can hear her. She knows too that there is nothing anyone can do for

David and is surprised at the strength of her impulse to save him. It seems that even the death of a murderer can provoke pity.

Another figure appears on the opposite bank. A tall, thick-set figure. Nelson. He is shouting something but Ruth can't make out the words. She starts to make her way towards him, around the edge of the pool. As she does so, the sky is filled with a sound like the beating of enormous wings. A police helicopter appears overhead, its rotors churning up the black waters. It circles the pool and then heads out to sea. The water is still once more.

On hands and knees, Ruth crawls along the shingle bank on the south side of the pool. It is further than it looks and she is beyond exhausted. The sound of the helicopter fades away and now she can hear human voices and, in the distance, dogs barking.

By the time she has reached the far bank, the police dogs have arrived. Actual bloodhounds, straining at their leashes and uttering low, booming barks that seem to come from another century. Ruth reaches Nelson just as he is looking, with dawning wonder, into the face of the girl next to him.

'Nelson,' says Ruth, 'meet Lucy Downey.'

CHAPTER 31

Ruth is walking along the sand. It is early March and although the wind is cold there is a faint promise of spring in the air. She is barefoot and the clam shells cut into her feet.

She is near the henge circle. The sand, rippling like a frozen sea, stretches far in front of her. She thinks of Ozymandias, 'the lone and level sands stretch far away'. There is something grand and terrible about the great expanse of sea and sky, something terrifying, yet at the same time exhilarating. We are nothing, Ruth thinks, nothing to this place. Bronze Age man came here and built the henge, Iron Age man left bodies and votive offerings, modern man tries to tame the sea with walls and towers and bridges. Nothing remains. Man dwindles into dust, less than sand; only the sea and sky stay the same. Yet she walks jauntily, with a spring in her step, stepping lightly over mortality.

She is due to meet Nelson, who is going to give her the latest news of Lucy. This is one legacy of that terrible night, three weeks ago. Ruth feels bound to Lucy and knows that this connection will last forever, whether Lucy wants it or not. Ruth may soon fade in Lucy's mind – indeed, she hopes many things will fade from Lucy's mind; one day she will become just the strange, large lady who comes with presents at Christmas and birthdays, bringing with her a faint memory of a dark night, a wild sea and the end of a nightmare. But for Ruth, that moment when she held Lucy in her arms was a turning point. She knew then that she would do anything to protect Lucy. She knew then what it is to be a mother.

Nelson told her about Lucy's reunion with her actual parents. 'We called them, didn't tell them what was up, just asked them to come to the station. It was four in the morning, God knows what they thought. The mother thought we'd found Lucy's body, I could see it in her eyes. We had a child psychologist standing by; nobody knew what would happen. Would Lucy even recognise her parents? She was very calm, just sat there, huddled in my jacket, as if she was waiting for something. We made her a cup of tea and she screamed. Hadn't expected it to be hot. Probably hadn't had a hot drink for ten years. She screamed and dropped the drink on the floor, then she cringed away from me, as if she expected me to hit her. That bastard ill-treated her, I'm sure of it. So I left her with Judy. Then, when I came in with the parents ... she made this noise, this little cry, like a baby. Then the mother said, "Lucy?" And Lucy just howled "Mummy!" and flung herself into her arms. Jesus. There wasn't a dry eye in the house. Judy was weeping buckets and Cloughie and I were both sniffing away. But the parents, they hugged her as if they'd never let her go. Then the mother looked at me, over Lucy's head, and said "Thank you." Thank you! Jesus.'

'Will she be alright, do you think?'

'Well, she's obviously seeing an army of psychiatrists but they say she's remarkably resilient. She has to learn to be a teenager, not a little girl. In some ways, they say, she's stuck at five years old but, in others, she's amazingly mature. I think she understands a lot more than we give her credit for.'

And Ruth, remembering the way that Lucy had used the bird call (the call, she is sure, of the Long Eared Owl) to lure David to his death, believes him.

They have not found David's body. It must have been washed out to sea and carried by the tide to another shoreline. Perhaps they will never find it and David's remains will one day join the Neolithic bones and relics that lie beneath this shallow sea.

They did find Erik though. The great shaman, who knew the marshes like the back of his hand, had drowned in a marshy pool just a few hundred metres from Ruth's cottage.

Ruth went to Norway for Erik's funeral. Despite everything, she found that she still had some love left for him – and for Magda. Erik had always said that he wanted a Viking's funeral. Ruth remembers him, by the campfire in full storyteller mode: 'The ship, its sails full in the evening light. The dead man, his sword at his side and his shield on his breast. The flame, that burst of purifying fire that will send him to Valhalla to sit with Odin and Thor until the world is renewed ...' So they had taken his ashes and put them in a wooden boat built specially by Lars, Magda's lover. They had set fire to the boat and sent it sailing out onto the lake, where it burnt all through the night and was still smouldering in the morning.

'You know,' Magda had turned to Ruth, her face lit by the glow from the boat, 'we were happy.'

'I know,' said Ruth.

And she did know. Magda and Erik were happy, despite Shona and Lars and all the others. And she, Ruth, still loved Erik, despite the letters and the adultery and the cold light behind the blue eyes. She seemed to have learnt a lot about love over the last few weeks. After Norway, she went home to Eltham where she went shopping with her mother, played Scrabble with her father and even attended church with them. She doesn't think she will ever be a believer herself but these days it does not seem so important to remind her parents of this. Somehow, when she held Lucy in her arms in that terrible cellar, she found a way back to her own mother. Perhaps it is just that she learnt the value of the maternal cliché, the love that is always the same no matter how many years pass and burns no less strongly by being expressed in time-worn phrases.

Erik was never charged with any crime. Cathbad was quietly cleared of the charge of wasting police time. The letters, with their haunting messages of life and death and resurrection, were never made public. Ruth thinks about them sometimes though. Thinks about why Erik and Shona wrote them, why Erik hated Nelson so much that he was prepared to distract him from his job of catching a murderer. Was it grief for James Agar that motivated Erik or was it arrogance, the chance to pit his wits against the police, that embodiment of a philistine state? She will never know.

Cathbad celebrated the dropping of the charges by performing a spiritual cleansing session on the beach, not unlike a Viking funeral, involving much dancing around a ceremonial fire. He invited Nelson but Nelson declined to attend. Despite this, Cathbad and Nelson have become, for want of any other word, friends. Nelson has a reluctant admiration for the way Cathbad remained calm in the storm, guiding him across the deadly marshes. And Cathbad is convinced that Nelson saved his life. He says so on every possible occasion, which somehow Nelson doesn't dislike as much as he should.

Ruth sees Nelson approaching over the sand dunes. He is wearing jeans and a leather jacket and he looks wary, as if he expects the sand to leap up and attack him. Nelson will never love the Saltmarsh. He always found it a spooky sort of place and now it will always be associated in his mind with Lucy's long imprisonment (under the noses of his officers!) and with death.

Nelson has reached Ruth who is standing, she thinks, at the start of the henge circle. There is nothing to show for it now though, just a few blackened streaks on the grey sand. The timbers themselves lie artificially preserved in the museum, far from the wind and the sand.

'What a place to meet,' grumbles Nelson. 'Miles from anywhere.'

'The exercise will do you good,' says Ruth.

'You sound like Michelle.'

Ruth has met Michelle now and, to her surprise, quite likes her. She admires the way that Michelle always does exactly what she wants, whilst retaining the image of the perfect wife. This, she feels, is a skill she could usefully learn, not that she is planning to be anyone's wife. Ruth suspects that Michelle, for her part, is simply dying to give her a make-over.

Peter has gone back to Victoria. Ruth is happy for him,

and is also relieved that it was David, not Peter, who sent the text messages. Her memories of him can stay intact.

'How's it going?' Ruth asks.

'Not too bad. There's a new corruption scandal brewing which may take the pressure off me for a bit.'

The discovery of Lucy Downey was, of course, a media sensation. There seemed to have been little else in the papers for weeks, which was one reason why Ruth escaped to Norway and Eltham. Nelson came in for his share of criticism; after all, Lucy was found in an area which had been searched many times by the police. But, then again, Nelson did get all the credit for rescuing Lucy. Ruth was more than happy for her part to be downplayed and Cathbad, too, had his own reasons for remaining in the shadows. Also, Lucy's parents consistently refused to criticise Nelson, saying instead that it was his tireless searching that had eventually resulted in Lucy's discovery.

'How's Lucy?' asks Ruth as they walk along the sea's edge. The tide is going out, leaving a line of shells and glistening stones. The seagulls swoop low, looking for treasure.

'Good,' says Nelson. 'I went round there yesterday and she was playing on a swing in the garden. Apparently she remembered the house and the garden perfectly. But she'd forgotten lots of other things. When she first saw a cat, she screamed.'

Ruth thinks of Flint who, fully recovered from his exertions, stayed with Shona while she was away. Shona, desperate to make amends, fed Flint almost entirely on smoked salmon. I should get another cat, Ruth thinks. Stop Flint getting too spoilt.

'Has Lucy said anything about what it was like?' she asks. 'When she was locked up?'

'The psychiatrist has been getting her to draw pictures. The most disturbing things you ever saw. Little black boxes, clutching hands, iron bars.'

'Was she abused by him? David.'

'Abused? Of course she was abused. But, sexually, there's no sign. I think he was quite squeamish about sex, actually. The psychiatrists think that if she'd started menstruating, he might have killed her.'

'How did he make that underground room? It had concrete walls and everything.'

'Apparently it was an old Second World War bunker. He built the hide on top of it.'

'Jesus.' Ruth is silent for a few minutes, thinking of the preparation that must have gone into creating Lucy's prison. How many years had David been planning this?

'Does anyone know why he did it?'

'The shrinks have got a million theories but it's all guess-work. Perhaps he wanted birds to be free but liked to keep humans in captivity.'

'For company, that's what he said to me.' Ruth thinks of what David said when she told him of her grief for Sparky: 'she was company'. With a shiver, she realises that when she and Peter saw him that day he must have been on his way to check up on Lucy. That was why he hated tourists and litter. He wanted everyone to keep away from the hide.

'Company,' Nelson grunts. 'Jesus. Couldn't he have joined a computer club?'

Why not indeed, thinks Ruth, looking out at the sea. Why does anyone do anything? Why does she remain here, on the

Saltmarsh, where so many awful things have happened? Why is Nelson still in love with his wife, although they have nothing in common? Why does Phil still not believe that the henge and the causeway are linked? Why is she fat and Shona thin? There's no answer to any of it. But, she thinks, smiling to herself as the cold water foams over her bare feet, somehow none of that matters today. She's happy with her life, here on the desolate coast. She wouldn't change any of it. She likes her job, her friends, her home. And besides, she thinks, smiling even more widely to herself; I'm not fat, I'm pregnant. She has no intention of telling Nelson, though. Not yet.

Nelson too is gazing out to sea. 'What's happened about the Iron Age girl?' he asks suddenly. 'The one who started all this?'

Ruth smiles. 'They're calling her Ruth, you know, after me. I call her the lost girl of the marshes. I'm writing a paper about her.'

'Do you know any more about why she died?'

'Not really. She seems to be from a wealthy family; her nails are manicured and we've done tests on her hair that prove she had good nutrition. But no one knows why she was tied down on the marsh and left to die. Maybe it was to ensure safe passage over the marsh. Maybe she was an offering to the Gods. But, really, we don't know.'

'Seems to me it's all a lot of guesswork,' says Nelson.

Ruth smiles. 'The questions are more important than the answers.'

'If you say so.'

And they turn and walk back towards the dunes.

ACKNOWLEDGEMENTS

The Saltmarsh and its henge are completely imaginary. There was, however, a Bronze Age henge found in North Norfolk, at Holme-next-the-Sea. For descriptions of this henge I am indebted to Francis Pryor's marvellous book *Seahenge* (HarperCollins).

The University of North Norfolk and the King's Lynn police force are also entirely fictional. Thanks to Derek Hoey and Graham Ranger for their insights into modern policing and to Michael Whitehead for supplying the Blackpool background. I am also grateful to Andrew Maxted and Lucy Sibun for their archaeological expertise. However, in all these cases, I have taken the experts' advice only as far as it suits the plot and any resulting inaccuracies are mine alone.

Thanks to my editors Jane Wood at Quercus and Dinah Forbes at McClelland & Stewart and to my agent Tif Loehnis. Love and thanks always to my husband Andrew and our children, Alex and Juliet.

Don't miss the next gripping Ruth Galloway Mystery

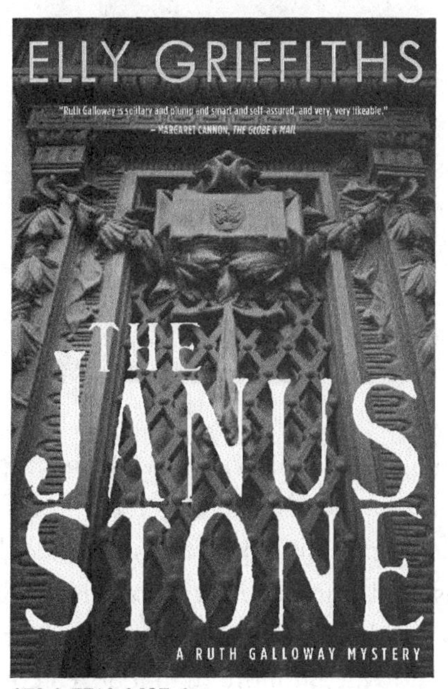

978-0-7710-3587-6
Hardcover

The Janus Stone, the second Ruth Galloway mystery, sees Ruth literally up to her neck in trouble. She's standing in a trench cut into the ground floor of an old Victorian mansion in Norwich once run by the Catholic Church as a home for children. The mansion is being demolished to make way for a condo development, and because a medieval church was originally on the site, the county council has ordered an archaeological survey before the new buildings go up. And now they won't go up, not until Ruth has finished her investigation, because she's staring at the headless skeleton of a child buried under the imposing front door.

Jerry Bauer

Elly Griffiths's Ruth Galloway novels are inspired by the work of her husband, who gave up a job in finance to train as an archaeologist, and by her aunt, who lives on the Norfolk coast and who filled her niece's head with the myths and legends of that area. *The Crossing Places* has been published worldwide, in more than a dozen countries.

Elly Griffiths lives near Brighton, on the south coast of England, with her husband and two children.